Southern Charm

Tinsley Mortimer

SIMON & SCHUSTER

NEW YORK   LONDON   TORONTO   SYDNEY   NEW DELHI

Simon & Schuster
1230 Avenue of the Americas
New York, NY 10020

First Simon & Schuster hardcover edition May 2012

SIMON & SCHUSTER and colophon are registered trademarks of Simon & Schuster, Inc.

For information about special discounts for bulk purchases, please contact Simon & Schuster Special Sales at 1-866-506-1949 or business@simonandschuster.com.

The Simon & Schuster Speakers Bureau can bring authors to your live event. For more information or to book an event contact the Simon & Schuster Speakers Bureau at 1-866-248-3049 or visit our website at www.simonspeakers.com.

Designed by Akasha Archer

Manufactured in the United States of America

10 9 8 7 6 5 4 3 2 1

Library of Congress Cataloging-in-Publication Data

Mortimer, Tinsley.
Southern charm : a novel / Tinsley Mortimer. — 1st Simon & Schuster hardcover ed.
  p. cm.
Summary: "The entertaining first novel by socialite Tinsley Mortimer about a southern belle thrust into the frenzied world of high society in New York City." — Provided by publisher.
1. Socialites—Fiction. 2. City and town life—Fiction. 3. New York (N.Y.) —Fiction.
I. Title.
PS3613.O7786255S67 2012
813'.6—dc23   2011044263

ISBN 978-1-4516-2747-3
ISBN 978-1-4516-2750-3 (ebook)

For BB, Bella, and Bambi

Oooooooh, I absolutely love the Plaza.

—Eloise

Contents

Prologue

Sometimes You Just Have to Go for Broke

One of my first memories involves two of my favorite places: the Plaza Hotel and New York City.

I was eight years old. My mother, Scarlett Macon Davenport, a proud Southern belle from her Aqua Net–lacquered bob down to her perfectly polished Chanel ballet flats, decided it was about time she and I got out of Charleston, South Carolina, and had ourselves a "girls' trip." Apparently, there was no better place in the world to do "girly" things—shopping, giggling, being all-around glamorous and frivolous—than the island of Manhattan.

She tracked me down in the sunroom of our family home, Magnolia Gate, a grand, Georgian-style estate just outside of Charleston. It was a bona fide plantation with red brick and white pillars and a mile-long driveway lined with, yes, magnolia trees. It had been handed down in my father's family for five generations.

When I wasn't playing tennis, I spent my afternoons in my mother's sunroom poring over her latest copies of *Vogue, Harper's Bazaar,* and *Elle*. I would carefully cut out the most beautiful photos and paste them onto large sheets of poster board, creating collages of inspiration like my mother did for her interior design clients.

"I've bought us two tickets to New York City, Minty," my mother said.

She stood over me with her hands on her hips. Although she rarely left home without putting on a dress, she was partial to cashmere turtlenecks and slacks when she was hanging around the house. That day her outfit was entirely white—"winter white," as she called it— except for her monogrammed velvet slippers, which were black with white lettering. She had her cat-eye glasses on, the ones that made her look smart and authoritative, like a chic librarian.

"We'll visit Santa Claus," she continued. "We'll go shopping at Saks Fifth Avenue. We'll stay at the Plaza, of course."

I was sprawled out on the floor barefoot, wearing a pink plaid jumper and wool tights. I had pink satin ribbons woven through my French-braided hair. I always had ribbons to match my outfit, which meant I always had pink ribbons. Up until that point, I hadn't been paying much attention to what my mother was saying. I was too caught up in one of my latest creations, a colorful mishmash pulled from the pages of an old *Mademoiselle*. Flat on the poster board, Lauren Hutton stared up at me from an Ultima II perfume ad, smiling. Next to her, I'd laid out a photo of Grace Jones, the fierce, exotic yang to Lauren's all-American yin. I was in the midst of cutting up a Brooke Shields Calvin Klein ad when I heard the words "the" and "Plaza." I put down my scissors.

"The Plaza *Hotel*?"

"Yes, Minty."

"The *real* Plaza?"

"As opposed to the fake one?" my mother replied.

"The Plaza." I stood up. "Where Eloise lives?"

A tiny hint of a smile spread across my mother's face.

"Where else would we stay, Minty?"

My grandmother gave me my first Eloise book when I was born and I have been obsessed ever since. In fact, they are the only books I have ever *truly* enjoyed reading to this day and I still leaf through their pages once a week.

At eight years old, Eloise had already made an indelible impact on my young life. I aspired to dress in a jumper like Eloise, to speak on the telephone like Eloise, to order room service like Eloise. I wanted to *be* Eloise, or at the very least make her my friend. But most of all, I wanted to live like Eloise.

Through my tiny, fictional idol, I had come to the conclusion that not only was the Plaza the most incredible, glamorous, over-the-top, wonderful, delightful place in the world to be, it was the *only* place to be.

And it just so happened to be in New York City.

I considered my options for about thirty seconds, during which my mother rolled her eyes and crossed her arms over her chest rather dramatically.

"Mary Randolph Mercer Davenport. Today?"

Mary Randolph was my grandmother's name. Mary was my "official" first name, but I'd been called "Minty" since before I can remember. No one can ever recall the specifics, but it has something to do with the fact that I'd loved candy as a child, especially the red-and-white swirly "starlight" mints.

"All right, Mommy," I finally said. "Let's go to New York."

A rosy flush spread over my mother's cheeks. She looked like a little girl about to open a present.

"You're going to just love it, Minty," she said, her voice taking on the hushed and sacred tone of our priest at church. "New York City is a magical place."

"Eloise lives there," I said.

"Yes," my mother replied. "Yes, she does."

———◦◦◦———

A week later, I stood next to my mother as she helped our longtime driver, Claude, pack up the car with her vintage Louis Vuitton luggage collection. By the looks of it, we were leaving Charleston for good, but many of the trunks were empty and would come back filled

4 Tinsley Mortimer

with Christmas presents for my younger sister, Darby, and me as well as the latest designer creations for my mother's spring wardrobe.

I slid into the back of the car, clutching a small Lanvin purse my mother had let me borrow for the weekend. I had filled it with Blow Pops and two sheets of sparkly stickers shaped like high heels and handbags.

"Well, good afternoon, Miss Minty," Claude said from the driver's seat, looking at me through the rearview mirror.

Claude was almost like a grandfather to me. He had weathered, sun-beaten skin so soft it felt like vintage velvet. It was the color of a sun-ripened peach, warm and ruddy. His lips were always curled up in a broad, white smile, but his eyes were solemn and thoughtful.

I liked Claude for many reasons, most of all because he always kept starlight mints in his pocket for me. If we were all driving together and my mother happened to be otherwise engaged, which she often was, Claude would extend his arm toward the backseat and present a mint to me in his open palm—a tiny secret between the two of us. I loved the mints so much that my mother often caught me sucking away at several at once, tiny rivulets of red running down the sides of my mouth.

"So, New York City, eh, Miss Minty?"

"Yes, Claude," I said in a very authoritative tone. I crossed my legs at my ankles, a mannerism that had been drilled into me since I was old enough to sit up on my own.

"What are you going to do there?"

"Eat candy," I replied. "And Mommy will shop."

Claude laughed.

From my perch in the backseat, the front of our house was obscured, but I could hear my mother's high-pitched Southern drawl making its way down the walkway. "And I will not have that child eating Froot Loops for dinner, Gharland. You hear me, now?

"Darby, honey," she said, addressing my younger sister. "You'll come next time. You'll have a nice time with Daddy."

Darby was six at the time and a bit too young to really understand what she would be missing, but she was putting up a fit anyway. I peered around the side of Claude's seat until I could make out my father, who was holding a squirming Darby.

"Next year, Darby," my mother cooed.

"We'll go to the movies, honey," my father chimed in.

My father was always an impossibly handsome man and still is today. He has deep-set eyes with a strong jawline and thick, dark hair that curls up a bit at the ends. Now it's nearly white, but back then it was the color of molasses, so intensely brown it almost appeared black. He's nearly six foot four with broad shoulders and the rounded stomach of a thrice-daily bourbon drinker. My mother always said, "He fills out a suit nicely," and he does.

My parents met at my mother's debutante ball in Savannah, Georgia, where she grew up. Their first introduction was far from romantic. As the escort of an infinitely less beguiling young lady (my mother loves telling this story, and with each telling the young lady becomes less and less beguiling) named Hayley Beaufort, my father was reluctant to attend the ball at all. So, he had spent the two hours from Charleston to Savannah shooting bourbon in the backseat of his friend's father's Mercedes and arrived on the scene in a state of inebriation so severe that he had to be carried into the men's room and doused with several rounds of water.

When he appeared in the ballroom over an hour later, he was slapped in the face by Hayley, given a stern talking-to by Hayley's father, and sent to sit at their table alone to atone for his sins.

My father had already established quite the name for himself as a notorious charmer and "finagler" (this is a word my mother still uses to describe him) who had made a sport of bedding young debutantes around Charleston and Savannah. He was known to feign undying love for a few weeks' time, taking the young ladies home to meet his parents, writing them intricate letters and sending flowers, jewelry, and clothing as tokens of his appreciation, and then flat dropping them when his interest inevitably waned.

He had recently done just this to one of my mother's closest and dearest friends, and my mother was not about to let a chance to reprimand him slip out of her fingers.

From the dance floor, she watched out of the corner of her eye as my father sat there, dumbfounded, his hair still wet from his dousing in the bathroom, his cheek still stinging. When the waltz ended, she walked right over and gave him a piece of her mind.

When she finished her tirade, he looked up at her and raised an eyebrow. "My God you're beautiful," he said. "What is your name?"

———◦◦◦———

Until that moment, when Darby wailed and screamed and punched my father with tiny fists, I had never seen him in anything less than perfect control. But that day he looked terrified, as if my mother and I were abandoning him to Satan's spawn.

"Newark!" Darby was screaming over and over. The correct pronunciation of "New York" eluded her, and she had resorted to shrieking the name of a far less desirable city in New Jersey. "*Newaaaark!*"

Claude caught my eye in the rearview mirror and we burst into a fit of laughter.

"Good Lord in the heavens above." My mother's slim frame appeared in the seat next to me. She had on large, black sunglasses. On her lap, she placed one of her signature quilted Chanel purses and folded her hands over it with such grace and care you might have thought it was a living, breathing entity.

"Let's get the hell out of here, Claude," she said.

Just as we were about to start backing up, my mother rolled down the window and allowed my father to stick his head in. This was a little ritual of his—a final word before the departure. He bent over with his left arm behind him.

"Y'all behave yourselves, all right?" he said, his blue eyes sparkling.

My mother turned and shot him a glance. "Ha!" she said. "We will do no such thing."

She rolled up the window and signaled to Claude.

As the car pulled out of the driveway, I could hear my father's laugh, low and bellowing through the thick glass of the Cadillac's tinted windows.

I don't remember much of the plane ride. I remember grasping my mother's hand as we navigated the long corridors of JFK. My mother stopped at one shop to buy her favorite Dior perfume and allowed me to spray myself with a bit of Shalimar, which made me cough and wheeze for the majority of the cab ride into Manhattan.

When the cab pulled up to the entrance of the hotel, the first thing I noticed was the row of perfectly groomed carriage horses. Then I saw the lights, the bellmen in pressed suits and hard round caps, the plush carpet, the sparkling glass, and the shimmering carved wood. I stood in the lobby and looked around, feeling as if someone had dropped me into a genie bottle.

"Welcome to the Plaza Hotel, Miss Davenport," a man said as my mother and I checked in.

He leaned over and handed me a lollipop. I almost told him I already had one in my purse, but I knew it would have been rude not to accept a present (the correct word was "present," not "gift," my mother always told me).

My mother caught my eye and smiled at me sternly, as if to say, *Go on and thank the man now, Minty.*

"Thank you, sir," I said.

The same bellman gathered our many bags and guided us toward a set of elevators. He told us that the Plaza had twenty floors and that we would be staying on the eighteenth floor in the Royal Terrace Suite, which featured a view of Central Park. I was only half-listening, of course. I was on the lookout for Eloise. I thought she might come running down the hallway at any moment and try to steal my lollipop.

"Is this your first time in New York City?"

We were in the elevator, climbing the floors one by one, and the bellman was posing this question to me, but I was not listening.

"Minty," my mother said. "Answer the nice man."

I must have jumped a little, because the man laughed.

"What are you thinking about now, little miss?"

I looked up, eyes wide and fueled by sugar. I answered with the first thought that came to my mind, which was the truth. "Eloise," I said.

"I thought you might be looking for her," the bellman said. Then he leaned down and whispered, just loud enough that my mother could hear as well. "You just missed her in the Palm Court."

I had *just* missed her? I had come all this way to New York City and just *narrowly* missed seeing and meeting Eloise?

"We'll look for her tomorrow, Minty," my mother said, stepping off the elevator. She exchanged a wink with the bellman.

I narrowed my eyes at both of them. The bellman directed us toward a door at the end of the hallway. It was heavy and old and had a brass plaque that read ROYAL TERRACE SUITE. He opened the door and deposited our luggage. Then he bowed slightly and let himself out.

My mother and I held hands and looked out the windows of the suite, past the sumptuous silk faille curtains and onto Central Park. I felt both awed and frightened by what lay past our window. The park seemed dark and sprawling, almost ominous without the benefit of daylight. "Time to go to sleep now, Minty," my mother said. "We have a full schedule ahead of us tomorrow."

As she tucked me in, she rattled off a to-do list for the following day: breakfast in the Edwardian Room, shopping at Bergdorf Goodman, a stroll down Fifth Avenue, a stop into St. Patrick's Cathedral, lunch at La Grenouille, more shopping at Saks. I drifted off into a deep sleep and dreamed about finding Eloise.

<hr />

Now, fourteen years later, I was back. Except this time, I'd left my mother in Charleston and my sister at Ole Miss. My parents divorced when I was in high school. My mother fought long and hard for Magnolia Gate and, in the end, won the right to stay there under the condition that the property would be left to my sister and me in her will. My father spends his days now playing golf in Palm Beach and has since gone back to his debutante days, breaking hearts. My mother often says, "You can't teach an old dog new tricks, and your father has always been an old dog."

I graduated from UNC Chapel Hill in the spring, cum laude, and immediately set my sights on New York City. It was the only place I ever wanted to be. Plus, I'd broken up with my high school sweetheart Ryerson Bigelow the year before, and I was still struggling with the fact that we weren't together. We'd fallen in love when I was a sophomore in high school and he was a senior, but we'd known each other for far longer. It just happened one day. I was walking home from school on a perfect fall day in Charleston. He came out of nowhere and tackled me into a pile of leaves. When I got my bearings again, I started hysterically laughing, and we kissed.

Later, he told me it was my reaction that made him realize I was different from the other girls.

"Anyone else would have been furious with me," he said. "You were such a good sport, I couldn't help but fall in love with you."

We were inseparable for six years after that.

And then, suddenly, we were over. I still wasn't quite sure exactly where things went wrong. He'd graduated from UVA and our relationship began to suffer. In the end, he told me he wasn't ready to settle down and get married. The last I'd heard he was traveling around Africa. I couldn't imagine staying in the South, where everything reminded me of my former life with him.

So I set my sights on a career in fashion—the only thing I'd ever been good at, besides tennis, of course. Luckily, New York was the center of the fashion universe. I was determined to turn my dreams into reality.

My mother was skeptical at first.

"New York, Minty?" she said. "What on earth are you going to do there?"

"Get a job in fashion!" I said, annoyed. She'd heard me say this a million times by then.

She shook her head. "Can't you do that in Charleston? We've got our own Madison Avenue right here on King Street. You could open your own shop and—" She paused. "This isn't about Ryerson, is it?"

"Mommy."

She crossed her thin alabaster arms over her chest.

"As long as you're not running away from something," she said, her eyes narrowing.

I scoffed. "It's been over a year, Mother."

"Very well then," she said.

It only took a few calls to some of her clients with apartments in New York before she was able to land an apartment in a "respectable" doorman building on the Upper East Side (although, she noted, "the address is east of Park Avenue, so we will have to do something about that eventually"). And a few weeks later, there I was, an official Manhattan resident at the ripe old age of twenty-two.

Did I have a job? Not yet. Did I have friends? Well, I was working on that. What mattered was that I was in New York City, and if I stretched out my bathroom window and turned ten degrees to the right, I could just make out the very top of the roof of the Plaza Hotel.

And maybe even catch a glimpse of Eloise.

Grin and Bear It

My mother always says it takes about two weeks to get "situated" in a new place. She told me this when I was headed off to sleepaway camp for the first time, and she was wrong. She mentioned it again when she dropped me off at Chapel Hill my freshman year. Again, wrong. And she reminded me of this two-week rule as I boarded the plane to New York.

"Give it two weeks, honey," she said. "Two weeks and you'll be just fine."

Maybe it takes *her* only two weeks to feel situated in a new place, but I guess I move a little slower. Two weeks after arriving in New York, my apartment felt more like a campsite than home. My bed was still technically a mattress on top of a box spring. I barely knew where the good restaurants were let alone where to go if I needed a cute outfit for a party.

Which brings me to my social life. I have always been good at making new friends. In the eighth grade I was voted "most outgoing." People tell me all the time that I have a way of making others feel at ease, of reaching out to the one person in the room who is feeling like an outsider and making them feel included, part of the group.

Unfortunately, *I* was that outsider now.

It's hard to meet people in New York. It's not like Charleston, where you walk down the street and pretty much everyone waves and smiles. In New York, if you wave and smile at someone you don't know, you look like a crazy person.

Sure, a few of my casual acquaintances were probably in the city, girls from camp or the daughters of my mother's clients who'd lived in New York the last time I checked, but I didn't really know these people. Cold-calling Mr. Pierson's second cousin or Harriet Gumble's sister-in-law's niece just didn't feel right.

I figured I'd start meeting new people when I found a job, but even that was slow going. In two weeks I'd gone on a handful of interviews, one at Oscar de la Renta, another at Macy's and one at *Glamour* magazine. The people who interviewed me seemed to like me well enough, but they all ended up saying the same thing: I needed more experience. So I bit the bullet and called my mother for advice.

"What you need, Minty," she said, "is an in."

"An 'in'?"

"A connection. Someone to help you get your foot in the door. God knows I can't do it from Charleston." She paused. "Think about it. You must know *someone*."

I thought for a moment. She was right. There must be someone I could call. But all of the friends I'd graduated with were starting jobs in Atlanta or Washington, DC. What about someone older? Did I know anyone who'd moved to New York a few years back? I pulled out one of my old yearbooks and flipped to the photo of the women of Pi Beta Phi, my sorority at Chapel Hill. There were faces I hadn't seen in years. Lots of pretty faces. And that is when it dawned on me: Emily Maplethorpe.

Emily was two years older and had acted as my "big sister" when I pledged PBP. She had light brown hair and a bright, warm smile. She also happened to be a bona fide New Yorker—the only one I'd ever met. She had grown up on Park Avenue; attended Chapin, one of the most exclusive girls' schools; and had moved back to New York after graduating from Chapel Hill. The last I'd heard, she was working as a publicist for Saks Fifth Avenue, which sounded very grown-up and fancy to me.

I remembered that she'd sent me an e-mail sometime in the late winter, something about a PBP reunion in New York. After searching through some old e-mails, I found it: Emily Maplethorpe, Public Relations Manager, Saks Fifth Avenue. I dialed her direct line.

She picked up on the second ring.

"Minty!" she said. She sounded out of breath. "How *are* you? Oh my God, it's been so long! What are you *doing*? Where *are* you?" I could hear her fingers typing away and phones ringing in the background. "Minty," she said, "I'm kind of busy, actually, but I'd love to catch up. Can I call you back later this week?"

"Oh, sure," I said. "I was actually calling to talk about jobs. I just moved here and I've been interviewing and—"

"Wait. You're in New York?"

More typing.

"Yes," I said. "I got an apartment on Sixty-first and Lexington and I've been trying to find something entry-level in—"

"Hold on," she said.

It sounded like a tornado was coming through her office, there was so much noise, buzzing, and shouting. About thirty seconds later she came back, even more out of breath than before. "Minty, actually, are you busy today?"

I almost laughed out loud.

"Not really."

"Wonderful," she said. "How quickly can you be dressed and out the door?"

———— ◆◇◆ ————

Emily explained she was in desperate need of a "seat filler" for a Saks charity luncheon. One of the VIP guests had dropped out at the last minute, leaving her with an empty seat, and she was panicking. She told me all I had to do was put on a cute dress, sit there, and look pretty, maybe have a glass of champagne and make conversation.

"This is right up your alley, Minty," Emily said. "You're a natural. It's that Southern charm." She hung up.

I caught a glimpse of myself in the mirror over my dresser drawers, bed head and footie pajamas and all. I looked more like a five-year-old at a slumber party than someone who might be invited to attend a charity luncheon at Saks Fifth Avenue. Call me naïve—and I was at the time—but I had never been to anything with VIPs and free champagne and "seat fillers."

Okay, so I could certainly put down a glass of champagne, but what in God's name was I going to wear? I immediately called Emily back.

She did not seem as happy to hear from me this time around.

"Minty! You've been to a million parties. Just wear a dress."

"But what kind of dress? Short? Long? Dressy or more casual?"

I had already pulled out the majority of the contents of my closet—everything from BCBG to Céline—and had started a pile on my bed, a vortex of ruffles, bows, and various shades of pink.

"Minty, I have to get back to work," Emily said. I heard the tap, tap, tap of her fingers on the keyboard. "I don't have time for this."

"But, Emily, I don't even know where to begin!"

"Just wear what you feel most comfortable in!"

Click.

I had less than two hours to be washed, primped, and ready to attend my very first New York event.

<hr />

When I walked into Saks, I felt like a kid in a candy store. That is, if candy came in patent leather, ostrich, and sumptuous suede. Ladies in sleek black suits offered me a sample of the latest designer perfume. Women popped in from work to fawn over the latest handbags: Burberry, Dior, Marc Jacobs, Prada. Even the elevators were glamorous—gilded and polished, lined up at the back of the store like gateways to heaven.

"Wow," I said out loud.

There's a Saks in Charleston, but compared to the Manhattan

flagship it might as well have been a Piggly Wiggly. It didn't buzz like this. It didn't sparkle like this. For a moment I was so dazzled that I almost forgot I had somewhere to go. I rushed for the elevator just as the doors began to close and pressed "8."

Emily greeted me straightaway. She looked different than she had in college. Slimmer. Sleeker. She wore black from head to toe and a little headset like you sometimes see PR girls wearing in the movies.

"Minty, honey," she said. "You look so . . . colorful."

"Thanks, sweetie," I said, smiling.

The outfit I'd eventually decided on was a bright pink Alice and Olivia baby doll dress with an empire waist, with black patent leather Mary Jane Manolo heels. I'd had only half an hour to do my hair, but I made sure every curl was perfect. I'd recently taught myself how to apply false eyelashes, the ones that come in long strips and make your eyes pop like a movie star's, and that morning I'd applied them liberally.

My outfit *was* colorful. But what's the point of getting dressed up to go out if you look like you'd rather be at a funeral?

Emily guided me toward the back of the floor. "How are you?" she asked. "I can't believe you're in New York!" She paused. "Wait, is Ryerson here?"

I looked at her, then down at the floor.

"Oh," she said. "I see. We'll get to that later." She narrowed her eyes and looped her arm through mine. "Come on, we have a charity lunch to attend."

The luncheon was being held in the midst of the designer collection section. About ten round tables were set up in a figure-eight formation, topped with cool silvery gray tablecloths and flower arrangements, bursting with some of the largest white peonies I have ever seen. The sparkle of the tables complemented the surrounding clothing. There were beaded gowns from Elie Saab hanging gracefully in one corner and structured cashmere trousers from Ralph Lauren in another. I had never seen so much amazing fashion in one place.

The guests ranged from an elderly woman in a colorful caftan and large, round, black-rimmed glasses to a twentysomething man in high-water pants and shiny brown oxfords. The guests stood in little clusters in front of the tables, holding delicate champagne glasses by the stems and staring over one another's shoulders. No one was making conversation. It was as if there was an unspoken agreement: they were there to observe and judge, not to interact.

I leaned in and whispered to Emily. "What exactly am I supposed to do?"

She gave me an exasperated look, then grabbed my arm and ushered me to the side of a photographer who was furiously snapping away. I watched him, mesmerized. He had longish hair and a weathered Irish face. He moved sporadically, instantaneously, like he had the power to disappear and reappear.

As I was standing next to Emily, waiting for some direction, he turned toward me.

"Oh, wow," he said. His eyes traveled up and down and zeroed in on mine. "Look at you! You're like a little doll—all prim and proper." He stepped back and held the camera up. "You're like something from a bygone era. I've *got* to get your picture. Do you mind?"

I just stared.

Did I mind?

Gosh, I wasn't sure. No stranger had ever asked to take my picture before. For one, who was this man? And why would he want to take my picture? What was he using these photos for? Where the hell did Emily go?

"Richard Fitzsimmons," he said, holding out his hand. "You're new to this stuff, aren't you, honey?"

I shook his hand and looked around again. No sign of Emily.

"Yes," I said, smiling. I always smile when I'm nervous. "Yes, Mr. Fitzsimmons. Richard? Sorry, so nice to meet you. I'm just—I'm a friend of Emily's and . . . Oh gosh, I'm rambling."

Richard just smiled. "I like the accent!" he said. "Sort of Scarlett O'Hara meets Delta Burke. Charming, just charming."

I was about to curtsy as a joke, but just then a waiter came out of nowhere with a tray full of little chicken skewers. He ran right into me. The peanut sauce landed squarely on my arm and began dripping toward my dress. I held my dripping arm out in front of me, mortified, watching the peanut oil run down my fingers and swan-dive toward the pristine silvery carpet.

Oh, shit! I thought.

Only I didn't just think it—I said it aloud as well. The moment I realized that I'd cursed aloud, I cupped my hand over my mouth, mortified. I gaped at Richard, shaking my head as if to say, "That did *not* just happen!"

Language—cursing—was my one bad habit. And here I was at a private luncheon in the middle of Saks Fifth Avenue, standing in front of some sort of society photographer, and I had just used a not-very-ladylike word. I pictured my grandmother, six feet below in the Charleston cemetery, clutching her Hermès Kelly bag to her chest and having a dead-person heart attack.

Richard cocked his head. Then he started nodding up and down until his whole upper body joined in on the motion, shoulders moving, chest heaving. He was laughing. Laughing at me, really. But there was nothing mean-spirited about it. He grabbed a napkin, dipped it in water, and helped me clean up.

"Much better," he said, examining my arm. He stepped back again, raised an eyebrow. "Photo?"

"Really?" I asked. I was still recovering from the chicken skewers mishap. He motioned for me to get in place, so I obliged. Oh well, why not?

I stood back a little and smiled toward the camera.

Click, flash! And it was over.

"Minty, there you are!" Emily had magically reappeared just as Richard finished taking the shot. She pulled me toward one of the tables at the center of the room.

"Wait!" Richard called out after me. He was holding his camera up in the air. I noticed a tiny microphone tilted toward me.

"Your name?" he asked.

"Over there," Emily said to me, ignoring him. She pushed me gently toward the grouping of tables in the back. "Table six, toward the corner on the right."

"Emily, dear, what's your friend's name?" Richard yelled after us. I turned around in time to see him wink in my direction.

Emily looked at him and laughed. "Richard, she's no one."

It was Richard's turn to laugh now. "Not for long," he yelled after us. "Not for long."

———❧———

I took my seat at the table next to a girl who was wearing really expensive clothes that didn't actually look expensive: a Dries Van Noten T-shirt that hung over her skin-and-bones frame, Helmut Lang jeans so skinny I swear they were child size, and some sort of bondage wedge that could only have been Alexander Wang. Her long, dark hair looked unwashed but smelled like lavender.

I tried to introduce myself, but she just looked at me and raised an eyebrow. So I tried again. "I'm Minty," I repeated, holding out my hand.

She didn't take it. Instead, she made that sound people make when they're not impressed: humpf. Was I hurt? A little bit. But I figured maybe she was just having a bad day. Or maybe she hadn't heard me. I always try to give people the benefit of the doubt.

"Minty," I said for the third time in a row, making eye contact.

She tilted her head and looked right back at me.

"Julie," she said flatly.

"Nice to meet you, Julie."

I always repeat a person's name out loud. It helps me to remember it and—as my mother has been telling me since I was basically an infant—people are usually charmed by the sound of their own name. It's an icebreaker, a peace offering. And if I were going to get through this lunch without stabbing my eyeball straight through with my salad fork, I needed all of the icebreakers and peace offerings I could get.

Julie grumbled, "You, too."

"Minty, I see you've met Julie Greene from *Harper's Bazaar*."

It was Emily. Wow, I thought, Julie works at *Harper's Bazaar*? I was beyond impressed (and jealous!). When Emily sat down, Julie perked up immediately. It was like we'd just gone from being enemies to old friends in a matter of seconds.

"Oh, you know Emily?" Julie asked.

"Yes," I said. "We were actually sorority—"

"Minty, honey," Emily interrupted. She leaned over me, speaking to Julie, and said in a very knowing tone, "Minty just moved here from South Carolina."

Julie raised an eyebrow. "Oh? How . . . nice."

She smiled at me like most people smile at small children.

"Julie handles the party pages for *Bazaar*," Emily explained.

"That's amazing," I said. "I've been reading *Harper's Bazaar* since I was five!"

Julie responded to my enthusiasm with a smirk.

Just then, our waiter arrived. Or, I should say, *waiters*. It seemed as if there was one impossibly good-looking and impeccably outfitted man for every two people. They placed the food down in front of us in one single swoop and promptly disappeared. In front of me was the most gorgeous arrangement of ripe, red tomatoes and buffalo mozzarella I had ever seen. Although the portions were so tiny!

"Olivier Cheng," Emily said, pointing at the dish.

Olivier who?

"Is this the appetizer?" I leaned in and asked.

"Eating is not exactly the main priority at these things, Minty," Emily explained.

Oh.

I looked at Julie, who was sipping slowly from her glass of water, her salad untouched. The small piece of bread that had been placed on the plate next to her salad had somehow migrated toward the center of the table, as far as Julie's tiny arm could reach. It was as if she didn't even want to smell the bread, let alone eat it.

A woman came over to the table and whispered something into Emily's ear. She wore a severe, pulled-back hairstyle and a very form-fitting shift dress. I wondered how she could breathe. Emily immediately put down her fork, got up, and followed the woman over to the other side of the room, near the elevators. Their pace was more of a slow run than a fast walk. Then, a group of young women carrying notepads joined them, followed by Richard Fitzsimmons and a trail of other photographers. The guests put down their drinks and glanced casually in the direction of the elevators as a hush came over the room. Julie sat up in her chair, yawned slightly, and checked her BlackBerry.

The elevator doors opened then and a woman exited, followed by a younger man in a tailored black suit and crisp white shirt. He stood aside as the photographers screamed, "Tabitha! Tabitha! Over here!"

It was like the biggest celebrity in the world had just entered the room. I strained to get a better look, but all I could make out were flashes and hands waving in the air and a glimpse of Tabitha's long, bright blonde hair. At one point I even saw Emily shouting at one of the photographers to step back. Her face was the color of rhubarb pie and she looked like she was going to pass out.

"Tabitha! With Tripp! Get together, you two! Come on!"

Tripp, I repeated to myself. I craned my neck for a better look. The broad shoulders; the dark, almost black hair; the piercing eyes and sideways grin. Oh my God, I thought. It was him. Tripp du Pont.

"You're whiter than the tablecloth," Julie said. "Are you okay?"

I gulped and nodded. "Sorry," I said. "I just saw someone I used to know."

She raised an eyebrow.

I watched as Tabitha and Tripp made their way toward their table. I couldn't believe it. After all of these years, there was Tripp du Pont. The last time we'd been in the same room together I was fifteen years old and I thought I couldn't be more in love with the dashing, sophisticated older boy from New York. I spent an entire Christmas break in Palm Beach with him, flirting poolside at the country club, meeting up on the golf course at night to steal a kiss. The last night of Christmas break we both attended a dinner party at the club. I was standing at the bar ordering a Diet Coke when I overheard Tripp's mother's friend asking someone about Tripp's girlfriend back home in New York.

I ran out of the room crying that night and never saw him again. Luckily, a few months later I met Ryerson. But now, seeing Tripp in front of me for the first time in seven years, on the arm of a glamorous older woman, no less, all of those first-crush feelings came rushing back.

I was so in shock, I hadn't noticed that Emily had returned to the table and was speaking to me. "This is huge for us. Tabitha Lipton!"

Tabitha Lipton.

I remembered bits and pieces of her story from reading the gossip columns. She was in her late thirties, an heiress to the Lipton tea fortune who had married a member of the British aristocracy. They were recently divorced, and she'd managed to take a good portion of his family's fortune in the end. And now she was stepping out with Tripp du Pont? *My* Tripp du Pont?

My stomach turned. He wasn't exactly *my* Tripp du Pont. But at fifteen, I thought he was the most perfect boy I'd ever met, and his betrayal felt like the end of the world to me. Truthfully, I'd never stopped thinking about Tripp. And to see him now without even the slightest warning . . . it knocked the wind out of me.

The waiters removed our plates.

"She hasn't officially been out since the divorce, you know," Emily continued, leaning over me so Julie could hear. "We'll set up another shot with Tabitha just for you in a few minutes, now that the rest of the photographers have left."

Julie nodded. "Fine."

I couldn't help but wonder if all editors were this grumpy. I pursed my lips, dying to tell Emily about my history with Tripp.

"Anyway," Emily continued, "you know Tabitha. I bet she'll talk your ear off."

It's a good thing Emily was speaking under her breath, because Tabitha had somehow made her way over to our table and was now standing behind Emily, holding a glass of champagne and waiting for Emily to notice.

I gasped a little, suddenly feeling like I needed a much better outfit, a nose job, and a professional blowout.

"Emily, darling," she said. "Where is *Bazaar*?"

I glanced over at Julie, who seemed even more annoyed than usual, then back at Tabitha, who was searching the room with an exasperated look on her face.

Caught in the middle, Emily attempted to appease both parties.

"Tabitha, you remember Julie Greene, don't you?"

She shot Tabitha a pointed look.

"Julie! Julie, darling, of course," Tabitha said. She waltzed over to Julie and took her hands. Julie pursed her lips and huffed. "How are you?" Tabitha continued, oblivious. "How is *Glenda*? The three of us must do lunch. It's been way too long. It's a crime!"

Julie's expression was just short of a sneer.

I glanced at Tripp and I think he smiled at me. But it was more like his eyes squinted first, and then his teeth showed a little, and then he turned red and looked away. I wanted to smile back, but then I noticed that Tabitha had a *What are you looking at?* expression on her face, and decided I should probably refrain from saying hi to Tripp. For now, at least.

Then Richard Fitzsimmons appeared out of nowhere.

"Girls. Girls," he said. He pointed at Tabitha, Emily, Julie, and then, much to my surprise, me. "The four of you. Let's do a picture."

Emily immediately refused, citing that she was under strict rules not to be photographed at her own events. "Okay, fine," Richard said. He looked at Julie, who was also opting out, minus an explanation. Which left Richard with Tabitha and me. I gulped and glanced at Tabitha, half-expecting her to laugh in my face.

"Darling," Tabitha said. She gestured toward me. "Come over here."

I shuffled over to her side feeling like a deer in headlights. I could see Tripp out of the corner of my eye, taking it all in.

"Look at her, Richard," Tabitha cooed, turning her body to the left so it formed one long, lean line for the camera. She placed a bejeweled hand on her jutting hip. "You're new."

"She's my latest discovery," Richard said.

I smiled meekly and looked at Emily, who was standing to the side of the spectacle with a curious look on her face. She twisted a strand of hair around her finger and tilted her head to the side. She squinted and released the tiniest of smiles.

I was taught how to pose for a photo the moment I could stand straight on my own, but when Richard lifted his camera, I don't know what happened—I froze. My arms hung at my sides, hands slack and motionless. The flash went off several times. With each pop, with each blast of light, Tabitha turned slightly or lifted her chin or smiled in a different way. I just stood there, terrified.

When Richard was finished, he kissed Tabitha on both cheeks and pointed toward me. "I've got your name, kid," he said.

All at once, everyone in the room knew that it was time to leave.

In the midst of waiters sweeping the tables of any remnants of food, I attempted to get a word in edgewise with Emily, but she was so preoccupied that I found myself the last person at the table, watching Tabitha usher Tripp toward the elevator.

I could have sworn he looked back at me, just once, but I couldn't tell for sure. And then—poof—Emily was thanking me for "helping out so last-minute" and I was in a cab headed home.

<hr />

The next morning, I woke up to no less than seven missed calls from Emily. Thankfully, she'd only left one voice mail: "Minty. The second you wake up, run out and pick up a copy of *Women's Wear Daily*," she said. "Call me as soon as you do."

I immediately made my way to the corner bodega, where I found a copy of the fashion industry's go-to daily newspaper. I leafed through the contents: a story about a new beauty brand, a report on the earnings of Louis Vuitton, a fashion shoot featuring jean trends for fall. And then I saw it: the "Eye" page. "Eye" was a special section that ran stories on industry events several times a week. In the center of the page was the photo Richard took of Tabitha and me at the Saks Fifth Avenue event. And there was my name next to Tabitha's! Well, at least an approximation of my name: Mintzy Darvenport.

Eeek. It wasn't the most flattering photo I'd ever seen of myself. I put the paper down and grumbled.

My phone started ringing.

"Minty!" It was Emily. "Minty, did you see it? Did you see *WWD*?!"

"Yes," I said.

I walked toward Lexington Avenue and waited for the light to change. I wasn't sure how I felt. It was cool to see my photo in a newspaper and to be standing next to someone like Tabitha Lipton. But I couldn't get over the fact that I looked, well, awkward.

"What's wrong?"

"They spelled my name wrong."

Emily laughed. "We'll have them do a correction."

"And I look kind of fat."

She laughed again. "That's ridiculous."

"I could have smiled better."

"Minty, sweetie," Emily sighed, "you're in *WWD*!"

I looked up as the light turned green. "Is it that big of a deal?"

"Yes, Minty," Emily said. I could hear the smile in her words. "It's that big of a deal."

The second I hung up with Emily, my BlackBerry buzzed. For a second I almost thought she was calling me again, but instead I found an e-mail notifying me of a Facebook friend request.

It said, simply, "Minty, is this you?"

The note was accompanied by Tripp du Pont's handsome profile photo.

2

Smile through the Pain

I couldn't help myself—I was excited that Tripp had reached out. I tried to look on the bright side of things. It was very possible that twenty-four-year-old Tripp was more mature than seventeen-year-old Tripp. Maybe he'd even learned from the mistakes he made with me. Then I remembered he had a girlfriend. Or at least I thought Tabitha was his girlfriend. So . . . should I take the friend request at face value? Tripp was never my "boyfriend," but we were certainly more than friends. And while he'd hurt me, there was always . . . *something* between us. Even the way he looked at me during the lunch. I was more confused than ever.

I called my mother.

"Tripp du Pont," she repeated. "If I do recall, not the most *solid* of citizens."

"Mother, we were teenagers."

"You were enamored with him," she reminded me. "And he spent all of Christmas break acting like your boyfriend."

"All right," I said. "He hurt me."

"Do not write him back," she said.

"But, Mother, it's been years. Maybe he's matured! I can't just ignore his friend request."

"What the hell is a friend request anyway?"

"Well, it's when—"

"Heavens, Minty, I know what it is. What I'm trying to say is . . . couldn't he have found you some other way? It just feels cheap to me. I say you make him wait."

"Of course I will make him wait."

"One week, Minty."

"One *week*?"

"One week."

"Fine."

"I mean it."

"Fine! One week."

I accepted the request approximately twenty-four hours later. I wrote him a quick, cute message about how I thought I'd spotted him at the Saks luncheon, how he looked nice and I hoped all was well.

I didn't disagree with my mother, but the thought of waiting an entire week was overwhelming. I figured that a day would be enough. It would seem as if I were simply busy, nonchalant, running around town with so many things to do that I hadn't had a moment to check my Facebook profile. A week just screamed "overthinking it" to me. I didn't want him to think I'd spent the last seven years dwelling on what happened between us.

Of course I liked the thought of his sweating it out even if just for twenty-four hours. I pictured him sitting by his computer, clicking the "refresh" button over and over again, pounding his fist onto his desk in frustration. So when I finally, officially accepted, I figured he might jump at the chance to perhaps drop me a line and, I don't know, ask me to dinner.

But there was silence.

A day later, Saturday morning to be exact, I was still waiting for a response when Emily called.

"Wake up," she said. "We're going to Swifty's for brunch. It's, like, a crime you've been in New York for almost two months now and you haven't been to brunch at Swifty's. Also, someone is coming who you need to meet, so we're doing it. We're going to brunch."

"Emily," I groaned. "The last thing I need right now is to be set up."

"Don't be ridiculous, this is not a setup. It's more of a . . . networking opportunity. And this person is rarely available, so I'd get my act together if I were you."

"On a Saturday morning?"

"Minty, this is New York."

"*Right.*"

I'd mentioned my desire to break into the fashion world to Emily at the Saks luncheon and she seemed to think it would be easy to find me something (which was surprising, seeing as I'd been on more interviews than I could remember in the last month). She said a friend of hers owned a PR firm and that she would check with her to see if they were hiring. I never thought she might actually make something happen.

"Gosh, Emily," I said. "I'm not sure I'm ready for this."

"Give me a break, Minty," she said, "I have been up since six A.M. for hot yoga and I'm currently alphabetizing my fall wardrobe by designer."

Her voice echoed like she was speaking through a bullhorn into a microphone. She must have had me on speakerphone.

"Hot yoga?" I said. "That sounds like torture!"

"It's a necessary evil, Minty," she explained. "Size two isn't small enough anymore. Just the other day, Marchesa sent me some samples for the Whitney Art Party, and—hand to God—they were size double zero. What am I supposed to do, send them back and tell them that nothing worked?"

"I think my left pinkie might be a size double zero," I sighed.

"Don't be ridiculous," she said. "Anyway, this networking opportunity . . . well, I wasn't going to say anything because I didn't want you to get all nervous and overthink as you tend to do, but it could lead to an actual job."

At that point, my idea of a "job" had nothing to do with the reality of an actual entry-level position: twelve-hour days filled with constant coffee runs and standing in front of the paper shredder so long you go to bed with a buzzing noise in your ear. Instead, I thought the perfect job in New York would be something extremely glamorous and would signal my acceptance into the exclusive club of New York career girls who ruled the city. In my imagination, these girls did little more than sit inside large, glass-walled offices all day drinking skim lattes from Starbucks.

"Meet me on Seventy-third and Lex at eleven. And don't be late," Emily said.

She hung up the phone.

⸺◈◈◈⸺

Swifty's was dark, with lots of oil paintings of dogs and pheasants and crisp white tablecloths.

For the one billionth time, I felt completely out of place. Nearly everyone was dressed like they'd just come from a ride at the stables. I had never seen so many shades of brown! I, on the other hand, was wearing a floral-print tea-length dress, platform Brian Atwood pumps, and a white overcoat with a ruffled collar. As I approached Emily, who was already seated at a table in the back, I could tell from the expression on her face that I had swung at the fashion fastball and missed.

Emily was wearing a camel cashmere sweater and khaki-colored stretch pants tucked into knee-high cognac riding boots. It worked on Emily but when I pictured myself in the same ensemble, all I could think was, Frumpety frump frump.

"You look adorable," she said.

But her tone did not say "adorable." It said "interesting."

"I have a hard time dressing for day," I admitted.

It was true. I don't even own that many items of clothing that might be described as appropriate for day. Every once in a while I find J Brand jeans and a pair of Delman flats in my closet and wonder how they got there.

"I remember," Emily said, smiling. "It's nothing a little trip to Bergdorf's won't fix." She leaned in. "So, quickly, what happened with Ryerson? I thought for sure you'd be married by now. You two were like the perfect little couple."

I looked at the ceiling. "Ryerson decided he had some soul-searching to do," I said. "That was over a year ago. The last I heard he's still . . . searching."

"I see."

"We were young," I continued. "I guess it just wasn't meant to be."

I had just picked up my menu, hoping for a change of subject, when I felt someone standing just over my shoulder.

"So *this* is the perfect candidate you were referring to?"

I turned around to see a woman as thin and spindly as a daddy longlegs, her wrists so slender they barely supported the weight of her Cartier Tank watch. Her hair was the palest silver gray, shaped into a perfectly symmetrical bob. She was probably in her late forties or early fifties, but her skin was smooth, without so much as a speck of sun damage. When she spoke, she pronounced each word in a loopy, soprano staccato, like one of those European ambulance horns. She was, in one word, intimidating. If I were allowed two words to describe her, I would add "hard."

"Ruth!" Emily exclaimed.

Emily immediately stood up. She and Ruth engaged in some form of multiple cheek-kissing that happened so fast, it was almost as if it didn't happen at all. When Emily turned to introduce me, I was already standing. From a very young age, I was trained to greet any new person at a table by standing up almost immediately and with as much enthusiasm as possible.

"And yes," Emily said, "this is your candidate—Minty."

I stared back at Emily, then Ruth, then back at Emily again. "Minty Davenport," I said, smiling my best smile and making eye contact with my potential future employer. "Pleasure to meet you, Ms. . . .?"

"Vine," Ruth said. "Ruth Vine. But please, call me Ruth." She glanced at Emily and winked. "Makes me feel younger."

"It is a pleasure to meet you, Ruth," I repeated, smiling.

Ruth's handshake was firm, a bit chilly. I noticed she wasn't wearing a wedding ring. I could instantly tell she was one of those New York power women my mother had warned me not to become: independent, unmarried, and proud of it.

"Please, please, ladies, sit down," Ruth said, motioning to the waiter to bring over an extra table setting. "Shall we order some wine?"

Emily nodded and shrugged. "Why not?" She grinned.

I agreed. In the South, drinking is an all-day affair, although it usually involves a little bourbon or Jack, not sauvignon blanc.

Ruth grabbed the chair from the table behind her and plopped down, swinging her body sideways so that her impossibly long, Wolford-stockinged legs extended directly into the center of the room. The waitstaff, forced to step over Ruth's legs, eyed her suspiciously.

"Darling, how is Bruce?" Ruth asked Emily.

Bruce was Emily's boss, the CEO of Saks Fifth Avenue.

"Oh, God," Emily sighed. "What am I supposed to say these days? Cautiously optimistic? It's a whole new landscape out there. We're adjusting."

Ruth's eyes twinkled. She leaned toward Emily, her shoulders squared, her whole body charged with conviction.

"Resilience, Maplethorpe, resilience," she said. She stopped and fiddled with the silverware at her place setting. "Jesus Christ, what am I saying?" she continued. "It's a fucking nightmare out there right now. I'm lucky to have the means to hire an assistant"—she glanced at me—"let alone run a healthy business."

The waiter came over and poured a generous amount of wine into each of our glasses.

"Which brings me to the blonde," Ruth said, ignoring the waiter and turning in my direction, her eyes two sharp, inquisitive darts. "Minty, is it? You Southerners. You crack me up. So what are you all about, Minty? Tell me your story."

I began, my voice a little shaky and low. "Well—"

Emily intercepted. "Minty's a PBP girl. Chapel Hill, cum laude, Charleston born and bred. She was my little sister at PBP, so I've known her for years. Her mother is a descendant of Thomas Jefferson and her father is the great-great-great-great-great-grandson of James Madison. Old-school southern-belle transplant, pretty much fresh off the plane." She grinned at Ruth, who managed a brief smirk in return.

I held up a finger. The James Madison part wasn't *entirely* true—he was actually my father's great-great-great-great-great-uncle—but Emily continued before I could get a word in edgewise.

"She'd be perfect for RVPR," she said.

Ruth . . . Vine . . . Public . . . Relations, I spelled out in my head.

"So, Minty." Ruth turned to me. "How do you feel about fashion?"

"Um, my all-time favorite thing?"

Ruth laughed. "And events? How do you feel about parties?"

"Tie for my all-time favorite thing?"

Emily's expression quickly turned serious and focused.

"She's one of the smart ones, though, Ruth. I can promise you, she *gets it,*" she said, implying that the majority of the girls who worked in fashion and events neither were smart nor *got it.*

Ruth nodded and pursed her lips.

"Let me have a look at you," she said, motioning for me to stand up.

I stood straight and proud, maintaining eye contact with Ruth as I smoothed down the skirt of my dress. I gave her another bright, sincere smile. I turned to the left, slightly, then to the right. I put my hand on my hip like a pageant queen.

Ruth seemed to think the whole thing was hilarious, because she let out a howl and slammed her hand down on the table. "You've got to be kidding me!" she said, glancing at Emily, who started to slink lower in her seat. "She's fucking adorable!" She motioned for me to sit down. "You're like a Kewpie doll . . . Anyway, let's get down to the nuts and bolts here. I'm assuming you can type?"

"Um, yes?" I lied, placing my napkin back on my lap. "I type very well."

Ruth furrowed her brow. "Whaddayou call a dress where there's a seam just below the bust?"

"Ahm-peer," I said, pronouncing "empire" correctly.

Ruth grinned. "Nice. Well done." She paused once more and

thought. "Okay, last one. What was the name of Vivienne Westwood's store on King's Road?"

Emily looked at me, bewildered.

I knew the answer to this one! I'd studied Vivienne Westwood in a fashion history course.

"Um . . ." I paused bashfully and whispered, "Sex."

"Excuse me?" Ruth turned her ear toward me.

"Sex," I repeated, slightly louder.

"What was that?" Ruth leaned closer still. She was starting to laugh, thoroughly amused by my inability to say the word "sex" at a normal decibel level.

"Sex!" I blurted.

This time the entire restaurant heard. Two brunching ladies toward the front turned in my direction and lowered their large sunglasses in order to get a better look at the girl who cried sex.

But the humiliation was worth it, because Ruth leaned toward me and said five fateful words.

"When can you start, honey?"

Emily and I released all the air in our lungs, filling the entire room with relief. Even the waiters, who were watching our table like we were the cast of a bad reality TV show, looked relieved. I wondered if they were going to start clapping or pouring glasses of champagne.

I placed my hand on my chest, feeling it flush with excitement.

I began, "Ms. Vine—"

"Call me Ruth for Christ's sake."

"Ruth," I corrected myself. "I'm thrilled to have the opportunity to work for you." I had to catch myself from leaning over to hug her. "Thank you so much!"

Ruth smiled, wrapped her fingers around her wineglass, and raised it in a toast.

"To Minty," Ruth said.

I blushed as we each held up our glasses and clinked them together one by one.

Be Cute and Quick

Tripp *did* write me back. But it took him an entire week, and an entire week in southern belle time is a lifetime.

The message itself was interesting. And by "interesting," I mean ridiculous and terrible and lazy. It may have been one of the worst messages—including greeting cards and e-mails and text messages—I have ever actually received. I had waited a week to read the words: "Oh, hey."

No more, no less.

I was so boggled by the nothingness of Tripp's message that I instantly began to rationalize. There were so many possibilities: A fire drill! Short-term memory loss! Carpal tunnel syndrome! Or maybe he was just an idiot. There was also that possibility.

Luckily, I was a busy girl. I was right in the middle of my first week as Ruth Vine's assistant. I was so busy that I barely had time to breathe, let alone worry about Tripp and his terrible messaging skills.

"Mintyyyyyy!"

After just three days of working for Ruth, I had already learned to tune out the sound of Ruth's voice screaming my name through the loftlike space of the RVPR offices. Lucky for me, the office intern,

Spencer Goldin, sat next to my cubicle and seemed to have my best interests at heart.

"Minty," he hissed, elbowing me in the side. "Minty!"

I jumped. I had been staring at my computer screen, nearly blinded by the Excel worksheet in front of me. It was filled with what seemed like a thousand yeses and nos and maybes and plus-ones and little notes in the last column marked by an asterisk that said things like, "May be filming in Vancouver but if in town will attend" and "Will only attend if hair, makeup, driver and stylist are provided." I was already in charge of my very own RSVP list for one of RVPR's most important launch events, which was both exciting and terrifying at the same time. Oh, and did I mention the event was happening that night? Gulp.

"Oh gosh," I said, jumping up from my desk. I could practically feel Ruth taking another breath in order to project my name through the loft. "Coming!" I shouted. "Coming, Ruth! So sorry!"

I scampered through the loft in my patent-leather Mary Jane Louboutins, already sad and scuffed from the constant back-and-forth. I could only take tiny steps in my black Theory pencil skirt, and my starchy white blouse was tucked in so tightly I could barely turn my upper body. The only hint of color in my outfit was a large Kenneth Jay Lane statement necklace made up of a cluster of red and orange brooches. Emily had declared that this was the perfect New York career girl outfit, but I thought I looked more like a cater waitress with great taste in costume jewelry.

"Minty, Jesus, you've got to get your ass here faster. My office is like twenty feet away."

Ruth liked to exaggerate. Spencer had actually measured the distance between Ruth's office and her assistant's desk, and it was closer to three hundred feet, or one hundred yards. So my constant back-and-forth was nicknamed the "hundred-yard dash," which was funny to everyone in the office but me.

According to office lore, Ruth purposely positioned her assistant's desk on the opposite side of the loft so everyone could watch whatever poor soul it happened to be that year (or, sometimes, that *month*) running back and forth, desperately trying to please her. "We've got less than four fucking hours to get our shit together on this Hermès launch and I haven't had a guest-list update from you since"—she paused, looking at her watch—"since something like almost a half hour ago."

She also liked to stress.

"So sorry, Ruth," I said. "I was just going through several new additions and I was just about to —"

"Save it," she said. "I don't need to know why you're not getting me the information I need. I just need to know the information."

"Okay . . . ?" I said, staring back at her blankly.

She stared back at me blankly in return.

"So?"

"Um . . ." I pursed my lips together. Shit. What did she want from me? "Oh!" I exclaimed, my hands covering my mouth. "One minute!"

I scampered back across the loft to retrieve the updated list. As I perched over my computer and pulled up the Excel sheet, my mind raced. I tried to skim through my e-mails. I knew there were several changes I still had to make, but there was no time! I could sense Ruth's mouth opening and beginning to form the word . . .

"Mintyyyyyy!"

"Coming!" I yelled.

Spencer looked up at me and frowned as I tiny-step sprinted back down the hallway.

"Where is it?" Ruth growled.

I handed over the guest list. I knew very little about what was going on that evening. I knew that we were throwing a party for a new Hermès scarf at the boutique uptown. I knew that this scarf featured some sort of drawing commissioned by an up-and-coming designer and that the collaboration was supposed to be very "cutting-edge" for the brand and would help get a lot of "buzz." Ruth used the word "buzz" a lot, as if *getting buzz* was the most important thing in the world. When I mentioned this to Spencer, he said, "Minty, for a publicist, getting buzz *is* the most important thing in the world." And then he shook his head and walked away.

According to Ruth, this "buzz" would then turn into press, which meant articles in magazines and newspapers, mentions on TV shows, write-ups on the most important blogs, tweets, and such. This, in a nutshell, was Ruth's job. This was the job of RVPR as a whole. Because buzz turning into press often turned into sales, and the bottom line for any company was, well, *the bottom line*. Ruth was very proud that our efforts contributed to the bottom line.

I only kind of grasped all of this, but the pace at RVPR was fast, and I had a feeling that if I didn't "get it," there would be no one holding my hand to make sure I was okay. So I opted for an approach I'd learned as an eager-to-please child: "Be cute and quick about it." In other words, you may not feel comfortable or prepared or even willing, but always put your best game face on and forge ahead or you'll be left in the dust.

"All right," Ruth said, "let's get going. The car is here, yes?"

The car . . . the car.

"Oh! God. Ruth!" I felt like my stomach was turning three somersaults. "I totally forgot. Oh my God. I'm so sorry." I stood there. Like an idiot.

"Jesus Christ," Ruth said, stomping over to her coatrack and grabbing one of the most gorgeous camel Max Mara cashmere coats I had ever seen. She threw it over her shoulders like it was a raggedy old sweater and motioned for me to start moving toward the door. "We'll grab a cab. Get your things and make sure you have a clipboard." She turned to face the office as I scurried toward my desk. "People!" she bellowed over the tops of the cubicles. "This is *Hermès*. I need your A-game. And I needed it yesterday."

She turned dramatically and stomped toward the elevator. I met her there, out of breath and overwhelmed but smiling. The elevator door opened and we were off.

<hr />

The Hermès store on Sixty-second and Madison Avenue smelled like money. There is no other way to describe it. I guess if I were forced to break it down, I would say it smelled like a combination of leather, heavy brass hardware, and money. But mainly money.

Walking in behind Ruth, who kept her sunglasses on indoors much longer than necessary, I felt cool and important by association. The salespeople rushed toward her and took her coat. One of them nodded in her direction and then scurried to the back of the store. No more than two seconds later, he emerged with a chic-looking woman who spoke in a French accent. He introduced her to Ruth as Virginie.

"Zee caterers ahr heeeere," Virginie explained.

Ruth nodded and flicked her finger in my direction with each bit of information. I stood to the side and jotted down notes.

"We are missing zee *fleurs* ahnd zee linens I dunno they are somewhere en route I am told," Virginie continued, speaking so quickly that there were literally no breaths, no punctuation marks, between her thoughts. "All in all vee are not een such bad shape but vee are cutting eet close madame."

"I see," Ruth responded, her exterior calm and collected. She glanced around the imposing space, filled to the brim with every single luxurious item you could possibly imagine: waitlisted Birkin bags, silk scarves so gorgeous they begged to be matted and framed, Collier de Chien bracelets stacked one upon another, nearly jumping onto my wrist and begging, *Take me home!*

"Why is the bar in the back corner, Virginie?"

"No clue," Virginie said, waving her hand around. "You say better in zee front?"

Ruth frowned. "Let's put it over here." She pointed at an area to the right of the stairs. "That way it's away from the chaos of the scarf display but still central. The point is to keep the traffic flowing. You don't want three hundred and fifty people beelining for the back of the store and ignoring Kevin's work," she said. "Still, you don't want them so close when they take their first sip of rosé Moët that they're spilling it all over his gorgeous designs."

There were so many details when it came to planning an event, all of which were second nature to Ruth. Did the cater waiters really need to be wearing those ties? Were flowers even necessary? Where would we store the gift bags? I tried my best to answer these questions with educated guesses: Yes? Maybe? Under the stairs?

Before I knew it, we had solved all of the last-minute problems. The event was set to start in five minutes, my feet were already numb from standing and running all day in my once-precious Mary Janes, and little half moons of mascara had collected under my eyes. I stood in the corner and tried desperately to tidy myself up with the help of a cocktail napkin and a glass of Pellegrino.

"Mintyyyyyy!"

Ruth's voice came bellowing from somewhere in the back room of the store.

"Yes?" I shouted, limping in the direction of her voice.

"I need you on the door," Ruth barked, emerging from the back room wearing a little headset and holding the clipboard I'd brought from the office.

I noticed the clipboard was already locked and loaded with a copy of the massive Excel list I'd been working on since my first day. Ruth shoved the clipboard in my direction and handed me a headset.

"But I thought Nina was handling the door."

Nina was one of the more senior assistants. I was told that maybe I would "shadow" her and observe the process of manning the guest list, but it wasn't even a possibility that I would handle the entire operation. What on earth was going on? I started to hyperventilate slightly.

"I just fired her. So, anyway, I need you to be wearing this at all times. There are going to be cancellations and additions and fires to be put out and they're all going to happen last-minute," Ruth explained, not missing a beat. She stared directly at me. This was Ruth's way of saying, "Are you in or are you out?"

"Okay." I gulped. "Got it." I grabbed the headset and put it on. I held the clipboard over my chest like it was a bulletproof vest.

"Right at the door. List only. No exceptions," Ruth said. "If you have any problems, you just radio over to me. But I don't want to be bothered with bullshit. Got it?"

"Yes, of course. Got it," I said.

The guests started arriving almost immediately, and the process seemed simple enough at first. I would just ask for their name, they would give it to me, I would find it on the list and then check them off. They would smile at me and enter the party. And that was that. But sometime around six thirty P.M., the guests started to arrive at a more rapid pace. Maybe it was my nerves or inexperience (or both), but it seemed like it was taking me longer to find names and the line of people waiting outside was growing longer and more impatient.

"Hellloooo," I heard one voice screaming from the back of the line. "Are you *kidding* me? Honey, pick up the pace!"

One man, who was wearing a floor-length mink coat and a pair of oversized, black-rimmed plastic glasses, insisted that he had received an invitation but had forgotten to RSVP and could I please just let him in? He said he was a friend of the president of Hermès and it would really be a problem if I turned him away.

As he made me flip through the list again, five more people tagged onto the back of the line until it was looping halfway around the block. I had no choice but to radio Ruth over.

She arrived in less than thirty seconds.

"What's the problem here, George?" she said, not so much as glancing in my direction. Ruth knew *everyone*.

"Oh, Ruth, hi!" he said, suddenly turning very shy and conciliatory. "How are you? I'm just explaining to this lovely young lady here that I received an invitation but I totally forgot to RSVP. Can you believe it? So sorry, I'm such a flake."

"You're not on the list, George, go home," she said.

She turned around and walked away.

I stared back at him, shocked. He returned my stare with a squinty-eyed sneer and stomped away, as if it were my fault that not only was he *not* on the list, but he was also *lying* in order to try to gain access to a private event. I couldn't believe it.

The next twenty or so guests went pretty smoothly. Rockefeller? Check. Gugelmann? Check. Hearst? Check. And everyone, for the most part, was lovely and polite. I thanked them for waiting. They obliged. And they all looked drop-dead gorgeous, I might add. I had never seen so much style in one place. Every outfit looked like it was straight out of magazine photo shoot. And then a youngish-looking Asian man stepped up. He was wearing a thin, drapey T-shirt; faded, distressed jeans; and limited-edition Nike Air Jordans. He had an air about him that said, *I am important enough to get away with wearing an outfit like this to a fancy party.*

"Kevin Park," he said, avoiding eye contact.

"Park, Park, Park." I searched my list. I flipped back to the first page and searched again. "Could it be under any other name? Maybe it's under Kevin?" I searched for "Kevin" and came up short.

In the meantime, he looked at me like I had five heads and a tail.

"I'm sorry, sir, I can't find your name," I said.

"You're kidding, right?"

A man behind him stepped forward.

"Sweetheart, we're late for the party. Let us in, will ya?" he said, raising an eyebrow and turning his head to the side. Kevin Park laughed.

"I'm sorry, I'm not allowed to let anyone in unless you're on the list," I explained.

I continued to flip through the sheets of paper, hoping for a small miracle. Ruth must have been checking up on me, because she appeared at my side just then, and (of course) immediately double-kissed Kevin Park and his friend.

"Is all okay, sweetie?" she said to Kevin, holding him by the shoulders.

He looked at me. "We were just having a bit of a hard time at the door."

Ruth looked horrified. "Oh, my God," she said. "Oh Christ, I'm so sorry. Come in, come in." She ushered them through the door while shooting me a look that said, *You idiot, can you do anything right?*

And that's when I remembered. Kevin Park. The *designer.* He was the whole reason they were *having* the party to begin with, and I had almost turned him away at the door. Oh my God, I thought. Could it get any worse?

"Lipton," a breathy female voice said in my ear.

I looked up to see Tabitha Lipton standing in front of me, in the flesh, the Tabitha I'd been photographed with (from the looks of it, she didn't remember me at all), *Tripp's* Tabitha. "Yes, ma'am," I said without thinking.

"Ma'am?" Tabitha repeated, chuckling. "Ma'am?!"

I'd somehow managed to insult her, and of course Ruth chose this moment to check on me again. "Tabitha, come on in, I'm so sorry," Ruth said, pushing me to the side. She turned to me briefly and hissed in my ear, "Get out of the way."

I glanced through the window and watched as one of the other assistants made her way through the crowd. Ruth had radioed for her to take my spot. Just before the other assistant made it to the entrance, she squeezed past a tall, dark-haired man who was taking off his coat. I recognized him immediately: Tripp. Of course. He must have been just behind Tabitha in line, I realized. Now I was totally humiliated.

Once the other assistant had the clipboard in hand, Ruth pulled me away from the line of people and into the street.

"You're dismissed for the night," she said. I could tell it was taking every ounce of restraint she had not to scream at me.

"Ruth, I—I'm so sorry, I don't know what to say."

"Go home, Minty." She stopped, took a deep breath and continued. "Get some rest. I'll see you in the office first thing."

She turned around and left me standing on the corner, shivering in the cold October night air with no taxi in sight and no money to pay for one. I'd left my purse and jacket inside, but what was I going to do? Ask Ruth if I could go grab them? My throat tightened.

I could feel the tears coming. They were definitely coming. I was grateful for the fact that there was no one around to see me cry.

"Minty?"

Tripp.

He was out of breath, as if he had been running after me. His cheeks were all ruddy and flushed. His blue eyes sparkled even more as a result.

"Are you all right?"

I noticed he was holding my jacket and purse. How in the hell did he—

"One of the girls . . . one of your coworkers I think?" he said before I had a chance to ask him. "She was coming out to give these to you and I couldn't help but overhear," he explained, smiling just slightly. He looked down. "You never responded to my message on Facebook."

I scoffed. "You mean, 'Oh, hey'?"

He stared back at me, wide-eyed.

"The message you wrote me sounded like you were writing a formal letter to your headmaster at boarding school or something!" He paused. "I was just trying to lighten the mood."

I narrowed my eyes. "The mood does not feel lighter."

"Minty." He tilted his head to the side and made a puppy-dog face. I couldn't help but smile.

Snap out of it, Minty! Teach that man a thing or two about how to treat a lady! This thought came out of nowhere, in my mother's voice, like she was sitting inside my head, her legs crossed, toe tapping. I stood up straight and brushed the tears away from my cheeks.

"Thank you for my coat, Tripp. And for my purse, as well." I took the coat and the purse. "It was very kind of you to get these to me."

"Oh come on, Minty." He grinned, looking down at me. "Is that all you're going to say? I haven't seen you in, what, how long has it been? Seven years?"

"Something like that," I said.

He laughed. "All right, I see," he said. "Still as *stubborn* as ever."

It took everything inside me not to smile again. It was impossible to deter Tripp du Pont. Where some men might turn away and give up, he forged forward until he got what he wanted.

"Anyway," I said, "shouldn't you be tending to your girlfriend?"

He raised an eyebrow. "Girlfriend?"

"Oh, come on, Tripp." I rolled my eyes. "Let's not go down that road again." He laughed, shocked I'd dared to go there. "That Tabitha lady?"

"Oh," he said, suddenly growing quiet and awkward. He looked around impatiently. "That's kind of a long story. But she's *not* my girl-friend."

Interesting, I thought. *Kind of* a long story? Classic Tripp.

"Right," I said.

"Let's get you home, shall we?" he said, resting his hand on the small of my back. "Where are you staying?"

Avoiding his hand, I stepped into the street as one off-duty taxi passed after another. "Sixty-first and Lexington," I said under my breath. "And I'm not just *staying* somewhere. I have my own apart-ment, you know."

"Got it," he laughed. "Listen, you're never going to find a cab this time of night. And it's raining. Even the gypsy cabs will be taken."

"I'll walk," I said over my shoulder, glancing down at my swollen, blistered feet.

Tripp smirked. "In those heels? You've got to be kidding me."

"It's only a couple of blocks."

"Don't be ridiculous, I have a car right here." He gestured toward a black town car that was conveniently pulling up to the curb. "Zeke will drop you off. Come on. It will take two seconds."

I clenched my fists and checked one more time for a taxi. Noth-ing. And the rain was starting to come down even harder. I couldn't believe it. He was going to win.

"Jesus, fine," I said. "But keep your hands to yourself."

He shook his head and opened the back door for me. "Point taken, Ms. Davenport."

Once we were in the car, I crossed my legs and positioned myself as far away from him as possible. He shut the door.

"I really could have walked," I said, staring out the window.

"Please," he said. "It's nothing."

When the car pulled up to my building, I felt like I couldn't get out fast enough. I was confused to say the least. On one hand, sitting next to him was intoxicating. He made me feel like I was fifteen again, discovering that someone like Tripp even *existed*, let alone liked me back. On the other hand, he hadn't earned the right to spend time with me yet. Call me old-fashioned.

Tripp looked out the window. "I actually grew up a few blocks from here, Sixty-fifth and Park. My parents are on Seventy-first and Park now."

"Oh," I said. "And where are you?" I put my hand on the door handle.

"Zeke will get that," he said, ignoring my question. With those words, Zeke, the driver, popped out of the driver's side and opened the door for me.

"Thank you," I said to Zeke. Tripp followed me to the awning.

"I'm in the same building as my parents, actually," he said, leaning toward me. "Super convenient," he laughed. "My father and I even walk to work together every day."

"You're working at your father's investment firm?"

"Yeah," he said. "But I'm definitely still the low man on the totem pole. You know, my father always said," he continued, lowering his voice and turning his chin down, "'All du Ponts have to learn the value of working your way up. You're not going to start from the top just because you can.'"

"I can see your father saying something like that," I said. Our eyes met and for a moment I was taken back to the first night in Palm Beach. We were at a dinner party with our parents. He whispered in my ear that he thought I was the prettiest girl in the room. I remember feeling dumbfounded—I'd secretly thought Tripp was Prince Charming incarnate for years but I couldn't believe he felt the same way. "So, anyway, thank you for the ride."

"My pleasure, Ms. Davenport."

"Good night," I said.

"Good night."

As I turned away, Tripp grabbed my arm. I felt my heart levitate. I couldn't control the way I reacted to Tripp. It was like he happened *to* me, and I was just a bystander, attempting to deal with the aftermath.

"I'm thinking I should get your number," he said.

I had hoped he was going to kiss me.

"I'm not sure that's such a good idea," I said.

"Come on, Minty," he said. "What else am I supposed to do, tap-dance? Stand-up comedy? Pull a rabbit out of a hat? Recite the alphabet backward while standing on my head?"

I couldn't help but smile.

"Fine," I said.

I recited my number out loud and watched as he punched it into his phone. He immediately hit the "call" button. My BlackBerry started to vibrate and I saw his number pop up on my screen for the very first time. "Just checking you're not trying to pull a fast one on me," he said, turning away and walking toward the car.

I watched him disappear into the backseat, wondering if I would ever have the chance to see that number pop up on my screen again. I immediately saved the number under "Tripp," feeling somewhat foolish about it, wondering if he deserved a spot in my contact list. The back door closed and the car pulled away. And he was gone.

Get Up to the Net

My mother was named after Scarlett O'Hara from *Gone With the Wind,* and she takes the role of Scarlett O'Hara's namesake very seriously. She is an old-school southern belle with old-school-southern-belle values.

My mother's dream for me was not only that I get married as soon as possible but that I marry "well." Tripp probably qualified as "well." My mother had always had a soft spot for him (I think he reminded her of my father, both the good and the bad), but she was also skeptical about my reconnecting with him, and for good reason. She stressed that I had to play my cards close to my chest.

"I'm just saying, I know what this boy does to you," she said to me during one phone conversation. "And I understand that he is a capital-C catch, but it's important you play this very carefully."

"Mother," I said, "calm down. We haven't even been on a date yet."

"But you want to go on a date with him, am I right?"

I was silent for a moment. "Yes."

"All right," she said, wheels turning. "Look at it this way. That boy has always had a thing for you. Let's say the first go-around wasn't the best timing. Maybe there's a reason you've found each other again.

And if you insist on carrying on with this New York City nonsense for longer than a few months, you should probably find yourself someone to make it worth your while."

"Mother, you're getting ahead of yourself, as always."

"Keep in mind, Minty," she continued, "I was married by the time I was your age. If you're going to spend all of your time daydreaming about making dresses, one of us has to focus on the practical things in life. Finding a husband. Having children. You're not a college kid anymore. It's time to get serious."

"Getting serious," it turned out, included a full overhaul of my lifestyle. My mother became borderline obsessed with decorating my apartment and it wasn't long before I was being bombarded with FedEx packages filled with fabric swatches and mood boards.

On the phone one night in early November, I let it slip that Ruth was closing the offices on Friday for some renovations. I immediately cursed myself, knowing my mother would jump at the opportunity to fly up to New York and spend the day with me. She'd been campaigning for weeks for us to visit the Decoration & Design Building so we could get started decorating my apartment. The D & D Building wasn't open on weekends, and it was the *only* place she would shop. As excited as I was to make my apartment a more comfortable place to come home to, I was also desperate to catch up on all of the sleep I'd missed in the process of trying to impress Ruth in the aftermath of the Hermès debacle. But she jumped at the chance to make a plan.

"It will be painless," she said. "Maybe even fun!"

"Mother, I need sleep!" I protested. "Please. We'll do it another day."

"There are no 'other' days, Minty," she said. "You told me yourself that Ruth woman won't let you take a day off before the holidays."

I pleaded with her to let me have the day to myself, but she showed up anyway. At seven A.M., no less.

"Good God, Minty, what have you been *doing* in this place?" Her signature drawl, high-pitched and twangy with a touch of an aristocratic lilt, jolted me from sleep.

When my eyes finally came into focus, I realized I wasn't dreaming. No. She was actually standing over my bed, perfectly dressed and accessorized in a Chanel tweed suit, tapping her foot on the parquet and humming to herself.

I grumbled and slowly came to. No call, no key, no doorbell ringing. How the hell did she get in? I turned over and buried my face in my pillow as I came to a frightening realization: she must have some sort of covert agreement with the doorman.

"Mommy," I whined, pulling the covers up under my chin, "what are you doing here? I was at work until God knows how late last night."

"We'll get to that situation in a moment," she said. "But, honestly, Minty, at least feign some excitement. I haven't seen you in months!" She sauntered over to my bedroom window, where she pulled back the curtains gingerly, as if the fabric was covered in something unseemly

"Minty, honey, these are all wrong," she said, her face scrunched disapprovingly. "What color is this? Chartreuse? Chartreuse in the bedroom! Honey."

I frowned. Her tone had gone from conciliatory to patronizing.

She peered through the windows onto Sixtieth Street and gasped. "Oh," she said. "What an *interesting* view."

My bedroom window looked down onto a perfectly normal New York street, but it was no Central Park.

"What do they call those little corner stores again? The ones where they play the ethnic music all day and sell overpriced cans of soup? I see you have quite the panoramic view of one of those very stores."

"Bodega, Mother," I sighed, sitting up. "Bodega."

"Well. At least you'll never want for scratch-off lottery tickets."

"Mother."

"Really, Minty." She moved away from the window and glanced around the room again. "Any stranger walking into this apartment would think you grew up in a hovel, not one of Charleston's most historic homes."

I sighed. I had been remiss in failing to create the proper environment, and Mother had found me out. And we were only in the bedroom. She still had my living room, kitchen, and bathroom to pick apart.

"Anyway, Mother," I said. "I should probably get dressed."

When I emerged several minutes later, wearing a plum sweater dress and knee-high suede Prada boots, she was positioned in the center of the living room, surveying its contents with disdain written all over her perfectly microdermabrasioned complexion.

She took off her Chanel ballet flats one by one and placed them to the side.

"Sisal, Minty?" She dragged a pedicured foot over the surface of the rug. Her cherry-red toes shone against the drab, oily finish of the cheap weave. I'd bought it because it was quick and easy and I needed a rug! I figured I'd have it replaced before she even had the chance to see it.

"It's just temporary, Mother!" I said guiltily.

She stared back at me, stone-faced.

"There is no such thing as temporary," she said. "Only second-rate."

The last part of that statement I said along with her, I knew it so well.

She glared back at me, annoyed and amused at the same time.

"Don't mock me, child," she countered with a wagging finger, a tiny smile creeping onto her face.

"Mommy," I said, slipping back into a little-girl voice, "I've been very busy. I don't have *time* to decorate. I barely have time to get dressed!"

She looked concerned for a moment; she tilted her head to the side and exhaled. I had seen this look before: serious, then focused, and finally morphing into the calm, resolved countenance of a woman preparing for action.

This is the thing about southern women (and my mother is a prime example of the species): They may come across as sugary-sweet and fluttery at first. They can be frivolous, fragile, trivial even. But not so fast. Beneath the perfectly coordinated ensembles; behind the hair blown dry to perfection; under the lipstick, with lips drawn in first with pencil, filled with a waxy garnet and finally blotted with the most delicate, most exquisite of handkerchiefs, southern women are all backbone. Suggest to my mother that she is not allowed to do something, even intimate to her that there is a possibility she will not be able to get her way, and may God have mercy on your soul.

"Enough with the excuses, Minty," she said.

I humphed and fell backward into my sofa.

"I just praise the Lord your grandmother isn't around to see this. You pick up and move to New York City, leaving behind your family and friends, your hometown, everything you have ever known—"

"Jesus Christ, Mom."

"—adopt some of the more uncouth habits of the North and casually use the Lord's name in vain." She paused dramatically, wiping her forehead with the back of her hand and raising her eyes to the ceiling. "All of that I can handle. All of that is just fine. But this"—she stopped and waved her arms around like Vanna White on steroids—"living in this . . . *situation* . . . with store-bought window treatments and a Bottega on the corner."

"Bodega."

"In *the midtown* of all places, overrun with frozen yogurt establishments and . . . chain retailers."

"I wouldn't exactly call Sixty-first Street and Lexington midtown, Mother. And you had a hand in placing me in this building, which is perfectly safe and in a respectable area."

"If I had known it was going to turn out like this, I wouldn't have let you come up here." She put her hands on her hips. "We've got to do something about this."

I was already dreading Monday, which marked my first Fashion Week meeting. Even though New York Fashion Week was in February, months away, we started planning before Thanksgiving in order to stay ahead of the curve. On one hand, it would have been nice to have a quiet, relaxing weekend to myself, but I couldn't help but agree with her—my apartment was in desperate need of a little TLC and I'd already put it off for too long.

"All right, Mother," I said, secretly excited. "Let's do it."

As Scarlett guided me through the countless showrooms of the D & D Building, she was in rare form (even for her). Fueled by the shock of my halfhearted decorating job, not to mention the words "Bed, Bath and Beyond," it was clear that she was on a mission to create a new life for me—the life she'd imagined I had been living in New York. She moved from Brunschwig & Fils to Manuel Canovas to Scalamandre like we were contestants in some sort of interior design version of *The Amazing Race*.

By the time we'd finished, it was almost four P.M. and I was starting to feel like the D & D had swallowed us whole. We had been in the Schumacher showroom for over an hour.

"Mommy, I'm sorry to interrupt, but the turquoise is just fine and if I don't eat something I'm going to pass out in that pile of silk taffeta over there."

She stopped dead in her tracks and turned to me, fabric in hand. "The *turquazzz*," she began, using the correct French pronunciation, "belongs on a pillow, not a wall, dear," she said, her tone serious, sober. "I'm thinking more along the lines of the chocolate brown grass cloth. It's a bit more dramatic, don't you think?"

I sighed. "Yes, of course. The chocolate brown."

She motioned to the salesperson, who looked more weary than I felt, if that were possible.

"And, fine, Minty," she continued. "We'll finish up for now and grab a bite to eat at Serendipity."

Serendipity is sort of a tradition for my mother and me. Ever since that first trip when I was eight, we made a point of going to Serendipity whenever we were back in New York.

Housed in the basement level of a tenement building and decorated like a turn-of-the-century parlor with white walls and Tiffany lamps, it's like something out of *Willy Wonka and the Chocolate Factory*. The speciality is Frrrozen Hot Chocolate, a large sundae glass filled with rich, chocolatey goodness and topped with an inordinate amount of whipped cream. I was trying to be good (I'd tried on one of Emily's size 00 samples a few days before, and let's just say it didn't exactly fit) but as we walked in and were shown to our table, I told myself, maybe just this once. After all, I'd earned it patiently listening to my mother explain the merits of wool over sisal and gold hardware over stainless steel for the last six hours.

"Well, that's a start at least," she said as we sat down. "I'm going to have to clear the next couple of weekends of course to install everything, but as long as the larger pieces arrive on schedule I should have everything set by Christmas."

"Christmas!"

Christmas was more than a "couple of weekends" away. I had not planned on a houseguest, let alone my mother orchestrating an interior-decorating job worthy of a four-page spread in *Architectural Digest*.

"Minty, calm yourself, I'll stay at the Plaza," she said, holding up a menu. She perused it briefly, lips pursed and eyebrows raised, and then placed it down next to her plate. "Shall we share the Caesar salad?"

This was her way of saying, "Shall we *not* order the Frrrozen Hot Chocolate?"

"But, Mother," I said. "We always get—"

"Focus, Minty," she interrupted. "You're a New Yorker now. I won't have those girls in size double zero dresses outshining you at one of those charity events."

God, I thought. She picks up on everything.

"Fine," I said. "Boring Caesar salad."

Mother flagged down the waitress. "We'll share the boring Caesar salad, sugar," she said to the waitress, shooting me a glance. "Dressing on the side, please."

Over dry lettuce and unsweetened iced teas, I filled her in on my new life. I admitted that New York was not the easiest place for a girl like me to adjust to. Everything was dirty, for one. I was going through shoes like they were disposable pedicure flip-flops and just the day before I'd almost been run over by a bike messenger. And then there was Tripp. Since the night he dropped me off in the town car, he'd been calling me nonstop and was practically begging me to have dinner with him. But I was still feeling slightly hesitant.

Tripp was technically my first love, the first boy I ever kissed. He was sophisticated, confident, charming, and smart. He made me laugh. But he had hurt me, however long ago. If we had any chance of rekindling any kind of romance, we had a lot to talk about. And the Tabitha situation was still so unclear.

I asked Scarlett her opinion on the matter.

"I wouldn't even give this Tabitha business a second thought." Mother paused, taking a sip of her tea and swallowing dramatically, like a motivational speaker taking a break in the middle of a speech. "God gave you a lot to work with, Minty Davenport. So start working with it!"

I couldn't help but smile.

"Thank you, Mommy."

She flicked her wrist at me. "Enough of this 'thank you, Mommy' and 'I don't know' and 'I guess.' Where has the Minty I raised run off to? The one who took the stage at the annual St. Gertrude's School recital when she was just eight years old and wowed the crowd by lip-syncing to 'Material Girl' in a custom-made Madonna outfit? The Minty who led her debutante ball? The Minty who took the St. Gertrude's tennis team to three national championships and went on to captain the tennis team at one of the top Division One universities in the country?"

"I see what you're saying," I began. "It's just—New York is a lot tougher than I think I was prepared for. It's a lot different. *I'm* a lot different. I'm used to fitting in somewhat easily. I've never had to think twice about what I was wearing and if it was appropriate and how much makeup I should be putting on. Here, it's like I can't get it right."

As I was speaking, I noticed that Scarlett had checked out slightly. She was on her phone, texting away to someone. This was not a rare occurrence, especially when she felt that she had already made her point, but it was disconcerting nonetheless.

"Mommy."

She looked up.

"Oh," she said. "Of course, dear. You're different and . . . well . . . welcome to life." Her phone buzzed and she picked it up, glanced at it, and tried to contain a smile. Then she put the phone down and focused again, staring directly at me. "You've got two choices here. You let this get the best of you and come home. Which, by all means, Minty, feel free." I responded by rolling my eyes and sinking back into my chair. "Or, you can get up to the net and volley that ball right back in their faces before they can even anticipate what's coming for them."

I smiled.

"Well, then." Mother motioned to the waitress. "Shall we get going? I already have a few deliveries scheduled for this evening and I'm going to need to be there to make sure everything runs smoothly."

"This evening?"

"Yes, Minty. Do you think I have nothing better to do than decorate your apartment? I have company arriving on Tuesday and three cocktail parties scheduled next week. If we're going to do this and do this right, we have no other choice but to work round the clock."

"I see."

We gathered our belongings and walked onto Sixtieth Street. The light was just starting to dim. There was a crisp, auburn glow that marks the calm before the weekend storm. Some of the higher buildings toward Lexington caught a bit of the sunset and looked as if they were illuminated by a spotlight, while at street level it seemed to be almost nighttime. Dusk had always been one of my favorite times of day, but dusk in New York is like something right out of a movie. As we walked west on Sixtieth, my mother surprised me by stopping on the corner to pull me toward her for a quick squeeze.

"What was that for, Mommy?" I asked.

She stepped back and gazed at me very dramatically. I was starting to feel a bit suspicious.

"I just want to have a good look at my little girl," she said. I tried to pull away, but she kept me locked in front of her.

"I've never gone this long without seeing you," she continued, staring at me so intently I thought she might go cross-eyed. "It's all going to come together," she said. Then she stopped, her eyes widening with what was clearly mock surprise. She directed her gaze behind me and slightly to the right.

"Oh my, look who it is!" she exclaimed.

I turned around and there was Tripp, looking handsome as ever in a wool overcoat and jeans. He was also attempting to look surprised.

Was she serious? Was *he* serious? Did this kind of thing really happen outside of an eighties sitcom? When Scarlett Davenport is your mother, yes.

"Tripp," I said.

"Minty," he replied.

"Oh"—my mother cupped her face in her hands—"isn't this just crazy? Tripp, sweetheart, how are you? It's been years!" She leaned in and touched his arm, lowering her voice. "You know, Minty will have my head for telling you this but we were actually just talking about you! Can you believe it? So funny the way things happen."

"Very funny," I said.

If it were possible, Tripp had less acting ability than my mother, because he broke character and just started to laugh, as if the whole thing was a big joke and there was nothing strange or creepy about the fact that he'd been communicating with my mother behind my back.

"Minty, honey," she said, stopping to get ahold of herself. "You have to admit we planned this all quite well."

"Your mother's the mastermind of the whole operation," Tripp said. His blue eyes twinkled once again, which annoyed me even more. He was like a little child who could get away with anything because he made it impossible to stay mad.

"Well, I really should be going," Mother said.

What?!

"That armoire is being delivered at six P.M. and if I'm not there to sign for it we'll have one ticked-off doorman on our hands."

"M-mommy, I," I stuttered, "I should probably help you?"

"Absolutely not," she said. She looked at me, then Tripp. "The night is young and you two obviously have some talking to do. Why don't y'all grab a drink around the corner and iron things out?"

Iron things out? I was starting to feel faint.

"Tripp, dear, don't make yourself a stranger, now, you hear? I don't want another seven years going by before our next chance meeting on a New York City street." She winked at him. She actually had the nerve to wink at him. And then she swiveled around and scurried away as though if she just walked quickly enough, I would forget she had ever been standing there in the first place.

"I forgot how amusing your mother can be," Tripp said.

"Amusing?"

"She's a pistol."

"Oh, Tripp."

"Anyway"—he looped his arm in mine—"she reminds me of someone I know." He smiled. "One drink, Minty Davenport," he said. "You owe me that much."

It's All in the Details

I believe in fate and just *knowing* within a short period of time that something is meant to be. In fact, my mother always swore she loved my father the moment she saw him, even though she also kind of hated him and definitely threw a drink in his face. She said that she was really just trying to get his attention at the end of the day, and she knew a man like Gharland Davenport wasn't exactly an easy target.

"Anyway," she explained, "sometimes love and hate are the same thing."

I understood what she was trying to say, but I never truly believed it until it happened to me.

Tripp took me to Nectar Coffee Shop on Madison Avenue. We ordered hot chocolate and apple pie. I was so in shock that it took me a good seven minutes to start talking, but there was nothing awkward about those first seven minutes of silence.

"I had to get your attention somehow," he finally said.

I raised an eyebrow. "I'm not sure I would call this 'getting my attention,'" I said. "It's more like, I don't know, cornering?"

He smiled. "A man's gotta do what a man's gotta do."

I stared back at him. That connection, however small, however undeveloped, remained. We both knew it. But was I really ready to rewind seven years and admit how much he'd hurt me? It seemed silly now in the grand scheme of things, but the scars were still there.

"I have to say, Tripp," I began, "I'm totally surprised by this."

He looked taken aback.

"Well," he said. "I'm not sure what you want me to say. I'm happy we ran into each other. I mean, I've been wondering about you for years. Probably since the last time I saw you. When was it? The Christmas party at the club?"

"Yes," I said. "It was the Christmas party at the club. And my memories of that night aren't exactly . . . fond."

"I see." He bristled. "I'm—I'm sorry about that."

"I know we were really young," I said. "And yes—it was such a short period of time. But I liked you so much—I even thought I might be falling in love with you—and you lied to me."

"I know," he said. He stared at his cup of coffee. "What else can I say? I liked you a lot too. If it helps at all I broke up with my girlfriend that spring. It had been winding down for a while. And I wanted to contact you, but then I heard you were dating Ryerson Bigelow."

I narrowed my eyes. "You know Ryerson?"

"I guess you could say that." Tripp smirked. "We've been playing lacrosse against each other since camp in the seventh grade." He rolled his eyes. "He was also UVA's top defenseman."

"I see," I said. Tripp was the top defenseman at Princeton.

"Anyway," he continued, "my point is, I learned my lesson—I should have been honest with you from the get-go."

Okay, I thought.

"Listen." He paused for a moment. "You're too good for me, Minty Davenport." He looked directly at me and smiled. "We both know that. And I screwed it up the first time around. But I want you to understand, I have no intentions of doing that again. I'm a different guy this time around. And all I ask is that you give me a chance."

My heart raced. The Tripp I knew at fifteen would never have said something so forthright. He would have played it cool.

I thought for a minute.

"Okay," I said, smiling softly.

Tripp exhaled. "Thank you."

"Not to say you're off the hook just yet," I continued, raising an eyebrow. "Tabitha Lipton. What exactly is going on there?"

It didn't take him long to unload the whole story. He admitted that he *had* been dating Tabitha Lipton, albeit casually, but when I came back into his life he couldn't pretend with her any longer.

"Listen, Minty," he said. "I just have a feeling about you, about us, and I think it's worth exploring. I don't know what else to say."

I didn't disagree with him.

That night, he dropped me off at my apartment and we kissed for the first time in seven years. Of course I'd kissed a few boys since Tripp, but what can I say? Every once in a while a person comes into your life and it's just . . . different. Years before, I was head over heels for Tripp. It was like I'd always pictured him in my mind and one day he appeared in front of me, an actual person. Now he'd come back into my life, new and improved. I wasn't going to question it anymore.

The next morning, he followed up with a text message, then a call the next day, and finally a delivery of a dozen white roses with a card that said: "Oh, hey."

———◦◦◦◦———

In the meantime, my mother took up residence at the Plaza Hotel. As I slaved away at RVPR, trying to balance the demands of being Ruth's assistant with the excitement of being wooed by Tripp du Pont, Mother was spending more time in my apartment than I was, orchestrating a most ambitious interior design project. One evening, I arrived home at midnight to find her in the kitchen on her hands and knees, inspecting the newly grouted tile.

"It's in the details, Minty," she said, looking up at me. All I could do was stare down at her, speechless. "Details, details, details."

It turned out this maxim could be applied to many areas of my life, especially my job. Ever since my disastrous performance at the

Hermès party, I was determined to prove myself to Ruth. I arrived at work an hour earlier than the other assistants (sometime between seven thirty and eight A.M. each morning). I smiled even when smiling was the last thing I felt like doing, which was usually the case. If I had to cry, I went into the handicap bathroom stall and did it very, very softly. I always carried Clé de Peau concealer and Visine so that when I emerged from the bathroom, I actually looked fresher and more alert than I did going in.

One morning, Ruth asked me to pick up some ballpoint pens for an event. I forgot which type was her favorite and had to ask before I ran out to buy some.

When I popped my head in her office to check, she turned very red, stopped breathing for a moment, and then buried her head in her hands. All I could do was stand there helpless, wondering if I should grab her a brown paper bag.

"Jesus Christ, Minty," she bellowed. "Do you think I have time for this crap? Fucking ballpoint pens? Get a fucking clue!"

Back at my desk, I wasn't sure whether to just make an educated guess or wait for Ruth to miraculously have a charitable moment and remind me on her own. I racked my brain for a memory of Ruth holding a pen and came up with nothing. So I made my way to the bathroom, where I spent approximately four minutes in the handicap stall trying not to cry.

When I returned to my desk, Spencer was there.

"Ruthless just left for lunch," he said, referencing a nickname Ruth had rightly earned in the industry. He used the nickname liberally, while the rest of us were too scared to use it even in the privacy of our own homes. "The coast is clear."

Spencer was a rare find in the fashion world, not because he was charming, clever, and good-looking, but because he was all of those things in addition to being straight (as he once swore in front of the entire office with his right hand on a copy of the Bible).

He had a boyish, prep-school look: dirty blond, sunburned hair and a ruddy complexion. He spent his junior year at Dartmouth abroad in Paris, during which he discovered Flaubert and the merits of the clove cigarette. When he returned to Hanover for his senior year, he decided he would become "a writer." He would move to New York after graduation and pursue a career at *Vanity Fair*.

Even if Spencer were years away from the *Vanity Fair* contributors' page as an RVPR intern, he was determined to schmooze his way up the ladder until his dream became a reality. Which couldn't help but make me think about my own goals. It seemed so far beyond my reach, but I dreamed of having my own fashion label one day. Hopefully the connections I was making at RVPR would bring me closer to that goal. Although sometimes I couldn't help but wonder, was I reaching too high?

"Minty." Spencer rolled his eyes as I sat down with a defeated look on my face. "You've got to stop taking things so personally."

"Forgive me if I'm wrong," I said, "but it's hard not to take it personally when someone tells you to get a—excuse my French—*fucking* clue."

"I grew up in New Jersey, where people in SUVs the size of a third-world country run you off the road if you're not going over eighty miles an hour." He paused and looked me straight in the eye. "It's not personal."

When Ruth returned from lunch, she was holding a small gift bag. I knew the blue shade of the bag well: Smythson. She walked into her office and summoned me via speakerphone. She always waited until she got back into her office to address me, as if she was following some sort of boss/assistant protocol.

Typically, I would have run to her office, but this time around, I couldn't help but walk slowly, like a prisoner walking the gangplank.

When I got to her office, there was something eerie about how calm she was. All I could think was, How am I going to explain being fired to my mother?

Before I could sit down, she rested her hand on the Smythson bag, which was in front of her on her desk, and slid it toward me. "Now,

I'm only going to say this once," she said, staring at me intently. "And if there is even a reason for me to want to say it a second time, well, let's just say I won't even have the chance to say it because you won't *be* here anymore."

"Okay," I gulped.

"Write. Everything. Down."

I picked up the bag and looked inside. There was a pink notebook. I found it curious, seeing as pink was not exactly Ruth's favorite color and, in spite of the fact that it was mine, I had never once worn pink in the office.

"Thank you, Ruth," I said. "I love it. I absolutely love it. I promise to write everything down."

"It had your name written all over it," she said, shooing me away.

When I got back to my desk, Spencer eyed my present suspiciously.

"Oh boy, she got you a Smythson?" Spencer grumbled. "That means you're in deep."

"In deep?"

"Well . . ." Spencer paused for a moment. "It's both good and bad. It means Ruth has a soft spot for you. It also means she's investing in you. Which—how shall we put this?—never ends well."

"Oh," I said.

One morning, about a week before Christmas, I arrived in the office extra early in order to get a head start on my growing to-do list.

I was praying to get out of the office at a reasonable hour. Tripp had invited me to a dinner at the home of one of his childhood friends, Baron Guggenheim, that evening. We had only been dating for about two months and I was a bit nervous about spending an evening with a group of native New Yorkers who had known one another their entire lives. I wanted some time to get ready.

The one saving grace was that Emily would be in attendance. It turned out that she and Tripp had several friends in common. While she seemed genuinely happy that I would be there, I could also make out a bit of hesitancy in her voice.

"I'm just warning you," she said. "It's a tough crowd."

Fine, but there was no way in hell I was going to play the role of helpless girlfriend swallowed up by a sea of piranhas. I wanted Tripp to see that I could not only hold my own with his friends but also win them over in spite of my lack of a preppy Northeast pedigree and Upper East Side connections. Emily might serve as a buffer, but as I learned at the luncheon back in September, she was no babysitter. Knowing Emily and her own unique version of tough love, she would probably give me several minutes of her time at the beginning of the party and then leave me to fend for myself, for better or for worse.

All I knew is that I wanted to feel prepared. I wanted to look my best, and there was no way that was going to happen if I was stuck at the office late and had to rush over to the party in my pencil skirt and pumps. I had never once asked Ruth for permission to leave the office in the three months I'd been working there. I figured if I promised to get all of my work done and asked her very nicely first thing, she would understand.

When I arrived at work that morning, it was no more than two seconds before my phone rang.

"I need you in my office," Ruth said.

"Okay." I hung up and grabbed my notebook.

When I walked into Ruth's office, I could tell something was amiss.

"Have you seen this?"

Ruth was holding a copy of the *New York Post*. The headline on the front page said something about a scandal with the NYPD. I wasn't sure. She held it up so fast, I could barely see the picture.

I tried to remember if I was supposed to read the *Post* first thing every day. I wondered if I had something written in my notebook about it and reflexively started leafing through the pages.

"Well." Ruth put the paper down and riffled through a few pages.

"You might want to." She folded the paper over and handed me "Page Six," New York's most notorious, ruthless, and widely read gossip column.

PLAYBOY DU PONT DUMPS TANTALIZING TABITHA FOR SASSY SOUTHERN DEB.

My mouth dropped open. "Oh . . . my . . . God."

Ruth stared at me. "Mmm-hmm."

The first paragraph read: "Move over, Tabitha the Tea Heiress, Minty Davenport is the new Belle of the Ball and she's not as sweet and innocent as she seems. Friends of Ms. Lipton say the socialite was 'shocked' and 'blindsided' by her breakup with Tripp du Pont, one of New York's most eligible bachelors. Sources cite Minty as the 'one and only' cause."

"Oh my God, Ruth," I said. "What is this?" I held the paper up to my face. "Why on earth would they . . . ? What?!" I skimmed the rest of the article, which could be summed up in one word: LIES! They made some reference to my "down-home" Charleston roots and mentioned that my mother "claimed" to be an "FFV," a descendant of one of the "First Families of Virginia." (This was true, actually.) Then they went on to describe my father as a "rug salesman."

"My father is not a rug salesman!" I yelped.

My paternal grandfather had once owned a well-known carpet company, but my father was a successful businessman in his own right! I didn't even know how they *got* that information, let alone managed to screw it up! Not to mention, they were making me out to be some sort of seductress, like I'd stolen Tripp away from Tabitha! I was mortified.

Either way, Ruth didn't seem to care.

"I'm not sure I signed up for this, Minty," she said.

I gulped. Neither had I!

"It's one thing for RVPR *clients* to show up on 'Page Six,'" she said. "It's another thing for RVPR *employees*."

"R-Ruth," I stammered, trying to wrap my head around what was happening, "you have to believe I had nothing to do with this."

"So you're telling me you didn't use one of my connections to get your name in bold print?"

"Oh God, absolutely not," I said, shaking my head. "I wouldn't even know the first thing about something like that."

A lump began to form in my throat. On one hand, I was dealing with the shock of public humiliation. Had Tripp read it yet? Was he freaking out? On the other hand, I was dealing with a boss who had me on probationary terms at best. And to top it off, she thought I'd set the whole thing up on purpose.

Ruth sighed. It seemed like she might, miraculously, believe me.

"All right, then," she said, staring at me. "I'm going to give you the benefit of the doubt. But I definitely have a phone call to make."

"Are you going to call—"

"Absolutely, I'm calling Farah," she said, referring to Farah Hammer, the notorious editor of "Page Six." "She fucks with one of my clients, she's going to hear about it. She fucks with one of my *employees,* well, that's a whole other level of retribution."

I grimaced.

"In the meantime, Davenport," she continued, "I want you to focus. As far as I'm concerned this is over and done with. Is that clear?"

I nodded. "Yes, of course."

<hr />

By nine that morning, word of the item had already spread. I ignored several calls from my mother, two e-mails from Emily, and a text message from Spencer, who was en route to work and had just picked up his copy of the *Post*. But when Tripp's number came up on my caller ID, I had to answer.

"Hello?"

"Minty."

I could hear car horns honking and various voices passing by. He was definitely on the street somewhere, navigating through a crowd and probably clutching a copy of the *Post*.

"Hey, sweetie," I said.

"Listen," he continued. "I'm assuming you've seen this 'Page Six' thing?"

"Ruth just showed it to me."

He sighed loudly.

"This is bad, Minty," he said.

"I don't know what to say, Tripp."

"Do you have any idea how they could have gotten this information?"

I felt my stomach churn. If he was, like Ruth, even *intimating* that I might have planted the story on my own, I wasn't sure I could handle it. My relationship with Tripp was so new. We'd never even had a fight. But he had to know that I would never do something so calculated, so desperate. What kind of person did he think I was?

"Are you serious?"

He paused. "I just . . . I thought I was getting away from this stuff the minute I ended things with Tabitha. Now they're picking up on you like you're fresh meat. It's the last thing I wanted to deal with today, that's all."

A siren zoomed by in the background. I couldn't help but wonder: Was seeking out press, even *negative* press, a frequent occurrence in New York?

"Listen." I took a deep breath. "It is unfortunate, but what are we going to do? People will have forgotten about it by tomorrow anyway."

I felt like I was lying not only to Tripp, but to myself as well.

"You're meeting all of my friends tonight."

"I know, Tripp."

"I just want everything to go smoothly."

If I could have made the article go away, I would have. But wasn't he supposed to support me? Wasn't it kind of his job, as my boyfriend, to make me feel at ease about the whole thing?

Thankfully, my mother's voice chimed in: *Chin up. Smile!*

"Honey, listen," I said, my tone of voice turning from defensive to conciliatory, "it's a little article in a newspaper. I can handle it, and I know you can, too. I imagine your friends are intelligent people who don't believe everything they read. And if, for whatever reason, they *do* believe everything they read, I'll just have to work extra hard to win them over."

When Tripp started talking again, I could tell he was smiling.

"Fair enough," he finally said. "But, Mints?"

"Yes, babe?"

"Promise me one thing."

"Of course."

"Promise me you'll never let this stuff get to us."

"What do you mean?"

"The gossip and the lies." He paused as a loud truck rumbled by. "This world can be vicious. I know it's all new to you, and I just want you to promise me that you won't believe everything you hear or everything you read."

I thought about this for a moment. Of course I wouldn't believe everything I heard or read, but why did he feel the need to get so specific? I didn't want to dwell on it, but there was already a tiny knot in my stomach. Was Tripp anticipating the fact that, in the future, he might have something to hide?

"Of course not, honey," I said. "Of course not."

"Good." His voice was sturdier, more assured. "Okay then, I really should be going. I'll pick you up at eight?"

"Can't wait," I said.

As I hung up the phone, Spencer walked in. He was wearing a dark navy overcoat, a scarf tied around his neck, and a 1930s-style fedora. Somehow, he pulled off the look. I couldn't help but smile.

"It was my grandfather's," he explained before I could even mention the hat. "It's legit."

"It sure is," I said, smiling.

"Anyway, stop trying to take the attention away from yourself, Miss Sassy Southern Deb."

I rolled my eyes. "Seriously, Spencer, I really don't want to talk about that right now."

"Just saying, I have a feeling one day I'm going to be writing about you."

"Spencer, please."

"No, I mean it," he said, his eyes traveling to the ceiling. "It won't be my Kennedy masterpiece. But it will be one of my career-cementing assignments en route to the Kennedy masterpiece. There will be lots of intrigue and extravagance and maybe a little bit of scandal, just for good measure." He paused and thought for a moment. "But I won't slaughter you. I'll put on the kid gloves. Because we'll still be friends."

Spencer was being totally serious and I couldn't help but laugh.

6

Never Let Them See You Sweat

Before dinner, I learned that Baron Guggenheim's family was *that* Guggenheim, the one with the museum. Tripp said that Baron's great-grandfather was a major art collector and his family were still patrons of the museum but they didn't have any real ownership anymore.

In the South, everyone claims to be part of some "old family," but they don't have names like Bloomingdale or Lauren or Trump. They have names like Winterthur and Piedmont and Carter, which are not necessarily connected to anything you can visit or buy in a store. There probably was a time when the Winterthur name was well-known because Mr. Winterthur owned a lot of land in South Carolina and Virginia, but that time is long gone. Southerners think it's better to have an "old" family name than a name currently being traded on the stock exchange.

In New York, "Guggenheim" was good enough, and Baron had certainly made good use of his name. According to Tripp, Mr. and Mrs. Guggenheim began spending December through March in St. Barth's when Baron was about seventeen years old, leaving Baron, who was an only child, to fend for himself in New York.

This could have been a sad, lonely story, but New York is not a sad, lonely place if you are a teenager of means. Baron loved the freedom and began throwing a "celebratory" dinner every year to kick off his parents' departure. Tripp had been attending the dinners for years now, and what had started as a thrown-together gathering of boys with pizza and beer purchased with fake IDs had morphed into a semiformal, catered event complete with an after-party at the club of the moment.

Hence, my anxiety.

By five thirty, I hadn't yet mustered up the courage to tell Ruth about the party and was nearly pulling my hair out over the fear that she would keep me there late. She never exactly told me I was free to go, but a little bit before six P.M., I heard her pass by one of the senior account executives' desks and mention she was leaving for a client dinner.

I waited seven minutes and then made my way toward the elevator, making Spencer promise he would call me if there were any emergencies or if Ruth returned for one reason or another looking for me.

Finally at home, I could focus on my grooming. The dress I chose was a light gray Peter Som. I figured it was feminine, but it wasn't pink or prissy. I paired it with my black patent Louboutin Mary Janes. One of my mother's favorite quotes is from Bette Midler: "Give a girl the right shoes and she can conquer the world." I always keep that in mind when putting together an outfit.

Next, I edited down the accessories: simple hoops, a vintage cocktail ring, and a set of bangles. In the end, I left the cocktail ring at home and instead wore the gold family crest ring my mother gave me when I graduated from high school. I like to keep my accessories as simple as possible.

I had a sudden inspiration for my hair and set some curls with a bit of hairspray, parted my hair on the side, and pinned it over. I was ready to go!

Just before I walked out of the door, I picked up the fifteen-layer caramel cake that I'd ordered specially from Caroline's, a bakery in

South Carolina that thankfully shipped to New York. I'd always been taught to arrive at a party with a present for the host, and caramel cake was my favorite.

As I lowered myself into Tripp's town car, I wondered out loud if the cake was too much.

Tripp looked up from his BlackBerry and placed his hand on my knee.

"They'll probably already have dessert at the party," he said. "It's catered and all."

I nodded, feeling slightly foolish. He was trying to be nice about it, but he was definitely suggesting I should probably do away with the cake.

"Why don't we just leave it here with Zeke," he said, stroking my face. "We can enjoy it later."

We pulled up in front of Baron's building at 812 Park Avenue. Tripp helped me out of the car and guided me through the lobby. The elevator opened up directly into the Guggenheims' apartment. Having an elevator that opens up into your apartment is the New York equivalent of a mile-long driveway lined with magnolia trees. The foyer smelled like priceless oriental rugs and dark wood, which was no surprise, as the entire place seemed to be covered in one or the other. In the center of the main room, visible from where we stood, was a gorgeous Christmas tree decorated in coordinating ornaments.

I stood aside as Tripp and Baron exchanged a familiar hug. Baron took my hands in his and stepped back, his eyes traveling over me.

"Minty, finally, what a pleasure," he said.

He was short, maybe my height if I didn't happen to be wearing four-inch Louboutins. In my heels I nearly towered over him, and I am no Amazon. He had a little belly, as if a can of beer took a pit stop just above his belt buckle, and round, ruddy cheeks. His hair was styled like a little boy's: straight, short, and parted to the side. He had the mischievous look of a person who was not exactly familiar with consequences or rules.

"Please, come in."

As Tripp and I handed our coats to the housekeeper, we saw

flashes going off to the right of the foyer, where people seemed to be gathering.

"You'll have to excuse the photographer," Baron said, guiding us toward the living room. "A friend of mine is an editor at *Harper's Bazaar* and she's been wanting to cover this party for years. I finally gave in."

Finally gave in? Wow, I thought, nonchalance is the unofficial currency of New York. As if having *Harper's Bazaar* at the party was a burden! I wondered if that grumpy Julie Greene girl was the editor. And then I saw her, hovering in the background looking unamused. She glanced in my direction briefly and turned away.

"I'm surprised we never met in Palm Beach," Baron said as we entered the living room. "I spent every Christmas down there until my parents bought a place in St. Barth's."

I wasn't that surprised we'd never met in Palm Beach. I was always too busy playing tennis or spending time with my extended family to really pay much attention to other kids. Besides Tripp, of course.

"Come in, come in."

We followed Baron into the large living room, which had views of Park Avenue and, beyond, the tops of the trees in Central Park. The camera flashed at Tripp and me, nearly blinding us, and I realized the photographer was Richard Fitzsimmons, who had taken that first photo of me at the Saks luncheon, the one that ran in *WWD*. It really is a small world, I thought.

"Richard!" I said.

Tripp looked at me like I was hallucinating as Richard lowered his camera and squinted in my direction.

"Hey, darlin', looking good," he said, stepping back to take another shot.

I posed this time, putting a hand on my hip. I'd practiced this in the mirror a few times since that first time at Saks, determined not to take another unflattering photo.

I wasn't sure if he actually remembered me, the greeting was so quick. But then he asked for my name and I immediately felt a bit foolish. What was I thinking?

"Minty," I reminded him. "Minty Davenport. It's great to see you!"

"Of course," he said, nodding probably just to be polite. "How could I forget a name like that?"

Tripp took my hand and pulled me away, looking a bit bewildered. "Come on," he said. "There are some people you should meet."

I looked around the room. To the left was a cluster of six or seven girls, each holding a glass of champagne. They looked very hungry and very glum. I smiled at them and instead of smiling back, they just stared until I looked away.

In the center of the room, the boys stood around wearing dinner jackets, one hand holding a glass of dark liquor and the other jammed in their pockets. They probably would have been happier at a sports bar like the Ainsworth drinking beer and shouting at a TV, but they knew deep down that parties like this were their future.

Tripp guided me over to the group of girls and began introductions. It happened so fast that the names were initially kind of a blur, but I remember Perry Hammerstein, a tiny, pixielike girl with a raspy voice and smudged eyeliner; Catherine Dorson, an alabaster-skinned former ballerina who was getting her business degree at Harvard; and, finally, May Abernathy, a gazelle-like creature with wispy auburn hair and saucer eyes. She was clearly the queen bee of the group, the way she stood with her shoulders back, like she should be holding a very long cigarette at all times. She was the only one who smiled at me, but the smile was tight and quick.

"You're from, like, Richmond, right?" she asked, her eyes circling around me and landing on my feet.

"Charleston, actually," I said.

"Oh," she said, sipping from her glass. "Is that in Virginia too?"

Perry laughed a very knowing, hearty laugh and said, "You bitch."

"What?" May turned to her, eyes wider than before. "How the hell am I supposed to know? I had a layover in Atlanta once on the way to Harbour Island, but it's not like I set foot outside of the airport."

Everyone giggled at this comment.

I glanced around the room and located Tripp, who was sitting next to Baron, engrossed in an animated conversation. I wasn't about to ask for his help but couldn't he at least support me for the first five minutes or so? I felt like I was the new kid at school who had just stolen the most popular girl's boyfriend.

"Minty, would you like a drink?" Baron was suddenly standing to my right. He put his arm on my shoulder.

I must have looked bewildered and, well, terrified, but I was grateful he took notice. I politely excused myself from the Mean Girls and followed Baron to the bar.

"Listen," he said, once we were out of earshot of May and her posse, "May is a little territorial at first, but she's not so bad, you'll see." He motioned to the bartender. "Dewar's on the rocks and a . . ." He turned to me, eyebrow raised.

I was going to need at least a little alcohol in my system to get me through the night.

"Ketel One, soda, extra lime, with a splash of cranberry," I said.

"She does that with every newcomer," Baron continued. "She's also friendly with Tabitha. So it might not be the smoothest transition. Give it some time."

As Baron and I waited for our drinks, May made her way over to the "boy section." She glanced at me briefly, then draped herself over a lanky guy perched at the end of the sofa. He had a mop of light brown hair and soupy, distant eyes. They actually looked like they could be brother and sister, save for the hair color, but it was pretty apparent that they were quite the opposite as he started stroking her leg and playing with her hair.

"Did May grow up with Tripp?" I asked Baron.

Baron handed me my drink and glanced over at May. She and her boyfriend were now talking to Tripp and two other guys.

"Ahhh, May," Baron began. "No, she didn't grow up here. She's American but grew up in Switzerland, went to school there, and spent the last couple of years in Europe traveling. She's dating Harry Van der Waahl."

I nodded.

"Like I said, she's a bit aloof at first, but she's a fun girl. I think you two would actually really get along."

May and I made eye contact again and she smiled this time. Okay, I thought. That's a little bit of progress.

"Anyway, let's go find your boyfriend, shall we?"

Baron took my hand and walked me over to Tripp, who was talking with Harry as May looked on, bored.

"I found something over by the bar," Baron said, winking at Tripp.

Tripp turned to me and smiled. "Babe," he said. "Have I introduced you to Harry yet?"

I was annoyed by this question because clearly he hadn't. Instead, he had deposited me in the shark tank and left me to be devoured.

"No." I smiled sweetly, extending my hand in Harry's direction. "It's so nice to finally meet you."

Harry took my hand and bowed slightly, like we were standing on a porch somewhere in Virginia in the 1860s.

"If it isn't the famous Sassy Southern Deb," he said.

"Behave yourself, Van der Waahl," Tripp warned him.

I was about to change the subject by asking May a question, maybe something about where she lived, or even complimenting her on her outfit, and then Emily appeared out of nowhere. "Hello, stranger," she said, smiling.

I had never been so relieved to see a person in my entire life. Having Emily to lean on centered me again.

"May." She leaned toward May and kissed her on the cheek, then did the same to Harry. "Harry. Good to see you. How is everyone?"

Once again, Emily was dressed in an outfit only Emily could pull off. She was wearing a pale beige sheath dress that clung to every tiny curve on her body, a structured gray jacket, and little suede booties. Her hair was pulled back into a loose, somewhat messy bun. She would have blended seamlessly into a Calvin Klein ad.

"Emily, how are you?" May said.

I couldn't help but notice that her demeanor was entirely different in front of Emily.

"Fine," Emily said. "Busy. How is everything with you?"

"Harry and I just got back from Majorca, incredible but exhausting."

Emily nodded knowingly.

I perked up. I'd actually traveled to Majorca the summer before freshman year of college. I had something to contribute! As I was opening my mouth to comment, Baron came over and asked us to start making our way into the dining room.

"*Bazaar* needs a photograph of us seated," he explained.

Tripp and I found our seats near the center of the table. We were seated opposite May, Harry, and Emily, a few places down from Baron. Catherine Dorson took the seat to my left. She actually smiled when she sat down—phew!

Catherine had heard that Ruth was one of the top events people in the industry and had a friend who'd worked for her a few years prior. She laughed when I admitted Ruth wasn't the easiest boss in the world.

"The fact that you've lasted two months is a huge accomplishment, actually," she said.

Tripp was discussing a recent Giants game with Harry when the energy in the room changed slightly. I wasn't sure exactly why, but I felt a chill, like everyone's eyes were on me, and then Tripp stiffened. Richard, who had just been in the corner packing up his camera equipment, suddenly started unpacking. Then I saw Julie get up from her seat. She tapped Richard on the shoulder and whispered something in his ear.

"Oh, yikes," May said. She looked past me, her eyes settling somewhere over my shoulder.

I saw Emily's mouth drop open. In fact, everyone seemed to be either looking over my shoulder or gaping at something or both. Except Tripp, who was suddenly enthralled with his filet mignon.

I turned around and watched as Tabitha made her way down the hallway and into the dining room. She was wearing what can only be described as a crotch-length Herve Leger bandage dress that barely covered her bony hips. Her shoes were sky-high, crystal-encrusted platform stilettos. She wobbled in them like she could tip over at any moment, her eyes so hazy she had to be either drunk or high or both.

"Oh my God," I said.

Tripp looked at me and tilted his head. "What?"

"Tripp, look," I said, my cheeks flushing. Did he know she was coming?

Tripp turned around. "Oh," he said indifferently, glancing over his shoulder.

I was shocked to see a seat had actually been reserved for Tabitha. She sat down, all the while pretending she wasn't being blatantly gawked at, and placed her napkin in her lap.

Tripp turned back. "Whatever."

I faced forward and took a deep breath.

Across the table, Emily was avoiding eye contact while May looked directly at me. I just took a sip of my water and smiled back at her. Kill them with kindness. That was really all I *could* do.

"She's obsessed with me," Tripp hissed in my ear. "I have no idea why she showed up."

"Was she invited?"

Tripp was silent.

"Baron knows her," he finally said.

"I see."

Within seconds, conversation began to flow again. Baron was fawning over Tabitha now, pouring wine in her glass and laughing like she was the most interesting person in the room. May and Harry started nuzzling each other and the rest of the guests seemed to lose interest in the fact that Tripp, Tabitha, and I, the love triangle of "Page Six" proportions, had found ourselves sitting at the same dinner table together.

When dessert was served, Emily excused herself from the table and quietly came around to my seat.

"Ladies' room?" she said in my ear.

It was the best idea I'd heard in a long time. I placed my napkin next to my plate and pecked Tripp on the lips.

We walked out, but Emily didn't take me to the ladies' room. We grabbed our coats from the coatrack and she led me up a flight of stairs and onto a roof terrace overlooking the city. It was one of the most beautiful places I'd ever seen, covered in vines and tiny white lights and populated by rows of sculpted evergreens.

"You don't mind if I smoke, do you?" she asked, pulling out a pack of Marlboro Lights. I had only seen Emily smoke on a handful of occasions, typically when she was stressed out about something.

"Of course not," I said. "Actually, this is one of those times I kind of wish I were a smoker!"

Emily grinned. "I'm going to tell you something," she began, taking a deep breath. "I wasn't even going to say anything, but then she showed up and, well, I think you have the right to know."

"Okay," I said.

"You know how Tripp told you that he and Tabitha were kind of a brief fling, that it was really casual?"

"Yes . . ."

"Well," Emily sighed. "The fact of the matter is, they've been on and off for years now. It's not like they were ever fully committed, but Tabitha is very territorial about Tripp. Before you came along, they were pretty hot and heavy."

"I see."

"I didn't tell you the whole story at first"—she paused, searching for the right words—"because I thought maybe Tabitha would just let it go. And it's clear that Tripp cares about you. He definitely seems to have fallen for you pretty quickly. But I just want to make sure he's being totally honest with you."

"Tell me about it," I said. "Like, he couldn't mention the fact that she might be here? He acted like it was an afterthought!"

Emily pursed her lips. "I think he might be trying to . . . downplay the relationship. Maybe it's because he's ready to move on . . . to move forward with you. But, it just concerns me that he's not laying all of his cards on the table. Especially since you two seem to be moving so quickly."

"Ugh." I buried my face in my hands. "You've got to be kidding me!" I was just starting to confide in and trust him. It was the déjà vu I'd feared all along.

I forced myself to pause for a moment. This information could very well have been hearsay—if I'd learned one thing, it was that there was a lot of gossip in New York, maybe even more than in a small town in the South! Which is saying a lot.

"Tell me about Tabitha," I said, taking a deep breath. "If I'm going to have to duke it out with this lady to get to the truth, I need to know what makes her tick. So far all I've got is . . . she's a socialite, she knows pretty much everyone, and she's out to steal my boyfriend."

Emily shrugged.

"Well, Tabitha is actually more of a businesswoman these days," Emily said. "She goes to a lot of parties, yes, but she often gets paid to go to them. Any time you see Tabitha walk a red carpet with a bunch of sponsors or show up at the launch of some product, you can bet she's getting paid. Even if she attends a fashion show, odds are they're paying her somehow, even if it's in free clothes. Tabitha is New York aristocracy. And in some circles, that counts for something. She adds a certain cachet."

I nodded.

"And there's her jewelry line of course."

"Jewelry?"

"Jewelry, accessories. I think there may be an evening clutch here and there. It's not really known that well in the States. I think it's sold at a little boutique on Madison. But supposedly it's huge in Asia and Germany. The last time I spoke to her, she was creating a less expensive version of the line for QVC."

I was impressed, and it must have shown.

"I know," Emily said. "Do you know how much money those direct-sell channels make? Oh my God, it's ridiculous."

"Interesting," I said. Apparently in New York, being a socialite—essentially getting dressed up and going to parties five nights a week—could be a job, one that could even be parlayed into a career in design. As ridiculous as it seemed at first, I couldn't help but admit that becoming a boldface name like Tabitha—being photographed at parties and building an image and a brand through that exposure—sounded like a great way to realize my dream.

"Listen, Minty," Emily continued. "I've known most of these people since I was born. I've seen them with runny noses and peanut butter and jelly stains on their school uniforms. And I still feel intimi-dated sometimes. I can only imagine what it feels like to experience it for the first time at twenty-two."

She waved her hand in the air and I looked around at the tiny white lights and vine-covered trellises. I took in the collection of to-piaries, covered in protective burlap for the colder winter months. I imagined that not many people have been on the rooftop of 812 Park Avenue. The air was so rarified it could almost have been bottled and sold, like a souvenir of the good life.

"I guess what I'm trying to say is, I've seen a lot of girls let this life-style get the best of them. They go out until all hours of the night and develop eating disorders just trying to keep up. The only way you're going to survive, the only way you're going to succeed, is if you stay true to yourself."

"So I should break up with Tripp?"

Emily laughed and took a drag of her cigarette.

"No! No, I'm not saying that at all, not yet at least," she laughed. "I'm saying . . ." She paused for a moment. "I'm saying, keep curling your hair." She pulled at one of my ringlets and smiled. "Keep wear-ing dresses and smiling and being polite. It might take a bit longer for people to warm up to you, but they'll remember you as a result. They'll remember you because you're different, because you stand out from the crowd of skinny girls in earth tones and no makeup, such as myself." She grinned. "And don't let women like Tabitha get in the way of any-thing you have your sights set on, be it Tripp or anything else."

"You sound like my mother." I laughed.

I always knew, deep down, that Emily was playing for Team Minty, but that night solidified it.

As Emily took one last drag of her cigarette and flicked it over the building's ledge, a couple stumbled onto the terrace, wrapped up in an embrace.

"I guess that's our cue to leave," Emily said, standing up. She glanced at her watch. "Anyway, it's after-party time."

Kill Them with Kindness

In New York, the clubs you go to—or don't go to—speak volumes. The good clubs have very long lines. But the even better, more exclusive clubs have smaller lines, because most people know they have no chance of getting into a top place unless they are officially on the list. And by "list," I don't mean some promoter's list thrown together with a group of NYU students celebrating a birthday. Those who are granted entrance into the best clubs are part of an elite group that rarely changes, much like the membership roster at an exclusive country club.

The Boom Boom Room at the Standard Hotel—where Baron was hosting his after-party—had one of the most impenetrable doors in the city.

"Supposedly Jessica Simpson tried to get in last week and they had to turn her away," Tripp explained as Zeke zoomed down the West Side Highway.

Emily had hitched a ride with us. I sat in the middle with my head rested on Tripp's shoulder.

"No way," Emily said with just a hint of disinterest.

"There was some sort of private party and she wasn't on the list," Tripp said, laughing.

Unlike in L.A., where clubs and lounges court every actor and actress with a YouTube profile, in New York, often the coolest clubs were the ones that *didn't* let celebrities in. Boom Boom was notorious for choosing class and connections over the latest cover of *Us Weekly*.

We pulled up to the entrance, which was an unassuming, industrial-looking doorway on West Thirteenth Street. There was a lone doorman standing outside wearing a large fur coat and looking like he had better things to do. To his right, a small group of women milled around, furiously typing away on their BlackBerries. They were probably trying to reach the person who had *promised* they were on the list. When we walked up to the doorman (Tripp referred to him by name, Sebby), he didn't even reference a clipboard or his BlackBerry. We just waltzed inside.

We walked through a dark hallway and into the elevator, which had mesmerizing, heaven-and-hell-inspired video art built into the walls. Finally, we were greeted by red-lipped models/cocktail waitresses, who ushered us into a hallway, which opened up into a huge room decorated in shiny gold finishes and sumptuous cream leather, like the inside of a genie's bottle meeting 1970s glam. I didn't know where to look, because the interior of the club was almost as stunning as the sweeping city views.

Tripp guided us straight to the center bar, where we ordered cocktails from a handsome, tattooed bartender with a mustache that was curled up at the tips. He and Tripp did a quick, familiar sort-of handshake, and he immediately began pouring our drinks. Once we were set, we found Baron and a few others holding court in one of the sunken banquette areas.

"You ladies take a seat here," Tripp said. He waited until we looked comfortable, then he touched the top of my head and gave me a quick kiss. "I'm going to find Harry. Be right back." He disappeared into the crowd.

Emily sat next to me quietly and sipped her cocktail. She hadn't said much since we left Baron's apartment. She leaned in, a bit tipsy.

Her eyelids were getting heavy and she pronounced each word slowly. "Forgive me for asking but I just can't help myself, have you slept together yet?"

My mouth dropped open and I slapped her on the knee.

"Emily Maplethorpe!"

"It's an honest, relevant question."

"Which I'm not going to answer."

"So you have?"

"No! Emily! Oh my God, I'm turning beet red."

"Oh, bummer, you haven't."

"Emily, we are ending this line of questioning immediately." I pulled away from her and crossed my legs in the opposite direction. "Honestly."

"It's probably good that you haven't," she continued, ignoring my protests. "I mean, a guy like Tripp is used to—how shall we say this—getting what he wants when he wants it. I imagine part of the reason he's so into you has something to do with the fact that he hasn't had the chance to actually *get into you,* if you know what I mean."

"*Emily.*"

Okay, so she wasn't just tipsy. She was drunk.

I turned around and Tripp was standing there.

"You girls look like you're up to no good," he said, smiling.

Sometimes when I looked at him, I had to stop myself from swooning. He was like a present-day JFK Jr. He'd often been compared to him in the press. He was taller, though, more of a presence. He had the swagger of a Division I athlete.

"Always," I said coyly.

Emily rolled her eyes. "Your girlfriend's being her old uptight, southern belle self again," she said with a grin.

"Girlfriend, eh?" he said, elbowing me playfully.

I gulped.

"I guess you *are* my girlfriend," he said.

I'd thought about this moment several times since Tripp and I started dating. How would it happen? When would it happen? Would it ever happen? But I definitely never questioned how I would feel when it happened. I thought I would be happy, elated even, and part of me was. But I couldn't get what Emily had said about Tabitha out of my mind.

He wrapped his arms around my waist. "You're my girlfriend," he said. He kissed my forehead, then my nose.

It didn't take long for the entire banquette to get wind of Tripp's declaration. Baron started clapping. Then everyone was clinking glasses like they were celebrating an engagement.

"Awww, look at the happy couple," Baron cooed.

Tripp ignored him.

"I'm going to marry you one day," he continued. His words were mixing together. He wasn't slurring, but he'd definitely had a few drinks.

"Tripp!" I punched him in the arm.

"I mean it," he said, "I love you."

I took that "I love you" with a grain of salt. It was late. He was slightly intoxicated. Maybe I was too? Before it could settle in, he kissed me and everyone started cheering. He gave me a final kiss on the lips and scooted out toward the bar.

"Maplethorpe, keep an eye on my girlfriend," he said.

Just then, Julie Greene appeared out of nowhere and inched toward my seat in the banquette. She was still wearing her coat and holding a tiny notepad. I'd always thought writing about parties sounded like the most amazing job in the world, but now I understood why Julie always looked so bored. Yes, technically, she got paid to go to parties, but she never got to let loose and have fun.

"Hi, Minty," she said. "Do you mind if I sit down for a moment?"

"Julie! Hi! How are you? Of course!" I patted a spot next to me. I was surprised she remembered my name, let alone wanted to strike up a conversation.

"Just need to know who you're wearing tonight and I guess . . . why don't you tell me what you thought of the dinner since you're a first-time guest and all."

"Well," I started, trying to come up with an answer that didn't sound too "aw, shucks," when I felt a tap on my shoulder. I turned around and there she was: Tabitha.

"Darling," she said, scooting her way into the banquette and elbowing Julie out of the way in the process.

I glanced at Emily, whose lower lip was practically dragging on the floor. Julie immediately got up and stood over us, aghast.

"Oh, hello," I said in my most polite tone. I glanced at Julie and mouthed a "sorry." She rolled her eyes.

"I believe we've met once before," Tabitha continued, "but I figured I should introduce myself in light of the fact that you're fucking Tripp du Pont."

I have to admit, it took me a moment to regain my composure. First, I was distracted by the use of the word "fuck" (not that I never use the F-word). And she had this completely calm look on her face, like I was just a tiny flea of a person she would like to exterminate before I made her itch any more.

"You must have mistaken me for someone else," I said with the sweetest smile painted on my face.

Tabitha laughed. "Very funny," she said. "But you're right." Then she leaned in and whispered in my ear. "I bet there are at least five sluts at this bar right now who would fit the same description." Then she turned around and walked away.

⸎

The next day at work, I felt like my brain was being squished in an industrial-sized vise. I hadn't even had that much to drink, but before I knew it, it was three o'clock in the morning and the Boom Boom Room was still going strong. How did people stay out so late and function the next day? A little something called "not having a desk job" probably had a lot to do with it.

"Someone looks like she's been kicked in the face by a Manolo and hit over the head with a bottle of Belvedere," Spencer observed as I dragged myself to my cubicle. "Ruthless had a breakfast meeting this morning."

"I know," I said, "why do you think I'm here at nine instead of eight?"

"My first guess was you overslept."

"Yeah, right," I said. "I have three alarm clocks and a mother who shows up at my apartment at seven A.M. to oversee the installment of window treatments and new hardware. There is no way in hell I'd ever oversleep."

"I need to meet your mother."

"Be careful what you wish for," I said.

"So." Spencer leaned over from his desk. "Fallout from the 'Page Six' drama? Catfights?"

"Why do I have a feeling you're writing this down?"

"Because I am. In my head."

I rolled my eyes.

"Minty, how many times do I have to tell you? One day, I'm going to be the next Truman Capote," he said, "except handsomer and far more straight. And you're going to be the next C. Z. Guest." He paused. "Except blonder and far more scandalous. And then I'm going to write a bestselling book about you and your life and we can both be fabulous together and operate on a plane somewhere above A-list celebrities and somewhere below the president of the United States."

"You are ridiculous," I said.

As Spencer was talking and I was pretending to listen, Ruth stepped off the elevator and stomped toward her office. She called me in immediately, of course.

When I arrived in the doorway of Ruth's office, she actually looked fresh and triumphant, the way she usually looked after she had placed a feature in *The New York Times*—or fired someone.

"I saw our friend Farah this morning," she said.

Farah Hammer, the editor of "Page Six."

"O-oh?" I stammered. I wasn't sure how I was supposed to respond.

"She's a cunt," Ruth said. She typed something on her computer. "But I have her in the palm of my hand." She swiveled back in my direction and pointed at me. "Fear of God," she said.

I looked up at Ruth and nodded. She was having a conversation ahead of me and I was attempting to catch up after stumbling a bit over the C-word.

"For example," she continued, "you do what I say because I have put the fear of God into you."

She was right.

"At the end of the day, it's my ass on the line at this company. And the only way I can trust that you'll actually listen and get the job done to my liking instead of spending the whole day tweeting or blogging or flirting on Facebook like Spencer does"—she took a breath—"is if I know that you're not only afraid but terrified. And that's my tactic with so-called journalists like Farah."

I wrote down an edited version of this statement in my Smythson.

"Which is not to say she isn't going to write about you again," Ruth continued. "God knows she has to now that you're dating that Tad von Trapp character." She glanced around her desk and found a pack of cigarettes. She pulled one out and lit it.

"I can't tell her what to write and what not to write. But. You're an RVPR employee. If she's going to write about you she's going to mention that fact, goddamn it, and she's also going to call me before she publishes even a sentence with your name in it."

I took a deep breath. The news was both comforting and horrifying. I had barely recovered from yesterday's story and here she was, anticipating countless more to come? What was Tripp going to think if every time our names popped up in the papers it looked like an RVPR publicity blitz?

"Okay," I said. "I guess that makes me feel better."

"I don't care if you feel better," she said. "You're lucky I'm letting you keep this job after the crap I had to deal with yesterday." She turned back to her computer. My cue to leave.

I made my way toward the door.

"Also, Davenport," she said.

I turned back at full attention.

"You're going to start taking on a more visible role. I'm making you my right-hand gal for all things Fashion Week. It's months away, I know, but we're working with five new designers this year and we're already drowning. You've got connections now. You can pull some strings. Get some of your friends or Trapp's, Tripp's, whatever, friends to show up—I'm talking boldface names only. I'm going to rely on you to help take things to the next level this season. Got it?"

"Got it," I said.

Back at my desk, I processed the information slowly. At face value, in the wake of the "Page Six" scandal, I could have been a detriment to RVPR. But Ruth was turning me into an asset. She was, quite literally, using me—and my relationship with Tripp—to get press for the company. And, in the meantime, she was forcing me to use Tripp's connections to bolster RVPR's Fashion Week guest lists.

After a few long minutes of thinking, Spencer turned away from his computer and waved his hand in front of my eyes.

"Why the long face?" he asked.

I tilted my head to the side and sighed. I wasn't exactly sure.

"Have you ever felt like your life is running away from you?" I asked.

Spencer thought for a moment.

"No. Usually I feel like it's not running fast enough."

"I just don't know if I can keep up."

"You've lasted over two months as Ruthless Vine's assistant," he said. He thought for a moment. "I'm pretty sure that's a world record." He placed his hands on my shoulders. "As long as you want to, you can keep up."

8

Practice Grace under Pressure

Spencer clearly didn't let anyone—or anything—intimidate him and it seemed to work for him. In fact, it seemed to work for a lot of people I'd met since I left Charleston.

So when Ruth handed me my first task in my new, more responsible role at RVPR, I forced myself to react positively instead of worrying about all of the things that could possibly go wrong.

I was in charge of creating and managing the guest list for the designer Kevin Park's boutique opening downtown, the same Kevin Park who had collaborated with Hermès a little over a month before. The same Kevin Park I'd failed to recognize outside of the party in the boutique, which, of course, eventually led to my being sent home and running into Tripp.

"Ruth, this sounds amazing," I began, "and I'm sure I can do a really great job. I just want to make sure you're comfortable with me handling the Kevin Park account, seeing as the first time I met him I—"

"Oh Jesus Christ, Minty," Ruth said, "enough. Not to mention, do you really think Kevin remembers that? Or *you* for that matter? Get over it."

Fine, I thought as I walked back to my desk. After all, I wasn't even sure if we would cross paths, since I'd be working behind the scenes. Either way, I was definitely nervous. Not only would the food, décor, and music need to be perfect, but each guest needed to be more famous and more fabulous than the last.

Of course, I'd barely managed a list before, let alone created one. Now I had to not only come up with a list of proposed guests but also call and e-mail them or their publicists until I got an answer. And, like Ruth said, a yes was never really a yes until that person actually showed up at the party.

If a real A-lister said they were coming, it was my job to make sure they had something to wear—like a free dress from Kevin Park—and someone to drive them there. Arranging a driver was really the only way an event planner knew a guest was actually going to show up.

"This should be second nature by now, Minty," Ruth explained later that day. "It's your job to not only make sure this happens but to recruit a few new people—It Girl types, starlets, you know the drill—who will catch the eye of photographers and press. It's a lot of juggling, but I'm counting on you."

Ruth used the phrase "counting on you" a lot. By saying that she was "counting" on me, she wasn't just asking me to complete a task, she was acting as if she had all the faith in the world that I had the ability to complete it even though she did not. I was scared out of my mind that I would fail and I also felt strangely guilty that if I *were* to fail, it would be somewhat of a personal offense to Ruth. Working for Ruth often felt like walking a tightrope naked over thousands of onlookers. Every once in a while she would light that tightrope on fire without giving me the slightest warning, and if I fell or screamed or even startled in the slightest, it was my fault, of course.

Spencer and I spent the entire week juggling both the Kevin Park event and Ruth's increasing anxiety over visiting her parents in Phila-delphia for the Thanksgiving holiday. While Spencer made calls to Ruth's hotel (yes, she was staying in a hotel room) to ensure that the room dimensions were up to snuff and the restaurant offered gluten-free options on its menu, I was running down to Magnolia Bakery in the West Village to find a pumpkin pie that looked as homemade as physically possible. Spencer and I personally tested three rounds of pies before one was deemed appropriate.

I spent the day of the Kevin Park event slaving away over final confirmations and car arrangements. It seemed that every time I set up a pickup time for a car, someone's assistant called and said they needed to change.

"Dude, you're on Style.com again," Spencer said, his eyes peeking over his computer screen in my direction. "From that Cinema Society screening."

The Cinema Society was an organization that hosted semiweekly screenings and after-parties for new films. The guest list was mainly made up of the film's director or directors, producers, actors, actresses, and various other celebrities. It was an honor just to be invited. Of course I was curious to see which photo Style.com had chosen, but I didn't have time. If I so much as shifted in my seat I could feel Ruth's eyes boring into me from wherever she happened to be on the floor.

Besides, I was on hold with the car service, once again.

Spencer let out a hoot. "You're ridiculous."

"What do you mean?"

"You're on Style.com twice in one month and you barely bat an eyelash."

"Yes," I said into the receiver. "I'm so sorry. Thank you." I was put back on hold. "Spencer, of course I care," I continued. "I'm just kind of busy right now and if I don't get this—"

"Jesus Christ," Spencer yelped.

He was waving a copy of *New York* magazine in my face.

"Spencer!" I swatted him away.

"'Party Lines'!"

I grabbed the magazine and skimmed over the page, which was mainly made up of pictures of people from various parties and events in New York. And there I was, wearing a light blue Dolce & Gabbana corset dress at the Cinema Society after-party. Spencer was standing over me, his mouth open.

"This is a big . . . fucking . . . deal, Davenport," he said.

Spencer pointed to Kirsten Dunst's boldface name on the page. "She's a celebrity, Minty. They didn't even run *her* picture. And they ran yours!"

I'd be lying if I said it wasn't really exciting. But I was so busy I didn't have the luxury of thinking about it. All I knew is that I had twenty-three more car reservations to change and less than an hour to make it happen. Just as I shooed Spencer away and turned to pick up the phone again, an envelope was deposited in front of me. I glanced up to yell at Spencer again, but it wasn't Spencer. It was a strange man in a navy blue outfit. I screamed and nearly fell off of my seat.

"The mail guy," Spencer deadpanned from his cubicle. "Right up there with Jack the Ripper and Freddy Krueger."

"Thank you," I said to the unfazed mailman.

The envelope was thick and square, the size and weight of a typical wedding invitation—or at least wedding invitations I'd seen over the years, which were mainly for Charleston weddings and were about as formal and over-the-top as they come. My name was spelled incorrectly: Mintzy Darvenport. Whoever sent me the invitation apparently read *WWD*. And maybe was only inviting me because I appeared in *WWD*?

"I have a feeling I know what that is," Spencer said.

"How on earth would you know just by looking at the envelope?" I asked.

He shrugged. "These things are like clockwork, Minty," he explained. "New Yorkers for Children Fall Gala, the Whitney Gala, the Apollo Circle Benefit for the Met, etc. etc. And then, everyone goes to Vail or Aspen and forgets about charity balls for—supposedly—the rest of the year. But the Frick always sends its save-the-date before everyone zones out for the holidays. The actual party doesn't happen until January, but think of it as an early Christmas present."

I'd heard about the Whitney Museum and New Yorkers for Children, but what on earth was the Frick? And how was anyone supposed to keep track of all of these parties?

"The Frick Collection is only one of the most venerable museums in the city," Spencer explained. "Once Henry Clay Frick's private home." He looked at me for a reaction, but nothing was ringing any bells. "Ugh," he said, disgusted. "You get invited to one of the most exclusive events of the year and you act like you might as well be going to a five-year-old's birthday at Chuck E. Cheese."

He held the invitation up to the light and gazed at it lovingly.

"If you love the Frick so much, why don't you go?" I asked naïvely.

Spencer glanced around the office, ascertained that Ruth was indeed on the phone with her door closed, and pulled his chair up next to mine.

"Mary Randolph Mercer Davenport."

Apparently he knew my full name.

"One doesn't just *go* to the Frick ball. One doesn't even just get invited to the Frick ball. One gets chosen." He straightened his posture and crossed his hands over his knees. "Wake up, Minty. You have been plucked from virtual obscurity and placed into the upper echelons of New York society." He broke character for a moment. "Albeit, on the lowest rung of the upper echelons, seeing as this is only your first time." He cleared his throat and resumed the deep voice. "But this is a momentous occasion nonetheless. One that should be taken *very* seriously."

He swiveled around in his chair, just in time for Ruth to emerge from her office looking like, well, a fright.

"Minty, why aren't you in my office right now?"

Ruth was standing over my cubicle with her hands on her hips. I looked at the clock: 3:02. We were supposed to meet at three P.M.

"Oh! Sorry!" I promptly deposited the save-the-date on the floor. "I was just— Oh. I was . . ."

In the last two days I'd left eighty-four voice mails and sent one hundred and twenty-one e-mails to various celebrity publicists and a few well-known socialites who hadn't responded yet. But apparently celebrity publicists didn't really answer their phones or respond to e-mails. The socialites just assumed we knew they were coming and often showed up unannounced. Regardless, I'd managed to confirm Jules Gregory, the daughter of an aging rock star; Tamsen Little, a well-known celebrity stylist; and Bernadette Flannery, a pretty downtown art dealer. They were not exactly Gwyneth Paltrow, but they were "boldface" names in their own right. Jules, for one, had been popping up on "Page Six" for the last couple of months and was rumored to be signing a deal for her own reality show.

At the last minute, I'd also added a few "fill-ins" like Spencer and two of his friends from college, who promised they would bring two attractive, chic girls. I also included Emily, who was thrilled when she heard I was helping plan a party for Kevin Park.

"I have a really good feeling about this, Minty," Emily had said. "If this goes well, Kevin could be an instrumental person for you."

I wasn't so sure what she meant by this.

"The fashion industry is New York's answer to Hollywood," she continued. "Designers hold a ton of power in this town. If you've got one in your corner—better yet, by your *side*—you're pretty much golden. I mean, name one social girl who hasn't served as a 'muse' to a designer. And let's face it, Kevin's style is perfect for you. His last collection was inspired by Eloise, of all people!"

"Really?" I probably should have known that already.

By the time I made it to Ruth's office to go over the guest list, I was already four minutes late. She grabbed the list from me and scanned it in record time. I sat across from her desk, leaning forward slightly, praying to God that I'd done something right.

"What the hell is your boyfriend doing on here?"

But I guess God wasn't answering my prayers that day.

I'd invited Tripp at the last minute, thinking it might be nice for him to experience one of my first big events, but his lack of enthusiasm was surprising. He'd said something about "trying" to make it, then when I called him that morning to ask again, he said he was sorry but it wasn't really "his scene." As a concession, he said he'd head to my apartment straight from work and would be waiting for me when I was done with my event. I was lukewarm on the compromise. If our relationship had one roadblock so far, it centered on the fact that he was not entirely supportive of my career. Sometimes I felt like he was a little threatened that I was going out a lot, meeting new people, and starting to carve out a niche for myself in New York.

Whatever his issue was, I guess it worked out for the best.

"Oh, sorry, that must be a mistake," I said.

She crossed his name off the list, pulled out a highlighter, and started marking up the list. Shoot, I thought. Ruth had told me it was "my" list to manage, but I guess she didn't exactly mean I could invite whomever I wanted.

"What is this, Minty's New York coming-out party?" She slammed the list onto her desk and several other pieces of paper flew up around it.

I gulped.

"I mean, seriously, Minty, I love Emily to death but she is no A-lister." She shook her head. "And this plus-two bullshit? Plus fucking two who?"

"Sorry," was all I could manage.

Ruth buried her face in her hands.

"I have *The New York* fucking *Times* and *Gotham* magazine covering this party exclusively, Minty. I can't have a bunch of nobodies showing up and making it look like a second-rate event." She put the list down and glanced at the clock. "Go back to your desk and tell your grade school friends and their third cousins once removed they're not coming." She glanced at the list again. "Tamsen Little is a good add. But I want to see at least three additional notable fucking people at this party who have accomplished something beyond taking you to dinner."

Back at my desk, I logged onto my Gmail Chat account so I could send Spencer a quick download of my meeting with Ruth. It was our way of communicating at the office without being overheard. I had just finished typing the word "bitch" when a message popped up.

Taking New York by storm, I see?

I gasped. It was Ryerson.

"Oh my God," I said out loud.

I honestly had no idea what to say. I hadn't heard from him in over a year. Why would he contact me now when we were thousands of miles away from each other? Come to think of it, I didn't even know where he was.

He continued with a second message when I didn't respond: *I saw your photo somewhere. I know it's been a while . . . but maybe the next time I fly through New York we can get a drink.*

And, finally: *I miss you, Minty.*

What?! I stepped away from my computer.

Spencer popped his head up from his cubicle. "All okay?"

"Um, yeah," I said, shaking my head. Spencer looked back at me, puzzled. "I'm just, um, kind of under the gun with this list."

I was partly telling the truth, of course. I didn't have a clue as to how I was going to confirm more top people at such a late hour. I picked up the phone and called Emily. Luckily, she said she had two people in mind—Georgia Bennetton, a socialite, and Olive Hudson, an up-and-coming actress. She thought she could get them to come if we would "gift" (a term for giving free things to celebrities) them a Kevin Park dress. It turned out Saks had just picked up Kevin's line, so Emily was able to pull directly from the floor. It really was the perfect solution. I was able to wrap up the list and make it down to the Kevin Park boutique just in time for the start of the event, all the while thinking in the back of my head, What the hell does Ryerson Bigelow want?

<hr />

The boutique, located on Mulberry Street in Nolita, was a modest (by fashion-empire standards), austere space finished in smooth concrete and bright white paint. The clothes were feminine—frilly almost—in bright, whimsical shades of pink, lavender, powder blue, and yellow. It was almost as if he'd stepped inside my head and created the perfect wardrobe.

When I walked in, everything seemed to be in good shape. Kevin and his team were en route from the showroom and all we had to do was make a few final adjustments to the flowers and wait for the guests to show up. Besides the fact that Emily was still coming (I couldn't exactly disinvite her when she was the reason we'd confirmed two more amazing guests), I was feeling pretty confident this time. All I could do was hope that Ruth saw the trade-off and respected my decision.

Thankfully, things were going so well from the get-go that Ruth took me off the door and asked that I circulate and make sure everything was running smoothly. Kevin, whom I hadn't met yet, caught my gaze through the crowd and motioned for me to come over.

"You work for Ruth, right?" he said.

"Yes! I'm Minty." I extended my hand. "It's so nice to meet you. I'm such a fan of your designs. I hope you're happy with everything . . . ?"

Kevin smiled. "Yes, I was just looking for Ruth." He glanced around the room. "You guys are doing an amazing job—I just saw Olive Hudson come in. I mean, she is one of my favorite girls! I have been dying to dress her. Please let Ruth know if I don't find her first."

Just then, Emily walked over with Olive and Georgia.

"Emily!" Kevin exclaimed, pulling her toward him. "Oh my God, I didn't know you were coming, this is amazing! Did you have a hand in getting these amazing girls in my clothes?"

Olive and Georgia smiled and Emily made introductions. As I was standing there—feeling relieved and proud—I saw Ruth come out from the back of the store. She immediately zeroed in on Emily and started making her way through the crowd, her expression tight-lipped and focused.

"Actually"—Emily smiled—"I have to give the credit to Minty here. It really was all her idea."

Kevin looked at me and beamed. "Genius, Minty. Just genius. I knew I liked you." He examined me closely, taking in my simple black sheath (ugh) and ankle boots. "Have I seen you somewhere before? You look familiar but . . . different."

"She's in work mode," Emily said, beaming, "but Minty's usually dressed like a Kevin Park ad. I mean, she could practically be your muse!"

His eyes narrowed and he lifted a finger to his lips. Then his face lit up with recognition.

"Oh, you're that southern belle! I'm always reading about you in 'Page Six.'"

I shrugged, slightly embarrassed.

"Yes," Emily said. "That's her."

"Kevin, honey, I see you've met Olive and Georgia?" Ruth asked.

"Yes, yes, I have," Kevin said. "Aren't they gorgeous? Dressed in the spring collection, no less."

"Genius," Ruth said. She turned to me. "Minty—"

"And I have to say, your girl Minty here is a lifesaver," Kevin continued. "Emily tells me she pulled some strings to get the girls here and even made sure they were wearing my designs."

Ruth paused, and for a moment I thought she might lose it. All right, so Emily was there, but I had technically pulled through in the end. And Kevin—Ruth's most important client at the time—seemed thrilled. Wasn't that really the only thing we cared about?

"She's my little protégée," she finally said, patting me on the shoulder.

I managed a strained smile in return, half-expecting her hands to travel up to my neck and strangle me right then and there. Okay, so she was basically bringing the credit back on herself, but at least she hadn't blown up in front of everyone.

"We've got to get her in some Kevin Park," he said, eyeing me again and putting a hand on his hip.

"Definitely," Ruth said. "Definitely."

———❦———

"Darling, how was the party?"

I jumped when I opened my door. I'd been expecting to see Tripp in my apartment, not Scarlett.

She was wearing a Ralph Lauren jacket and wool pants with a silky white blouse. Her hair was pulled back with a red headband.

"Mother, what are you—"

"You just missed Tripp, darling, we had the nicest conversation," she began, waltzing into the living room. "He said to tell you he'd speak to you in the morning." She paused. "Mind you, I didn't know he had a key to your apartment!" She narrowed her eyes at me.

"Mother, please."

"Anyway, it was so good to see him again, I feel like it's been ages. We got to talking about the holidays and I've been thinking. You know, Thanksgiving is going to be blink-and-you'll-miss-it."

We were planning on spending Thanksgiving in Charleston, but with my work schedule I would only be able to spend a grand total of twenty-four hours there.

"And then Christmas is right round the corner," she said. "We'll see all of the extended family at Thanksgiving, of course. So I was thinking we could maybe do Christmas in New York with just our immediate family. We could invite your father. It would probably be a lot more relaxing than boarding a flight to Palm Beach for another whirlwind trip."

But I loved spending Christmas in Palm Beach. It was a family tradition after all.

"Christmas in New York?! Dad?! What the hell are you talking about?"

Even though my parents were divorced, they were still close friends. Dad usually spent the holidays with his third wife. So if he was to be invited to spend Christmas with us, it could only mean one thing: marriage number three was headed down the tubes.

"We could even include Tripp somehow," she continued, ignoring me. "Maybe for Christmas Eve dinner? Didn't you say something about how his family only celebrates on Christmas Day?"

"Mother."

"It's just that, I'm here and you're here and God knows you're so busy with this public relating business you've gotten yourself wrapped up in. Darby has four goddamn weeks off from Ole Miss; I barely know what I'm going to do with her and I imagine your father will be no help at all."

"Mommy, I'm not so sure that this is the best idea."

"Well, why on earth not?"

There were many reasons why on earth not. Tripp had met my parents before, of course, but the thought of his joining us for Christmas Eve dinner was still intimidating. They were not exactly Norman Rockwell normal. My father, for one, had an uncanny ability to make my mother look like the most stable, least manipulative person on the planet. And then there was Darby, who would definitely spend the entire time asking Tripp if he had any single friends and then would force us to go out after dinner. I was getting a headache already just thinking about it.

"I just feel like it would be a lot."

"Five people? A lot? Sweetheart, you act as if we're not going to be in Charleston in a few days with approximately fifty of our closest relatives."

"I'm just . . . ," I began tentatively, "I'm just not sure it's the right timing. I mean Tripp and I have only been together a few months and I don't want to overwhelm him or anything, especially in the middle of Christmas when he'd probably rather be spending time with his family."

The look on my mother's face was one of utter disappointment.

"So, we embarrass you? Is that what you're trying to say?"

I couldn't help but roll my eyes.

"You can roll your eyes at me all you want, miss, but if this boy is even slightly serious about you, I'm sure he'll be thrilled to join us for Christmas Eve dinner."

"I'm not saying he wouldn't be thrilled, Mother," I began. "It's just . . . a lot to throw his way. I don't want to overwhelm him."

"Overwhelm him?" She was the one to roll her eyes this time. "Your father and I were married after six months together. I think I knew within the first few weeks of dating he'd be the father of my children. And I was younger than you!"

"Mommy, that was a different time."

"Oh please," she said. "Not that much has changed about falling in love. You must have some idea about how you feel about him. About whether or not you see a future with him."

I was quiet. Of course I did.

"So it's settled, then," she said, reading the look in my eyes. "We'll have a Christmas Eve dinner with Tripp."

I gulped.

In Charleston, I knew Ryerson's entire family before we were even dating. But New York was different. I was worried the invitation would scare Tripp away. I was thinking I could just lie and say I'd invited him and he was unable to attend. But then I remembered Tripp and my mother were already in cahoots.

"Mother . . . ," I began, my voice tempered and calm.

I walked farther into the living room until I was standing over her. I attempted to maintain my composure.

"Yes, honey?"

The way she raised both eyebrows, cocked her head, and smiled sweetly told me I already knew the answer to my question.

"You didn't *already* invite Tripp to Christmas Eve dinner, did you?"

She tilted her head back and opened her mouth slightly. It was a classic Scarlett Davenport stall tactic, as if she was trying to recall, amongst the thousands of invites to Christmas Eve dinner, if she had extended one to my boyfriend. She pressed a finger to her lips and hummed.

"Well, I believe I may have," she finally said.

"Mother!" I threw my hands up in the air.

"Oh, Minty." She waved a hand in my direction. "You have got to stop being so dramatic. I will have you know that Tripp was ecstatic to know we were planning—excuse me, thinking about—spending Christmas in New York and responded immediately to my invitation."

"Unbelievable, Mother. Truly unbelievable."

The thing with my mother is, you can fight her and lose or you can just surrender to whatever master plan she's cooked up and hope for the best. I was done fighting with my mother. We would have Christmas in New York.

———◈◈◈———

As I was going to bed that night, Tripp called.

"Hey," he said. "Sorry I missed you earlier."

"Sorry my mother is a crazy stalker!" I said.

He laughed. "Listen," he began, "I was hanging out before Scarlett got there and I went to log on to my Gmail account. For some reason your Gmail account was open and I guess I saw something I shouldn't have."

"What do you mean?" I asked. I was so brain-dead at that point I couldn't even begin to imagine what he was talking about.

"Ryerson Bigelow?" he said.

I racked my brain. Oh my God, I'd totally forgotten about Ryerson's messages!

"Oh, Tripp," I said. "Please. That was so long ago. I honestly don't know why he's contacting me after all of this time."

"He clearly 'misses you,'" he said in a singsong voice.

I rolled my eyes. Something about Ryerson—beyond the fact that he was my ex—really got to Tripp. Boys could be so competitive.

"Tripp," I said. "Please. Ryerson and I are ancient history. Do we really have to talk about this now?" I was afraid I was going to fall asleep midconversation.

"Ancient history or not," he said, "you wanted to marry the guy at one point."

"But I didn't," I groaned. "And now I'm with you."

He was silent.

"Listen, sweetie," I said, "I'm exhausted. It's so dumb. I didn't even respond!"

He sighed. "All right," he said. "I'm sorry I even saw it in the first place."

"Well, try to forget it," I said. "I know I have." I thought for a minute. "Besides, I can promise you Ryerson is not invited to Davenport Christmas Eve dinner."

Tripp laughed. "He better not be!"

"I'm glad you're coming," I said.

"Me too."

"I have to be up early to fly to Charleston tomorrow," I reminded him, yawning.

"Okay," he said. "I love you."

My eyes popped open. Tripp had said "I love you" that night at the Boom Boom Room, but this was the first time he'd said it, well, not under the influence. If it hadn't happened to be past eleven o'clock at night, it was what I would have called a "daytime I-love-you." Either way, I could tell he was sincere. It felt good.

"I love you too," I said.

9

Never Keep a Lady Waiting

In New York, when it rains it doesn't just pour, it torrential-downpours for five minutes straight then stops, leaving you soaked, shocked, and standing in the middle of the street with a broken umbrella.

After the Thanksgiving holiday, it was like someone pressed the "fast-forward" button at work. While we were always focused on pleasing the journalists who helped make our clients' brands successful, we became obsessed with making sure they were very, very happy during the holidays.

Like with everything else in New York, there was a class system when it came to giving presents to the writers, editors, TV reporters, and producers at the media outlets we worked with. A-list presents (typically the designer bag of the season or an expensive watch) went to top editors like Julie Greene and producers at programs like the *Today* show, while lesser-value B- and C-list items (scarves, fragrances, spa gift certificates) went to newspapers, general-interest magazines, and, finally, a short list of freelancers who happened to have great relationships with Ruth.

We were so busy organizing the presents that I basically blinked and Christmas Eve was literally two days away. I was so preoccupied that I almost missed a very important e-mail sent to my personal account. Luckily, my mother had just called and was eagerly awaiting my approval on some jpegs of fabrics she'd sent, so I quickly logged on. And there it was, an e-mail from someone named Laila Zimmerman.

"Dear Minty," it began, "I'm writing on behalf of Kevin Park. He enjoyed meeting you at the boutique opening back in November and was curious if you'd be available to join him for lunch tomorrow before he leaves for St. Barth's. Apologies for the late notice, but please let me know ASAP if you are able to make it. Also, Kevin would appreciate it if you refrain from mentioning this meeting to Ms. Vine." It was signed, "Laila Zimmerman, Assistant to Kevin Park."

I stared at the e-mail as I held a glossy white bag in one hand and a metallic gold pen in the other. What on earth could Kevin Park possibly want from me? Of course I was incredibly flattered, but either way, how was I going to manage sneaking out of the office for two hours unnoticed on Christmas Eve?

I solicited Spencer for some advice.

"Just tell Ruth you have a doctor's appointment." He grinned. "Like, the *lady* doctor or something—it will throw her off."

"Gross," I said.

I was skeptical, but Ruth must have been distracted because she gave me the go-ahead. And thank goodness, because I wasn't going to pass up an opportunity at one-on-one time with New York's hottest up-and-coming designer. I e-mailed Laila back and told her I was thrilled and would love to meet with Kevin. She responded immediately and said she'd made a reservation for the two of us at Morandi, a restaurant near the Kevin Park showroom in the West Village.

⤙❧⤚

That night, I ran out and bought a pale lavender dress from Kevin's resort collection. I paired it with gray suede booties from Brian Atwood, light gray wool tights, and a charcoal-gray wool coat. I even called my mother over from the Plaza for final approval. I wanted everything to be perfect. I had no idea what he wanted to discuss, but I had a feeling it wasn't the weather.

When I arrived at Morandi, a Tuscan-inspired restaurant situated on a tiny sliver of Waverly Place, Kevin was already seated.

He noticed my dress immediately.

"You see," he said. "You're exactly the kind of girl I design for. You live a cosmopolitan life but you're not afraid of color. You're not afraid to be feminine."

I was flattered.

He didn't waste any time in getting to his point.

"So," he began, "in a nutshell, I've been looking for a new brand ambassador, someone who's not a celebrity but has a bit of a . . . higher profile than your regular girl-about-town." He took a bite of his fish and looked at me.

I raised an eyebrow. Was he suggesting that I fit the bill? I was out and about more than ever now, and the invitations—to product launches, trunk shows, store openings, charity cocktail parties—were definitely starting to increase, but I didn't know if anyone would say that I was "high profile" just yet.

"You're on the verge of It Girldom," Kevin said. He laughed. "Okay, so that's not even a word, but you know what I mean. I could help take you to the next level. And you could help *me* sell some clothes."

"Gosh, Kevin," I began. "I am so flattered. I mean, the only thing in the world that would make me hesitate for one second is . . ."

Kevin waved a hand in the air.

"Ruth? Let's be honest, you've got to be miserable there."

I was silent. Of course I thought about quitting RVPR at least twice a day. I had regular breakdowns and my mother thought I was crazy for staying as long as I had. Tripp was acting as my on-call therapist and had already talked me off the ledge more than a dozen times. Lately, if I called him hysterically crying because Ruth had berated me in front of the entire office for answering her phone the wrong way or had sent me back to the salad place for the third time because the arugula wasn't crisp enough, he just told me to quit. It was becoming pretty clear that maybe RVPR wasn't the right fit for me.

"Ruth can be very demanding," I finally said.

"We all know that's an understatement." Kevin smiled. "I guess my point is, a girl like you needs to be out and about in fabulous clothes, not sitting in a cubicle slaving away on a guest list. And this position would allow you to do that. In fact, that's pretty much the job description."

"Going out and wearing your clothes?" I asked. I thought he must be joking.

"Well, yes," he said, his tone suddenly serious. "If you're going to all of the best parties, wearing my dresses and being photographed by Richard Fitzsimmons, appearing in *WWD* and getting mentions in 'Page Six,' that kind of visibility is priceless for a small brand like mine."

"Wow," I said. "I really don't know what to say!"

Of course I *did* know what to say, and it was *Yes!* How could I pass up such an opportunity? I genuinely liked Kevin. He clearly wanted to support me and see me grow in a way that Ruth never would. This "job" he spoke of sounded like more fun than work. The thing was, I'd only ever heard about one person quitting RVPR for another job and the word "blacklisted" was used several times when her name came up. Ruth was great at firing people, but she was not so great at letting them move on.

"Just be honest with her," Kevin said as we walked out of Morandi. "If there's one thing Ruth understands, it's ambition. You can't exactly remain her assistant forever."

"True," I said.

"So do you accept?"

"Of course!" I said. "Yes, I absolutely accept."

"Great," he said. "We'll discuss the details after the holidays."

"Absolutely, Kevin," I said. "I'll talk to you soon."

He gave me a big hug and sent me on my way. Funny, regardless of Kevin's assurances, I felt like I was about to walk the gangplank.

Maybe I was being silly. After all, assistants weren't so hard to come by, especially in the fashion PR business.

———❦———

When I arrived back at the office, I had my game face on.

"Ruth's been looking for you," Spencer said.

"It's not even two o'clock yet," I said.

"Don't shoot the messenger," he replied.

I didn't have a good feeling at all. As I knocked softly on Ruth's door, she screamed from inside for me to enter.

"Spencer said you were looking for me?" I asked, peeking my head inside.

She gestured toward the seat in front of her desk and I sat down.

"Over the course of a few months," she began, "I've watched you morph from a simple, wide-eyed girl from Charleston into a self-absorbed . . . how shall I put this . . . party girl. And your priorities have become very skewed, to put it lightly."

I scoffed. What was she talking about?

"Ruth, I'm sorry, but I just don't know where this is coming from," I said. I felt my stomach flop and churn. Minutes before, I had been so confident and focused, ready to put my foot down, and now I felt like the tables were being turned. Could she possibly know that I was about to quit?

"Face it, Minty," she continued, "you're not exactly dedicated to this job. You seem to be dedicated to attending charity events and cocktail parties though. And the whole doctor's-appointment thing? Do you really think I bought that?"

Oh God, I thought. Did she somehow know I had met Kevin for lunch? She was Ruthless Vine, after all.

"I know you were at Morandi today," she said. "And don't even try to deny it or act surprised. You were there. With Kevin Park."

"I—I—" I stuttered. "Ruth, I don't know what to say. He asked me to lunch and I wasn't sure how you would react. I actually wanted to talk to you," I continued. As the words came out, I was amazed that she was even allowing me to speak. "Kevin and I had a really good talk and—"

"Save it," she said. "You think I'm going to let you quit before I tell you you're fired? Fat chance." She picked up the phone and pressed one button. "Yes, as soon as possible. Thank you," she said, hanging up the receiver.

I looked around. What the hell was going on?

Within thirty seconds, two large men were standing in Ruth's doorway.

It was like something out of a nightmare. Before I could even get out of my seat, they were "escorting" me toward my cubicle, where I was then ordered to empty the contents of my desk drawers into a cardboard box and exit the building as fast as humanly possible. Ruth stayed in her office the entire time. I think she may have even been on the phone laughing about something. It was all such a blur, all I can remember is Spencer staring at me, bug-eyed and drooling, like I had just been convicted of murder and was being carted off to Rikers Island.

"Do you have everything you need, ma'am?" the man to my right said.

Ma'am? Now I knew how Tabitha felt! I looked around my desk. No one else in the office seemed to be paying much attention to the spectacle. Even Spencer, at this point, was staring intently at his computer screen.

"Yes, yes, I think so," I replied. My voice sounded like it was coming from somewhere else, somewhere completely removed from my body.

For several minutes, I stood on the corner of Prince and Broadway holding my cardboard box, literally staring into space, dumbfounded. As I glanced at my BlackBerry out of habit, it started vibrating: Tripp.

"How was the meeting with Kevin?" he asked.

Kevin, I thought. It seemed like two years ago.

"It went really well," I said, staring down West Broadway. "He offered me a job."

"Babe," he said, "that's great!"

"And then Ruth fired me." I exhaled. Saying those words felt like both a relief and a disappointment.

He paused for a moment. "Well. Let's be honest, that's also great."

I couldn't help but laugh. He certainly put things in perspective.

"Listen," he continued, "they're letting us out of work early. I thought we could meet up before dinner with your parents. Have you been to see the tree yet at Rockefeller Center?"

I laughed again. I'd basically been sleeping at the office for the past month. I barely had time to breathe, let alone brave the crowds at Rockefeller Center. At the same time, I couldn't believe it was the day before Christmas and I hadn't seen the tree yet. When I was growing up, my mother always took me to see it during our yearly holiday shopping trip. Now I *lived* in New York and the thought hadn't even crossed my mind!

"No," I said. "But I would love to."

Tripp told me to meet him ASAP on the corner of Sixth Avenue and Forty-Eighth Street. The streets downtown were ridiculously crowded with last-minute holiday shoppers. After unsuccessfully trying to hail a cab for almost ten minutes, I gave up and hopped on the subway, something I'd never done before. I was kind of terrified.

I must have looked pretty pathetic on that train holding my cardboard box, because some random guy came up to me and stuck a dollar in it. He smiled as he walked away, which I guess meant he was joking, but I didn't find it funny.

As I stepped out of the subway and onto Sixth Avenue and saw Tripp standing on the corner, I felt an immediate sense of relief. Yes, my life was moving fast and changing even faster, but Tripp was a reassuring constant. As flighty, noncommittal, and distant as Ryerson had been in the end, Tripp was the opposite: steadfast, determined, and focused. He wasn't always totally supportive of my ambitions, but he made it clear that he wanted me in his life. And now he was taking me to see the Rockefeller Center Christmas tree. It was the perfect ending to a roller-coaster day.

"You all right?" he asked as I walked up and fell into his arms. He took the box for me and glanced inside. It contained nothing more than some pens, a tape dispenser, and a few celebrity weeklies. "Do you really need this stuff?"

"Chuck it," I said into his coat lapel.

He stepped away and threw the box into the nearest trash can. "Better?"

"Much better," I said.

———✦———

We stood in Rockefeller Plaza amidst throngs of people holding up digital cameras, posing in front of the tree or just taking it all in with their families. As crowded as it was, there was a collective goodwill in the air, a spirit of generosity. People came from across the world to see the almost-one-hundred-foot-tall tree. And it's definitely worth experiencing in person. Seeing those thousands of tiny lights up close . . . there's nothing else like it. Tripp held my hand and all I could think was: I've never been happier.

I remembered the first time I visited the tree with my mother. It was our second trip to New York and she'd just taken me to get a pair of red patent leather Mary Janes. She took a picture of me in front of the tree wearing the new shoes. That photo is still in our house today, framed in the living room. I was caught up in this memory when I heard a woman next to me gasp.

"Oh my God!" she said.

I glanced over and realized she was pointing frantically in my direction. I wondered if I had a spider on me and started to swat at my coat reflexively. Then I realized what she was pointing at. Tripp had kneeled down in front of me and was holding a little red box. As I glanced down, he opened it to reveal a gigantic sparkling Cartier engagement ring.

"Holy shit," I said, covering my mouth. "Tripp!"

"Minty Randolph Mercer Davenport—" he began.

I stared at him.

"I've thought about this moment since we were fifteen."

Oh my God. I cupped my hand over my mouth.

"It took me seven years to find you again. I just don't see any point in waiting another minute."

It was one of the most beautiful rings I've ever seen—emerald cut, flawless, platinum band. I actually had to turn away when I looked directly at the ring because one of its facets caught the light and nearly blinded me it was so dazzling. And then it hit me: Tripp was proposing. He was actually proposing marriage to me after three months of dating, in the middle of Rockefeller Center, no less. Part of me thought, This is ludicrous, but the rest of me felt like it was the most normal thing in the world. And that is when I knew what my answer would be.

"Yes!" I nearly screamed. "Yes, yes, yes!"

He looked up at me, bewildered but smiling. A small crowd had gathered around us. Someone started clapping.

"I haven't asked you the question yet," he said.

"Go on and ask it!" a random male voice chimed in. Everyone laughed.

"Will you marry me?"

I almost screamed. "Oh my God, Tripp, absolutely, yes!"

He slipped the ring on my finger and I felt completely different. I'd officially finished the transformation from Minty Davenport of Charleston, South Carolina, to Minty du Pont of Manhattan. The ring was like a seal of approval stamped with a 10021 zip code.

Someone took our picture and before I knew it Tripp was ushering me into his town car. Zeke had somehow managed to pull up at exactly the right time.

"Your parents are waiting uptown," Tripp said, taking my hand. We zoomed up Sixth Avenue to the Upper East Side.

10

Better to Be Overdressed
Than Underdressed

When Tripp and I walked into my apartment, my entire family—Scarlett, Gharland, and Darby—was waiting with expectant looks on their faces, each one of them decked out in a perfectly coordinated holiday outfit. I noticed immediately that Darby had on the coolest knee-high Isabel Marant boots that I'd been drooling over for months. She always had a knack for looking sexy without being over-the-top.

The entire living room was decorated to perfection, right down to the fresh spruce garland lining the fireplace and Christmas tree lit up in the corner. I gasped, overwhelmed. Scarlett must have been working on all of those finishing touches while I was at work.

"Hi," I said sheepishly, walking into the living room.

Everyone stared back at me blankly.

"Well," Mother began, breaking the silence. "I'm going to grab us each a drink. And when I come back let's have a look at that diamond! Even though I've seen it already, of course." She winked and disappeared into the kitchen.

I glanced at Darby and my father, who just smiled and shrugged. "Y'all knew?!"

My father frowned. "You think Tripp would have asked for your hand in marriage without checking with me first?"

Of course, I thought. Wow. I just couldn't believe he'd been planning this and I had no clue.

"Daddy, it's so good to see you," I said, running over to him. In the excitement of the moment I'd completely forgotten to even greet him. We hadn't seen each other in months!

He wrapped me in his arms and picked me up off the ground so that my feet, platform booties and all, were left dangling over the carpet. I inhaled his familiar scent: cigars and bourbon. He placed me back on the ground and twirled me around, just like he did when I was a little girl.

There was a prolonged silence, which was typically my mother's cue to make a grand entrance. I looked over my shoulder and, like clockwork, the kitchen door opened. I was sure she'd been standing on the other side for the last five minutes waiting for our conversation to die down; her timing was too perfect.

She was carrying a tray of vodka sodas and two bourbons. She distributed each drink to its rightful owner and we each took a seat in the living room.

"Did I miss anything?" she asked. "Y'all haven't started planning the wedding without me, have you?"

"No, Mother," Darby said, rolling her eyes. She turned to me and whispered, "Congratulations, Tripp's a stud."

I poked her in the ribs.

"BTW," she continued, "I think I got fat. Mom barely gave me a hug."

I couldn't help but laugh. It was a running joke between my sister and me that the skinnier we were, the bigger the hug. She was being ridiculous though—she looked exactly the same.

"Darby," Tripp said. "I haven't seen you since you were, what, maybe thirteen?"

He went in for a hug.

She made eye contact with me over his shoulder and I almost burst out laughing, her expression was so priceless.

"Shall we toast to Minty and Tripp?" Mother said, raising her glass in the air. We followed suit. My father pointed his glass of bourbon in Tripp's direction.

"Just keep in mind," he began, "I had my eye on you back when you were a seventeen-year-old smart-ass and I've got my eye on you now."

Everyone laughed nervously.

"To Minty and Tripp," he finally said.

I couldn't believe it; Tripp and I were engaged.

———◆◆◆———

Over dinner that evening, my mother suggested we set the wedding date for the second weekend in June. June! That gave us about five months to plan, and five months in wedding time is equal to about three minutes.

Since my eighteenth birthday, Scarlett had booked the Charleston church and country club for the second weekend in June each year. Of course, she had been canceling (and rescheduling) steadily for the last several years, but she happened to be close friends with both our priest and the manager of the club, so they paid no mind. Of course, there were about a million other things to do. There was the engagement party, which Tripp said his parents, Phillip and Bebe, had already offered to host. Let's be honest, the very concept of anyone else sticking their nose into my mother's wedding-of-the-century extravaganza turned her alabaster skin a deep shade of crimson and warranted some alone time in the powder room, but when she emerged, she seemed gracious and accepting.

"I'm sure Phillip and Bebe will do a lovely job," she said over a dessert of chocolate mousse. "Perhaps Bebe and I could meet for some coffee in the next week or so to discuss?"

"Mother," I said.

Tripp raised an eyebrow and smiled.

"Fine." She patted her lips gingerly with her napkin and placed it back in her lap. "I will leave the engagement party up to the du Ponts."

Which was a blessing in disguise, because if my mother were going to pull off the wedding she'd always envisioned, there was a lot to accomplish in a short period of time. Such as booking a roster of names that read like the Who's Who of weddings, including the famed Peter Duchin band for music; the photographer Denis Reggie, who captured JFK Jr.'s wedding to Carolyn Bessette; a show-stopping cake by Sylvia Weinstock; calligrapher Bernard Maisner to place the finishing touches on the save-the-dates, invitations, escort cards, and place cards; and Glorious Food for the catering. Oh! And there was the dress, of course.

Within days of Tripp's proposal, I was receiving regular e-mail updates from my mother about the status of anything and everything, right down to the glassware, napkins, and chair covers. It was enough to put even a bridezilla over the edge, and I was teetering. It's not that I wasn't genuinely interested in making my wedding the most magical night of my life, but I was also overwhelmed. The wallpaper glue in my apartment was probably still drying and already I had to start thinking about the reality of finding a new place with Tripp. I was about to start my new job with Kevin Park. It was a lot to take in, but at the end of the day, I wouldn't have had it any other way. I was marrying the man of my dreams. So what if it wasn't the most convenient timing? Is there even such a thing?

———◈◈◈———

In the midst of all of the craziness, the night of the Frick ball snuck up on me. It turned out Spencer was right; it was extremely hard to score an invite to the Frick. Guests were chosen by a committee of "young fellows" of the museum, which consisted of some of the most powerful young men and women in Manhattan. As I ran through the list of names on the invitation, many of them jumped out at me: Trump, Rockefeller, Charriol, Aston. I was so flattered to be included as part of that group!

I wanted the evening to be perfect. Tripp and I hadn't attended an event together since we got engaged, and while some of our close friends obviously knew, the Frick would be our first official "coming out" as a couple.

The theme was the French Revolution and I planned on taking it seriously. I checked with Kevin about borrowing one of his dresses, but most of the spring collection had been lent out to various celebrities for awards season and everything that was left wouldn't have been appropriate for the theme anyway. The style of that era was pretty specific: corseted bodice, full skirt, exposed shoulders, very dramatic. Luckily I already owned a gown that fit that exact description. It happened to be my debutante gown. I figured no one in New York had seen me in the dress, so why not?

I made an afternoon appointment at the Oscar Blandi salon, where my stylist Ludmilla created what she referred to as a "deconstructed Marie Antoinette." It was one of the most over-the-top updos I'd ever seen, complete with carefully placed roses that matched my gown. I couldn't wait to get dressed!

As I was walking through my front door, Tripp called.

"I'm not sure I'm going to be able to make it tonight, Mints," he said.

What!?

"Um, excuse me . . . ," I said, "why not?"

I was trying to remain calm. I had an updo to maintain, after all.

"Something's come up," he said. "Work is crazy. I just don't think it's going to happen. I'm really sorry."

"You've got to be kidding me." I took a deep breath. "What am I going to do, go alone?"

I could hear him typing, which meant he was only half-listening to me.

"Isn't Emily going?"

Yes, Emily was going. But, like the majority of the people going to this thing, she had a date! What was I supposed to do, walk around the Frick Museum with Emily and her date and—oh—my engagement ring? How was I going to explain to people that my new fiancé had better things to do?

"Tripp, this is one night, a few hours. You've known about it for weeks!" I said, trying to control my temper.

"Give me a second." He put me on hold.

Of all things he could have done in that very moment, he put me on hold.

When he came back, I was at my wit's end.

"Mints, I'm sorry," he said. "I'm just . . . swamped here. See if Emily can pick you up on her way or something. Mints?"

What could I do? He clearly wasn't leaving me with any other choice.

"Fine," I said.

I know I should have said something far stronger, but I was so surprised and confused—all I could come up with was a weak, limp "fine." Not to mention, I wasn't brought up that way. In stressful times like this, I reverted to my upbringing, falling back on politeness when I should have stood up for myself.

I looked in the mirror and took a deep breath. Black mascara tears were streaming down my cheeks. "Deconstructed Marie Antoinette" was a *nice* way of putting it. I looked more like Marie Antoinette after the guillotine. How was I supposed to show up to the Frick without someone to lean on?

I called Emily. Maybe she could explain to her date that I was having a mental breakdown and she had no other choice but to come to my rescue.

"Ugh, Minty, Nate is going to be pissed," Emily said in an exasperated tone, referring to her date.

"Emily, I don't know what else to do," I whined. "I really need your help."

She huffed and puffed for a moment, but she eventually came around. "All right," she finally said. "I'm going to tell Nate I'll meet him there. I'll be over in a few."

"I owe you, Em!" I said.

"You do."

Emily arrived at my apartment wearing a breathtaking, dove-gray

J. Mendel floor-length gown. Her hair was pulled back into a tight bun and she'd applied the prettiest shade of petal-pink lipstick. She was like something out of an iconic painting that inspires entire fashion shows.

"Oh, your hair," she said.

I patted my updo.

"I wanted to look authentic! Am I going to look stupid?"

"You are too much," she said. "I have to be honest, not everyone dresses in theme for this thing, but why not? It will get people's attention, that's for sure. By the way, Nate was a good sport about meeting us there."

"Oh, Emily," I began, "I'm so sorry I got so wrapped up in my little catastrophe that I didn't properly thank you."

Emily looked like she was tolerating me, but just barely. "Minty, we have about ten minutes to get this show on the road," she said. "Attending the Frick ball is like your societal debut. I'm here to help you get it right. So let's see your dress."

My debutante gown was a white silk princess style with a cinched waist, cap sleeves, and a skirt so full I kind of felt like the lady in the large dress from *The Nutcracker*. After I put it on, I turned around in the mirror and glanced at the back, which dipped down to just above my waist. Emily nodded approvingly, but at the same time I could tell she was a little amused with my choice.

"That dress will *definitely* get you noticed."

I shrugged.

"Come on," she said. "Your subjects are waiting."

When I walked up the steps of the Frick that first time, I suddenly understood all of the fuss. It was like walking into Edith Wharton's New York, when society lived in houses instead of apartments and an entire staff of servants inhabited a wing of the mansion. Situated on the corner of Seventieth Street and Fifth Avenue, the Frick was impressive for a museum, let alone a private home. "Mr. Frick designed the house with the idea that he would leave it—and his art collection—to the public when he died," Emily explained as we entered the main foyer.

She guided me toward the coat check. I realized I was already starting to get a few stares, especially seeing as I could barely get through the crowd without forcing couples and groups of people to part down the middle and navigate around me.

"You're causing quite the stir," Emily said as we walked into a large room where all of the guests were gathering.

"Really?" I asked, adjusting uncomfortably, and glanced around.

Emily lifted a glass of champagne off one of the trays being passed around and took a sip. We stopped in the center of the room next to a huge column, one of several that lined the sunken atrium in the center. There were only a few other girls who had taken the theme to heart. One walked by us wearing a dress with a huge hoop skirt. Her makeup was like a mask, and her hair was piled high with extensions. She looked like she'd stepped off the stage at Lincoln Center.

"That's Yasmin Beak," Emily said, noticing my mesmerized expression. "She's some sort of artist. She shows up at a lot of these parties looking like a freak with the same makeup: powder-white skin, black liquid liner, and red lips. She adjusts the outfit accordingly, of course."

"Well, she's stealing some of my thunder," I said, laughing.

We walked farther into the main room, toward the fountain in the center of the atrium. Guests, dressed in floor-length gowns and tuxedos, milled around the fountain and sat on the benches surrounding it. The art collections were through a large doorway toward the back, but not many people were taking the opportunity to check out the sixteenth-century portraits. The real live people were far more interesting to behold.

"This is amazing people-watching!" I said.

Emily laughed. "I'm sure a lot of people are saying the same thing about you."

"Oh God." I took a sip of champagne and straightened my posture. My mother was always on me about my posture.

We stopped next to one of the fanlike fern plantings and tried to look nonchalant. Or, at least, *I* tried to look nonchalant. Not the easi-

est task considering my getup. Of course, Emily had done this type
of thing a thousand times before. I wondered when it started to get
easy—when it started to feel comfortable. I hoped never! It was all so
exciting and glamorous and fun.

We passed by a well-dressed couple standing with an impossibly
thin, petite woman. She was wearing a floor-length, boho-inspired
dress. Emily smiled and waved.

"That's Amanda and Barry Greenway," she said as we passed by,
motioning toward the couple. "They've been together forever. She's a
well-known interior designer. Oh! And supposedly he's gay and they
have some sort of arrangement."

"Emily!"

"And the other chick is Beth York. She's the fashion director at
Marie Claire. Generally nice and gracious."

I nodded, taking it all in.

"Harriet Blake," she said, motioning toward a chic-looking woman
with platinum-blond hair and a slim man with tanned skin and
slick, dark hair. "She's a stylist. Works with Kate Bosworth and Keira
Knightley."

Suddenly a tiny, almost birdlike man with a shock of white hair
swooped in front of Harriet Blake and snapped a few photos. He was
wearing a simple black jacket, but it wasn't a tuxedo or a blazer. It was
made out of the same type of flimsy fabric they use to make doctors'
scrubs. He didn't ask permission to photograph her ahead of time like
Richard Fitzsimmons would have, but his movements were so effort-
less that she barely noticed. I could tell after he scooted away that she
was flattered and excited to have had her picture taken by this man.
Who was he?

"Bruce Williams," Emily whispered into my ear. "He covers parties
and street fashion for *The New York Times*. He's a legend!"

"Oh!" I said. "I've heard of him. 'Sunday Styles'?"

"Yes." Emily nodded. "That's him. He has a different style from
Richard. But it's hard to pinpoint what he's going to go for. He goes for
what he likes. It's totally singular."

"I want him to take my picture," I admitted.

Just then, the DJ started playing dance music in the next room, a large, circular space with ornate wood paneling. I peeked in and noticed a few couples milling around the perimeter, contemplating making their way onto the dance floor. Bruce followed them inside.

"Classic tactic," Emily whispered. "The first people on the dance floor are pretty much guaranteed to have their photo taken by Bruce."

I turned around then. I'm not sure why. I felt someone behind me or someone coming toward me and I was right. It was Tripp, sheepishly straightening the bow tie on his tux. He'd made it to the Frick after all.

"Tripp," Emily said flatly.

"Emily," he replied. He pecked her on the cheek. "It's nice to see you again."

"Likewise," she said.

I stared at him. "You made it."

"I was able to move some things around," he said.

I noticed Emily rolling her eyes.

"Can I have this dance?" he said in a mock-serious tone.

I glanced at Emily, who waved me away. I was actually surprised—Tripp had always hated dancing.

"Go on," she said.

He pulled me onto the dance floor and started twirling me around, gigantic dress and hair and all. I was immediately brought back to the days when my parents forced me to go to cotillion in order to prepare for my debut. I spent hours waltzing awkwardly with pimply-faced boys who definitely would have rather been playing video games. But we had no other choice. We were supposed to know how to dance properly, so we danced. I'm not saying that Tripp danced like a thirteen-year-old boy, but it was pretty clear he hadn't updated his moves since his own cotillion days. He had a few crowd-pleasing moves that he kept coming back to, like the Pretzel and dipping me. Before I knew it, his hand was behind my back and my head was nearly touching the floor. And what was that? A camera flash? It happened so fast I barely had time to process it, but as Tripp pulled me back upright, I saw Bruce Williams scampering away. He was quick!

I turned to Tripp. "Did you see that?" I asked.

He looked at me blankly. "What?"

"Bruce Williams!"

"Who?"

"Bruce Williams." I poked him in the arm. "The *New York Times* photographer. He just took our picture!"

Tripp shrugged. "Oh."

"You don't think that's exciting?"

"What, some photographer taking our picture? Please, Minty." He pulled me off the dance floor and toward the bar.

I stood to the side and frowned. It *was* kind of thrilling. Like Emily said, Bruce didn't take just anyone's photo. It was a major compliment! I didn't understand why Tripp felt the need to be so dismissive.

"Please, yourself," I said, swatting at him. Suddenly I wasn't so thrilled that he'd decided to show up out of the blue.

Tripp walked off toward the bar.

I looked over and saw Emily standing a few feet away with an attractive Wall Street type—it had to be Nate. They looked happy, flirtatious even. I swear I saw her bat her eyelashes a few times. Could this be more than the "platonic friendship" she was making it out to be? After watching them for a few seconds, I couldn't help but wonder, where was the romance and happiness I'd been looking forward to that evening? I was dressed like a princess, after all. Where was my prince?

Tripp handed me a champagne.

"You know," I said, "I'm not feeling so well after all."

He looked surprised but also relieved, like he was just waiting for me to say the word.

"You want to get out of here?"

To be completely honest, I wanted *him* to get out of there so I could enjoy the rest of my evening. Tripp's appearance should have made everything perfect, but instead I just felt deflated.

"Yes, let's go."

We walked over to Emily and Nate and explained we were going to head out.

"Early morning," Tripp said.

"I see," Emily said. She gave me a quick hug. "I guess I'll see you on Sunday?"

Sunday, Sunday . . . I stared back at her blankly.

"Mandarin Oriental? Spa day?"

"Oh!" I jumped. "Oh yes, of course! I have to stop in to meet with Kevin for a bit in the morning and I'll head over there right after."

Tripp stood to the side, looking impatient.

"Break a leg," Emily said. "Can't wait to hear all about it."

Sticks and Stones

Can Break Your Bones

One thing I'd learned so far about New York people is that they are always working. It begins with the workday, which flows into after-work drinks with colleagues, which flows into after-after-work dinner with more work-related people. And weekends are just an opportunity to get more work done.

Sundays are official "unofficial" workdays, even in the fashion industry, and especially in the weeks leading up to Fashion Week, which happens twice a year. When I started working for Kevin, he was days away from his show and beyond crazed, but he asked that I come in for a quick meeting the Sunday after the Frick ball to go over my contract. It was the only spare moment he had.

Walking out the door, I grabbed my copies of *The New York Times* and the *Post* to read in the cab. As I headed down Fifth Avenue, I opened up the *Times* "Styles" section and there, as the centerpiece photo of Bruce Williams's column, was a very large photo of Tripp dipping me on the dance floor at the Frick ball! I skimmed the page. Underneath the photo was a caption with our names, and mine was spelled correctly this time! I couldn't believe it. As the cab pulled up to Kevin's office building, I quickly folded up the section, grabbed the rest of my stuff, and hurried out of the cab. The *Post* would have to wait for after the meeting.

When I arrived at Kevin's office on the tenth floor, his assistant ushered me into an open, airy conference room adjacent to his studio. He was sitting at the table with his director of public relations, Jenny Severs, a perky brunette with a sallow complexion and big saucer eyes, and Jenny's assistant, Lane Beekman, who was so busy taking notes, she barely looked up when I walked into the room.

"Sooo," Kevin began, smiling. "How are you?"

He looked at me a bit longer than I was comfortable with, as if my response might not be so positive. I smiled back at him.

"Great!" I said. I didn't know whether to mention the *Times* or not. I wasn't one to brag. I decided to let them bring it up. Or maybe they hadn't seen it yet?

"Good to hear, sweetie," he said, nodding his head solemnly. "So, let's get down to business, shall we?" He turned to Jenny. "I hate to say this but we're a bit strapped for time!"

"First off," Jenny began, "welcome to Kevin Park."

"Thank you," I said. "I'm so excited!"

Jenny smiled and slid a folder across the table. "I've put together a press strategy that's pretty straightforward," she said.

I pulled the folder toward me and opened it up gingerly, not sure whether I should look at it in front of them or not. Kevin had already quoted a pretty generous salary, so I was curious about what else they could be offering. I started reading from the top.

"I hope you'll find it satisfactory?" Jenny asked.

This kind of thing always made me uncomfortable. I glanced down at the bottom of the page and there was a "clothing allowance" in addition to my salary, which could be used toward clothing purchases in any of the Kevin Park boutiques and for shoes from a list of approved designers such as Christian Louboutin and Manolo Blahnik.

And, I must say: OMG.

It was a lot of money, especially considering the fact that, as far as

I could tell, they didn't even expect me to come into the office every day. In a nutshell, I was expected to attend all Kevin Park events and make myself available for press opportunities such as magazine profiles and television spots. There was also the possibility of my appearing in upcoming Kevin Park advertising campaigns.

"We have yet to launch a formal campaign," Kevin explained, "but hopefully that's next up on the agenda and if we do, of course I'd love for you to be the face of the line."

"Wow," I said. "This is amazing!"

Kevin looked at Jenny and smiled. I couldn't believe this was actually a job. I almost felt like I should be paying Kevin, not the other way around!

"Feel free to take everything home and look it over in detail, by the way," Jenny added. "And of course let me know if you have any questions. But maybe we can go over a few dates while we have you here?"

Lane handed me a calendar for the month of February with several dates highlighted. The first thing I noticed was the Kevin Park fashion show at Lincoln Center. I'd secretly hoped I was going to be invited. I'd only been to a fashion show once in my life. My cousin Virginia was working for Ralph Lauren at the time. My mother and I were due to be in New York for a few days before I went back to school and Virginia mentioned she could get me backstage. It was such a cool experience, being in the thick of everything, the makeup artists and hairstylists working in a frenzy to get the models finished in time.

I could barely see the models from where we sat, but it was such a treat nonetheless. Afterward, I turned to my right and I saw legendary *Vogue* editor André Leon Talley had been standing next to us the whole time. I was starstruck! And I couldn't believe someone of his stature would deign to watch the show from the nosebleed seats. It was like the fashion equivalent of seeing a celebrity on the subway. Virginia explained that sometimes he preferred to watch the show from the bleachers because they were more "low-key."

I couldn't believe how much had changed since that day. I was actually getting *invited* to fashion shows, with my own seat and everything. "I'm so excited to go to the show," I said.

"Oh, honey," he said, "you won't just be *attending* the show, you'll be walking in it."

"What?" I couldn't help but nearly jump out of my seat, and not in a good way. "You're kidding, right?"

Kevin laughed. "Not in the slightest. It will be your big debut. I'm thinking I'll have you walk in the grand finale dress."

"Kevin, you're crazy!" I said.

My phone started vibrating. Mother. I ignored it.

"So, anyway," Kevin said, standing up, "Jenny will schedule a few minutes for you to come in tomorrow to make sure everything is perfect with the dress. We have your measurements on file already so it should be all set, but there are always a few last-minute adjustments."

"I'll e-mail you first thing in the morning when I have a better idea of how the day is going to pan out," Jenny said.

"Sounds good!"

<hr>

As I was walking out of Kevin's studio, I called my mother back. She was due to arrive in New York Tuesday evening, a few days before the engagement party, so we could iron out some wedding details and do a little dress shopping. Maybe she had another activity to add to our itinerary, I thought.

"Oh, Minty," she said, "this is just awful."

I frowned. What was she talking about? Did she see my photo in Bruce Williams's column and hate it? Was it my hair?

"Mommy," I began, "it was a theme party. I was dressed up like Marie Antoinette!"

There was silence.

"I'm telling you," I said, "a lot of people at the Frick were dressed up in theme!" Okay, not a lot of people, but she didn't have to know that. I stood on the corner of Washington and Jane and hailed a cab. I had less than twenty minutes to make it up to Columbus Circle to meet Emily for our spa day.

"The Frick?" She paused. "Oh, no, sweetheart. I am not talking about the Frick."

"Columbus Circle, please," I said. The cab took off. "What are you talking about then? You didn't see the photo of Tripp and me in 'Sunday Styles'? It's amazing!"

"Sweetie, I'm sure it is and, God, I would have looked at it if I hadn't been dealing with this 'Page Six' thing all morning."

"'Page Six'?" I looked down at my lap and realized I'd left both of my newspapers at Kevin's office. Shit. What the hell was in the *Post*? I could tell from her tone that it was bad. Like, epically bad. I closed my eyes.

"Just tell me," I said.

She sighed loudly.

"Check the Internet, honey," she said, suddenly sounding rushed. "I've got the Hendersons and the Gregorys coming over for brunch. Up to my ears in errands. Oh, and your sister is calling on the other line. Gotta go. Bye."

"What on earth?" The cab approached a newsstand on the corner of Sixth Avenue and Forty-seventh Street. "Sir," I said, "do you mind stopping here quickly? I need to pick up a copy of the *Post*."

He swerved over to the right, nearly sending me flying across the seat. "Make it quick," he said. "There's no standing on this corner."

I rushed over to the newsstand, threw a dollar at the guy in the window, grabbed a copy, and ran back to the cab, which, thankfully, was still waiting on the corner. I barely had time to close the door before he sped off again and I was thrown backward into the seat. I didn't care. I just wanted to know what the hell was going on!

I skimmed through the headlines: BLOOMBERG'S BLUNDER, NIX TIME FOR THE KNICKS?, GIRL SAVES RAT FROM SUBWAY AND KEEPS AS PET, and so on. Finally, there it was, the headline simple enough: PARTY OVER FOR SOUTHERN DEB?

The item started with the news of my departure from RVPR, saying that I'd been "replaced" by a "pretty young thing" named Alexis Barnaby who'd been recruited from the offices of a rival fashion PR firm, where she had been working as an intern while taking classes at FIT. There was a direct quote from Ruth, who said that I had grown "too big for my britches" but that she wished me the "best of luck."

For a second I was almost relieved. I wondered why my mother thought this was so bad. Why did she sound so shocked? And then I reached the final paragraph. *No stranger to the late nights and indulgent lifestyle of Manhattan's elite, bachelor du Pont may know how to play the role of doting fiancé, but there's evidence he's spreading the love beyond the boundaries of his commitment to Miss Minty. As recently as only a few weeks ago, he was seen escorting a certain comely cougar back to his Upper East Side bachelor pad.*

I closed the newspaper. I might have developed a tough skin over the last couple of months, but I wasn't made of Teflon. There was something so official about seeing the words printed in black and white. It was almost like the *Post* was confirming a sneaking suspicion I'd had deep down for some time now. As the cab pulled up in front of Emily, who was waiting on the corner, my phone buzzed: Tripp, of course. I noticed he'd already texted me several times, *CALL ME.* Half of me wanted to call him and hear what he had to say. The other half needed some time to process the whole thing. I put my phone back in my Lady Dior bag.

"Em," was all I could say as I rushed over to her.

We hugged.

"Let's get inside," she said.

Once we made it up to the thirty-fifth floor and checked in, Emily and I met in a little seating area overlooking the park and waited for our therapists. We had one of the most amazing views I'd ever experienced in New York.

Emily broke the silence, clearly trying to keep the conversation lighthearted and fun. "First of all, the 'Sunday Styles' photo is *beyond*. You've arrived, Mints," she said with a smirk.

I stuck out my tongue and let it hang there for a moment. Literally, that was all I could bring myself to do. I didn't even have a raspberry noise left in me.

"Are you okay?"

"I just read the *Post* in the cab over here," I said. "I just keep hearing the words 'comely cougar' over and over again in my head."

"Oh God, you *just* read it?"

"Yes. I had my meeting with Kevin first thing this morning! I glanced at the *Times* and that's it. No wonder Kevin asked me if I was doing all right when I walked into his office! I can't believe this!"

"Well, look at it this way," Emily said. "They say it's better to be on 'Page Six' than to *not* be on 'Page Six'!"

There was some truth to what she was saying, but it wasn't what I needed to hear at that moment. I needed to hear the *real* truth, and I had a nagging feeling that Emily was hiding something.

"Just spill it, Em," I said.

She looked down at the floor.

"Listen," she sighed. "It's not that I know anything. It's just that yes, I've heard things. And I'm not saying Tripp is a bad guy or that he doesn't love you. But, like I've said in the past, he's not always honest about everything."

"Emily, just tell me! I'm ready!"

"I saw him that night," she blurted. "I'm pretty sure it's the same night they're talking about in 'Page Six.' About a week before Christmas, May Abernathy had a little get-together at her apartment on Gramercy Park." She paused for a quick breath. "I can't remember why you weren't there. I think you were working late or something? Tabitha showed up and I was going to tell you, I just didn't know if it was worth it. I mean honestly, Minty, I'm not even one hundred percent sure anything happened!"

"Wait a minute," I said. "Slow down. So Tabitha was just *at* this party or you saw them leave together or what?"

Emily was silent.

"Em."

"It was pretty late," she said. "And I was a little tipsy myself. Tripp said good-bye and walked to the door by himself. But Tabitha followed him."

"She *what*?"

"She followed him to the door," Emily said. "And yes, I saw them leave together."

If Tabitha really wanted to sneak around with my fiancé, she could just as easily have texted him and set up a time and place to meet in private. Was she hoping it would get back to me somehow? Probably. I pictured her curling up with her Sunday *New York Post* and smiling to herself, satisfied. Before I had a chance to respond, our therapists came out and handed us each an "organic purification tea" which was supposed to jump-start the detoxification process. I felt like I already had toxins oozing out of my pores between Tripp, Tabitha, and "Page Six."

I sipped my tea, which tasted like licorice and dirt.

"Just take a deep breath, first of all. It's a stupid newspaper."

"But what about the tiny little fact that my fiancé might be running around behind my back?"

"You don't know if it's a fact yet. You have to talk to him first." She paused. "Have you talked to him yet?"

I thought about my phone, far away in the ladies' locker room where I didn't have to think about it for at least another three hours—more if I finished up my treatment in the sauna and vitality pool. In fact, if I played my cards right, I could probably extend my spa visit into an entire spa day.

"No," I said. "I'm not sure I'm ready to talk to him, especially after what you just told me."

"That's fair," Emily said.

"What bothers me the most," I said, "is I don't even know this woman. I've seen her a few times from afar and that's about it. Tripp swears she's obsessed with him, that she practically stalks him. Maybe that's true but at the same time I feel like she's out to get *me* as well. It just all feels so . . . deliberate. It's like she's trying to get caught or get Tripp in trouble."

"The thing that you need to remember about Tabitha," Emily said, taking a sip of her tea, "is that she'll do what it takes to stay on top. No matter what."

12

Gossip Is an Unladylike Endeavor

As I hailed a cab outside of the Mandarin Oriental, I summoned up the courage to check my phone. No less than fifteen missed calls from Tripp. The last text message had come in a few minutes ago, around two thirty P.M.

It read: *Headed to the racquet club. This is bullshit. I love you.*

The racquet club, is that right? I thought. Here I am barely able to hail a cab because I am so humiliated and Tripp is burning calories.

Yes, I could have gone home. I could have retreated back to my perfectly appointed apartment and fielded calls from my mother, who was probably still dealing with her own backlash in Charleston, where for whatever reason many people we knew seemed to read the *Post* these days.

"Take me to Fifty-third and Park."

I'd never been to the Racquet and Tennis Club on Park Avenue before. Tripp often went there after work to play racquetball and go swimming, but it was an old-school club. Meaning, women were technically not allowed.

Nonetheless, I walked right up the steps and into a main room that looked like it had been decorated by an old white man. There was a lot of white marble, leather furniture, maroon paint, and brass fixtures. Granted, I still had my sunglasses on and was sporting a less-than-fresh hairdo, but pretty much everyone in the room turned to look at me as I walked up to the reception desk.

"Yes?" A man in a white coat and bow tie glared down at me like I was the pizza delivery guy.

"Hello, sir," I began, my southern manners kicking in. I took off my sunglasses. "I was wondering if you could help me. You see my boyfriend—my fiancé, excuse me—is a member here and I'm desperate to speak to him. It really is quite the emergency situation or I wouldn't be bothering you, you see." I almost curtsied at the end, I was so wrapped up in the role of damsel in distress.

"Your fiancé?" he repeated. "Last name, please?"

"Yes, sir," I replied. "du Pont."

The man stared back at me. Then he looked down at a board in front of him, which listed all of the members' names. Then he looked back up at me again.

"Of course," he said. "Mr. du Pont the Third, I imagine? Both the elder and the younger are currently in the club."

"Yes, the third," I said.

"I see."

He picked up the receiver of his phone.

"If you don't mind waiting, miss, I can put in a call to Mr. du Pont and let him know you are here."

You see, that wouldn't do. The whole point of my coming to the racquet club in the first place was that I wanted Tripp to be taken off guard. I wanted him to feel uncomfortable. And since I'd felt the depths of humiliation as a result of his actions, whether they were criminal or not, I wanted him to have a taste, as well. I wanted him to know what it felt like when someone you loved and cared about truly let you down. In a very public way, no less.

"Hmmm," I said. "You wouldn't happen to know if he's playing racquetball, would you?"

The man, distracted by an incoming call, barely looked at me.

"I believe he's taking a swim," he said, picking up the receiver and greeting the person on the other end of the line with a grim hello.

A swim, I repeated in my head. Perfect.

My behavior in the following moments is not advisable. For one, I had the perfect opportunity. The stuffy guard was tied up on an important call. I'd lingered long enough in the foyer for the original gawkers to lose interest, so no one was so much as glancing in my direction. Not to mention, I am not the most imposing person in the world. I stand five foot four on a good day. I knew it was going to be a challenge to make my way up to the top floor (Tripp had mentioned once that the pool facilities took up most of the top floor of the building) but it wasn't impossible.

I slunk toward an empty elevator, which I boarded just as the doors were closing. As far as I could tell, no one took notice. I pushed the button for the fourth floor. At that point, I didn't have a plan. All I could think about was finding Tripp.

The doors opened and two men stopped short and gaped at me. Suddenly I felt very self-conscious.

"Minty! What are you doing here?"

Tripp was standing just inside the entrance to the pool. He had a towel wrapped around his waist and was drying his hair with another towel. I walked over to him with my hands on my hips.

"There are no women allowed on this floor, Minty," he said in a hushed voice. "We really need to take this somewhere more . . . private. I'm going to get in trouble for this."

He put his hand on my shoulder but I swiped it away.

There was a minute where I felt slightly guilty and thought maybe I should leave. But then I remembered I had been humiliated in one of the most widely read newspapers in the country. Tripp could stand being humiliated in front of a few old guys in a pool.

"You know what, Tripp? I don't care!" I said. "I spent the whole day basically wanting to *die* because of you."

Some of the men stopped swimming to listen. Tripp placed his hand back on my shoulder and started guiding me toward the exit.

"It's bad enough that you might be cheating on me with that . . . *slut*. But I have to read about it in the newspaper on top of it? You can't even be honest with me?"

There was complete silence. Not even the trickling of water or the slightest splash. That is when I noticed there was something off about this pool. It wasn't just the fact that it was small or a little steamier than most. It wasn't that it was populated by all men, most of them in their twilight years, no less, and that I was the only female in their midst. No, there was something else. I glanced around me. The men who had been hanging around the deck of the pool when I walked in were each holding something—a kickboard here, a flipper there—in front of their nether regions. They were definitely looking at me strangely, as if I'd interrupted something private, something sacred. And—oh—there it was. How could I not have noticed? Behind the kickboards and the flippers there was nothing.

"Oh my God," I said. "Is everyone naked?"

That's when Tripp started pushing me toward the elevator bank.

"Minty, we need to get you out of here," he said.

"Get your hands off of me!" I shrieked. I squirmed and struggled. "Why is everyone naked?"

"Minty," he said, still holding me by the shoulders. I'd never seen him so mortified. He could barely breathe. "They're naked because they're supposed to be. It's a tradition. That's why they don't allow women up here."

I'd not only managed to break into one of the most exclusive clubs in New York, I'd probably just laid eyes on some of the most powerful you-know-whats in the city, as well. And I'd barely even noticed because I was so busy yelling at Tripp.

I started laughing. No, I *really* started laughing. Like, huge, hearty, bellowing, no-holds-barred laughter. I laughed so hard that I had to steady myself against Tripp, who was pretty wet and slippery.

He just shook his head. "We've got to get you home," he said.

More laughing.

"Listen." He shook me gently, but enough that I gulped and stared up at him. "You make your way down to the main hall and I'll be there in less than five minutes. Got it?"

I nodded, stifling a huge grin.

"I just have to put some pants on," he said.

"I'll say," I squealed, snorting inadvertently. I burst into another fit of laughter. I couldn't help it. I'd flipped a switch.

And, anyway, it was Tripp's fault to begin with. So there.

I agreed to wait for Tripp in the foyer under the condition that he prove that the "Page Six" article was an unfounded, nasty rumor and nothing else. He was furious about the spectacle I'd made, yes, but what could he say? I had reason to be angry. And when I got angry (which was not often, mind you), I committed to the role.

"Thank you for taking care of my fiancée, Jim," Tripp said to the man behind the front desk as he retrieved me.

Jim responded with a withering smile. However, several men whom I recognized from the pool walked by (fully dressed, thankfully) and actually nodded and waved at me!

Tripp suggested we walk to my apartment.

"Listen," he finally said after several silent blocks. "First and foremost, you have to believe me, none of this stuff is true. I'm going to fix this, but I need a moment to regroup. I'm going to drop you off at your place and we'll meet up for dinner at Philippe at nine o'clock."

I began to protest. I was in no mood for a romantic dinner.

"Please, Mints," he said, "give me a chance to explain."

I groaned. I was so exhausted, all I wanted to do was curl up in bed, but if Tripp promised this dinner was going to make things right, then, I decided, I might as well give it a shot.

Philippe was the restaurant Tripp took me to on our first "real" date, a few nights after the ambush coffee date my mother managed to arrange. There are several things I love about Philippe, besides the fact that it reminds me of Tripp and me. It's dark, romantic, and decorated in shades of deep red, white, and black. The food is *so* yummy. They have the most amazing lobster spring rolls I've ever tasted.

I walked in a few minutes after nine (southern girls are never exactly on time for a date, but never more than fifteen minutes late!).

I was wearing a little black Diane von Furstenberg dress I'd had for ages. It was one of my favorites, just short enough without showing too much leg. I'd paired it with four-inch silver metallic Brian Atwood pumps and a colorful Miu Miu clutch. I kept the jewelry simple. I didn't want any piece competing with the real point of my being there in the first place: my engagement ring.

Tripp was seated at "our table" toward the back of the restaurant. It was pretty late and a Sunday night so it wasn't very crowded. Seeing him for the second time that day was confusing. He looked so handsome that my first reaction was to run away and hide; I couldn't believe I'd made such a fool of myself at the racquet club! But he deserved it, didn't he? Even if the rumor wasn't true, Emily had seen him with Tabitha. There was something going on, and if Tripp and I were actually going to go ahead with this marriage, I needed to know that he was capable of telling me the whole truth.

"Hey," I said, sitting down.

"You look a little better than this afternoon," he said, laughing.

I scoffed.

He laughed again. "You look gorgeous."

"Thanks," I said.

"By the way," he continued, "I'm pretty sure every guy at that pool went home smiling tonight. Most of them probably can't remember the last time they were naked in front of a chick."

"Eww." I groaned. "I didn't know they were going to be naked!"

"Sure," he said, "sure."

Our waiter came over and took our drink orders.

"I know what I want to eat," I said. "Should we just order now?"

Tripp waved the waiter away. "Let's wait a minute," he said. "I need a moment to try to redeem myself here."

"A moment?"

"Okay, more than a moment, but just hear me out, all right?"

"Fine."

"I already said this in the five thousand text messages I sent this morning, but, first and foremost, the 'Page Six' thing is a lie," he began. "Obviously, this isn't the first time they've printed something about me that's unfounded and just mean, but it's starting to look suspicious."

I raised an eyebrow. "What are you saying?"

"I know you're kind of new to this game," he said.

I rolled my eyes.

"But," he continued, "'Page Six' doesn't just make things up. They have sources. So, nine times out of ten if they keep going with a certain rumor, it's coming from a person who they believe to be a reputable source. And the only person I could think of who has both the means and the will to trash me like this is Tabitha."

"Well," I said, "duh."

Tripp looked at me and shook his head. He was bouncing his right leg up and down so feverishly the table was rattling.

"Mints," he said, "I've always been honest with you about Tabitha. Yes, there was a moment in time where we casually dated. But, like I've said in the past, it was never serious and it ended the second I saw you."

I admit it: that part melted me just a little.

"The thing is, May Abernathy had some people at her apartment and Tabitha showed up. You were working late for Ruth and I spent the whole night wishing you were there."

There it was! Okay, maybe he *was* planning on telling me the truth.

"I didn't speak to her all night. In fact I actively avoided speaking to her. I didn't want her to get the wrong idea. I didn't want anyone at the party to get the wrong idea."

"Okay."

"So, when it came time to leave, I slipped out without anyone noticing. Or at least I *thought* no one noticed. But as I was waiting for the elevator, Tabitha came over with her coat on and it was clear that she wanted to come with me. I told her absolutely not. I reminded her that I was engaged to you and she had to respect that."

I nodded.

"And, well, she agreed," he said. "She said she just wanted things to be normal between us, the way they were before you came along, even before she and I dated, when we were just friends."

"Interesting," I said.

"Now," Tripp continued, "we did leave together. I dropped her off at her apartment on my way uptown. But we did not go home together." He took a sip of water.

I nodded again.

"Will you please believe me?" he said, pouting a little.

I sighed. "I just feel like everyone in the whole world thinks I'm an idiot, staying with you while you're running around behind my back."

"But you realize," he said, "all that matters in the end is the truth. And I'm telling you the truth."

Maybe it wasn't as bad as "Page Six" was making it out to be. Maybe it just *looked* like something was going on.

"Mints, you've gotta believe me," Tripp continued.

Who was I going to believe? The man I was about to marry? Or a gossip column? I knew who I *wanted* to believe.

"What do I have to do to prove to you that nothing is going on?" he asked.

"Oh, Tripp," I finally said.

The funny thing is, I wasn't really angry anymore. I just felt . . . spent.

"Seriously." He reached across the table and grabbed my hand. "I'll do anything. I'll marry you right here and now if that's what it takes."

I rolled my eyes.

"I'll get up tomorrow and go down to city hall and marry you, first thing," he said. "If that's what it takes to prove to you that Tabitha means nothing and you mean everything and"—he paused—"that I want to be with *you,* then that's what I'll do."

"City hall?" I asked. "Do people actually do that?"

"All the time." Tripp smiled.

I stared back at him. Part of me did find it kind of romantic. And an even bigger part of me was flattered Tripp was willing to do something so drastic, so spontaneous, to prove his love. But was he serious or just trying to appease me?

"You're not serious, are you?" I asked.

"Dead serious," he said.

"Tomorrow?"

"First thing tomorrow," he said.

The look in his eyes was calm, focused, centered. He seemed so confident. Part of me just wanted to see if he'd actually go through with it.

"Fine," I said. My stomach flip-flopped. "Let's do it then."

I expected my answer to throw Tripp for a loop, but instead he cracked a tiny smile, like he'd won.

"Really?" He grinned.

I thought for a moment. Honestly, no, not really. For one, my mother would have a fit. She was in the midst of planning an over-the-top Charleston wedding and Tripp and I were about to go behind her back in the worst of ways. What would we tell his parents at the cocktail party we were supposed to attend in a few days? Would we smile and thank people when they congratulated us on our "engagement" and then tell them, oh yeah, we were actually already married? Minor detail?

I shook my head.

"Come on," he said. "It'll be our little secret."

It was almost like he was daring me, and somehow I was feeling more and more up to the dare. In the end, I couldn't help but think that maybe getting married—and having it be "our secret," our one thing we could really call our own in the midst of the frenzy that was becoming our lives—was the answer. Maybe it was a step toward warding off the Tabithas of Tripp's past. Maybe it was my way of securing my future, a binding contract to ensure that Tripp would magically morph into the man I needed him to be. He would become someone I could rely on, someone I could trust. What can I say? I was young and naïve. I was in love.

"What do you say?" he asked. "We got a deal?"

"Deal," I said.

13

Mother Knows Best?

Sure, a lot of engaged couples live together, but in my family—and Tripp's family—living together before marriage is a no-no. So Tripp and I ferried back and forth between each other's apartments.

After Philippe, Tripp and I went back to his place and went to bed in silence. There had been the initial excitement, the adrenaline rush after he suggested a city hall marriage. But the walk home was a different story. I couldn't help but wonder, how was I going to explain this to Emily, who clearly had her doubts? To my mother, one of the most traditional people on the planet? And was this really the best solution for all of the problems we'd been having?

The sun streamed in through the window of Tripp's bedroom and I groaned. Could the city hall idea have been a dream? Or the result of two glasses of wine too many?

I sat up in bed. Tripp was sitting at his desk on the other side of the room in a pair of sweatpants and nothing else, scrolling through something on the Internet.

"Babe, what are you doing?" I asked, rubbing my eyes.

He turned around with a Cheshire Cat smile on his face.

"Oh, you know," he said, "just perusing the New York Department of Health website. There's something about waiting twenty-four hours after you get the license to do the actual ceremony, but I found a loophole. So I'm just working that out and then we should be all set." He shrugged his shoulders and grinned. "I've already called in sick to work. Oh! And I ordered breakfast in, by the way."

I guess I wasn't dreaming. I guess it wasn't the wine talking. "You're crazy," I said.

He turned around, a serious look on his face.

"Crazy about *you*," he said.

I narrowed my eyes.

He got up, came over to the bed, and leaned over me, his arms on either side of my waist. "Come on," he said. "This will be fun."

I thought about it for a minute. "You're still crazy."

He leaned in and started tickling me.

I yelped and squirmed.

"Stop it!" I screamed. "I will *not* marry a tickler!"

He pulled away.

"Will you marry someone who does this?"

He kissed my neck.

I shrugged my shoulders.

"Will you marry someone who does this?"

He moved down my chest.

"Maybe," I said, giggling.

"And what about someone who does this?"

His hands traveled underneath the elastic waistband of my boxer shorts.

"Oh . . . um . . . yes . . . definitely," I said.

The buzzer rang and Tripp jogged out of the bedroom. I watched him disappear. He had the broad shoulders of a star quarterback. No complaints here.

When he returned, he was carrying a tray overflowing with waffles and bacon and eggs. He'd even managed to pour two glasses of orange juice.

I was famished and immediately dove into the waffles. "So I'm thinking we get up in a bit and get dressed," he said. "And just hop in a cab. Apparently it's kind of a first-come, first-served basis."

"Okay," I said through a mouthful of waffle. It all felt kind of fun, make-believe. I started brainstorming my outfit. What did they do in the movies again? For some reason I was picturing a woman in a chic little white suit and a tiny veil. I kept only a few items of clothing at Tripp's—a little work-appropriate dress from Theory, a few Vince sweaters, and some J Brand jeans. I guessed I was wearing a work-appropriate dress to get married. There was no time to scour the city for a tiny veil. I frowned.

"What's wrong?" Tripp asked, looking up at me.

"I won't get to wear a tiny little veil," I said. "Like in the fifties? Those little hats with the veil attached? I feel like that would be perfect for this type of thing."

He shook his head.

"Now *you're* the crazy one," he said. "You'll have plenty of time to wear a veil in a few months."

———⊷◈⊶———

About an hour later, we stepped out of a taxi in front of the city clerk's office. I didn't realize the inside of the courthouse was so expansive. A nice lady in a uniform directed us to the third floor, where we filled out forms, paid a fee, received our marriage license, and were promptly told we had to wait twenty-four hours to get married.

"What?!" I said.

The woman behind the desk did little more than look back at me and make a face.

"Policy, ma'am," she said.

"Actually," Tripp said, looking assured, "we have a judicial waiver. It was called in this morning by Judge Beekman."

She raised an eyebrow, impressed. "Give me a moment," she said. "I'll go check in the back."

"Don't worry," Tripp whispered as we were waiting, "Beekman's a cool guy. I gave him the long and short of it and he took pity on me and promised to keep it hushed. I think he enjoys knowing more than my father or something. Old squash-team rivalry."

When the woman returned, she had a blank look on her face. "Nothing from Beekman's office," she said.

Tripp rolled his eyes.

"You're sure, ma'am? I'm sorry, what is your name?" he asked. His voice was an octave lower.

"Barbara," she said, pursing her lips.

"Barbara," Tripp repeated, holding out his hand.

She shook it halfheartedly.

"I'm Tripp and this is my fiancée, Minty."

I smiled my biggest, brightest smile.

"Tripp and Minty?" She raised an eyebrow. "Priceless."

"Barbara," Tripp continued, "I'm going to try to get Judge Beekman on the phone. Hopefully, it's just a mistake and he can call it in. Is there a direct number he can call? Just to speed up the process a little?"

Barbara wrote a number down on a piece of paper and slid it toward Tripp. "Be my guest," she said.

Tripp and Judge Beekman had a brief, heated discussion over the phone while I stood to the side wringing my hands and wondering if this little delay was a sign that we shouldn't get married like this. I could only make out a few words like "trust" and "fair" and "old enough." By the end of the conversation, Tripp was red in the face and exasperated. Then there was a brief silence. Finally, Tripp said, "Okay" and "Thank you," which was semi-promising, I guessed. He hung up the phone.

"He tried to talk me out of it," he said.

I crossed my arms over my chest. "Why?" I asked. "Didn't you just talk to him this morning?"

"He said the more he thought about it, the more he realized it wasn't a good idea. He called it a 'hasty move.'"

"I see," I said, gulping. It was hasty. But that didn't necessarily mean it was bad. "Maybe," I continued. "But 'hasty' is also a word old people use when young people are trying to do something romantic."

Tripp laughed. Barbara finally managed to crack a smile.

"Well," Tripp continued, "the good news is, he finally agreed to help us out. He should be calling right now."

"Well," Barbara said, "y'all can have a seat over there"—she pointed to a hard, cold bench in the hallway—"and I'll let you know when the waiver comes in."

"'Y'all'?" I repeated. "Are you southern?"

She softened a bit. "Mobile, Alabama," she said.

"Charleston." I beamed.

We smiled knowingly at each other for a moment. It was funny how even in the midst of downtown Manhattan in one of the coldest, most unfriendly buildings I'd ever been in, there was something comforting about hearing that little twang. I took it as a sign. Maybe Barbara was a good-luck charm.

After about an hour, Judge Beekman came through for us and we finally got the go-ahead. We then stood in line for another hour or so, watching couple after couple disappear behind the closed doors and emerge looking happy and married. Actually, some of them looked tired and annoyed. Others looked really young and scared. The experience wasn't turning out to be as romantic as I'd anticipated.

By the time our names were called, we were exhausted. The actual "ceremony" took all of three minutes. Tripp and I signed another piece of paper, walked into a little room in the back, and swore that the information we were providing was accurate. And that was it. The judge looked at us, pronounced us man and wife, and sent us on our way. Tripp and I stood there for a minute wondering, Should we kiss? So we pecked quickly in front of the man, who looked on with a bored and impatient expression on his face.

We walked out of the clerk's office and past Barbara's desk.

"Y'all went through with it, didn't you?" she asked.

"We sure did." I smiled.

"Thank you again for all of your help," Tripp said.

"Oh, honey," Barbara said. "Don't thank me."

"Well," I said, still smiling, "we appreciate your help."

"Tell ya what," Barbara said. "I've been married three times. You come back and thank me in ten years. If you still feel like thanking me, that is."

She was kidding, kind of, but her words still settled strangely with me.

On our way home, Tripp and I sat in the back of the cab in silence. I'm not sure if it was Barbara's comments or the "wham, bam, thank you, ma'am" ceremony, but being married didn't exactly feel the way either of us had expected it to feel.

"We're married," Tripp finally said.

"I know," I said.

I wasn't sure how else to respond.

Part of me loved that we'd done something so rebellious, so reckless. But there was also a small part of me that felt like maybe we had done it for the wrong reasons. I guess I thought that if Tripp agreed to marry me then and there, I'd have proof that he really, truly wanted to marry me. But why did I feel like I needed proof?

We pulled up to my apartment. I wanted to change quickly before we headed out for an early celebratory dinner at Daniel. We only had a few hours before my mother got back into town . . .

Oh, no! Mother! I glanced at my watch.

"Aren't I supposed to carry you over a threshold or something?" Tripp asked, swooping me up in his arms.

"Tripp! Stop!" I said, squirming. "Scarlett!"

He kept moving though, past my doorman, into the elevator and right up to my front door. He somehow managed to pull the keys out of his pocket, unlock the door, and push his way through in one single motion.

"She's going to be here any—"

There she was, standing in the foyer with her arms crossed over her chest, her luggage stacked neatly by her side.

Tripp almost dropped me on the floor, he was so surprised.

"Tripp, honey," she began, her eyes big and suspicious, "what are you doing carrying your fiancée over the threshold like that? Don't you think that's—" She stopped and glared at the piece of paper—our marriage certificate—in Tripp's hand. "What is that?" Before he could even react, she snatched it away and held it up to the light. She read it carefully, then put it down on the side table and stared at us. "Y'all are joking, right? Is this what I think it is?"

Tripp calmly put me down. He looked like he was standing in front of a firing squad.

"Mommy," I began.

She narrowed her eyes at me. "Don't 'mommy' me." She turned to Tripp. "What on earth is going on here?"

"Um, um," Tripp stammered. "We just— I— we just thought it— I don't know, Mrs. Davenport."

I rolled my eyes. Amazing backup, Tripp.

I took a deep breath and tried to fill in the blanks. "Don't over-react, now, Mother," I began. "That *is* a marriage certificate. Tripp *was* carrying me over the threshold. We *did* happen to go down to city hall today and get married—"

She opened her mouth to speak.

"—*but*," I continued, holding my hand up in the air, "it's just a formality. It's just a piece of paper. We'll still have the wedding. You and I will still go dress shopping and check out some of the shows and everything will be just fine."

She was breathing heavily now, her nose flared around the nostrils, her red lipstick somehow more intense. The whites of her eyes expanded until her pupils were barely visible. "Are y'all goddamn crazy?" she screamed. "Just a formality? Just a piece of paper? Jesus Christ, Minty, have you lost your mind?" She threw the certificate down on the floor. "What in God's name were you thinking doing this in secret like it's some shotgun wedding?" She pointed at me. "Your father will walk you down the aisle, ya hear? God save me, some days I despise that man with all of my heart, but your father will walk his baby girl down the aisle!"

"Y-yes, ma'am," Tripp stammered. "Absolutely. Honestly, we—"

"Don't you say a word, Tripp du Pont." She narrowed her eyes at him. "I expect this kind of dramatic behavior from Minty, but you should have known better."

I scoffed. "Mother!"

She ignored me.

"This is a travesty," she said. "This is a disgrace!" She threw her hands up in the air. "I can't even look at the two of you right now."

And with that, she grabbed the handle of her Louis Vuitton suitcase, threw her Chanel purse over her shoulder, and bulldozed past us, until she reached the door, where she turned around, very dramatically, and made her final statement.

"I will have you know that I am furious. I am beyond reconciliation at this point. But I will be staying at the Plaza, and, Minty, I will see you tomorrow backstage at the Kevin Park show."

14

You Catch More Flies with Honey Than Vinegar

Lincoln Center was buzzing with activity.

When I'd been Virginia's guest at the Ralph Lauren show, all of the shows were held in tents in Bryant Park, but as I climbed the expansive steps past the main fountain, I couldn't imagine them happening anywhere else.

I immediately saw Kevin backstage, looking frazzled and standing next to a rack being loaded and organized according to which model was wearing what.

"Oh my God, Kevin," I said, giving him a kiss, "I don't know how you do it. Have you even slept?"

He laughed. "Not in three days," he admitted. "I'm pretty sure I have nothing but Red Bull running through my veins at this point."

"Did you get my list of confirmations?" I asked. One of my first assignments was to make sure Kevin's front row was sprinkled with some of the latest and greatest It Girls in the city. In the last week, I'd confirmed eleven people, ranging from a model/DJ to an avant-garde lingerie designer.

"Yes! I nearly died when I saw Kelsey Montgomery on the list!" he exclaimed, referring to an up-and-coming artist who'd recently been featured in the Whitney Museum Biennial.

"I'm so happy," I said, clapping a little. It was nice to know I'd made a contribution to the show's success.

Kevin guided me toward a corner where a few models were lingering, some slipping in and out of tops and skirts, others just texting in their underwear, waiting for the next look. They were so relaxed, so detached, it occurred to me they probably could have been naked and they wouldn't have cared. I nearly tripped over one who had curled up on the floor in nothing more than boy shorts and a tank top.

"Actually, I'm not sure who is more exhausted at this point, us or the models," Kevin said. "They've been doing castings all week. They're probably not eating much. And it's only the first day! Some of these girls have four, five shows in a day. They really run themselves into the ground."

"Yikes," I said. "I'd feel bad for them if they weren't all stunningly beautiful with perfect bodies."

Kevin laughed. "Now let's get you in the hot seat."

He motioned for me to stand on a little platform and told me to strip down to my underwear, as if it were the most natural thing in the world to do. I'm pretty modest by nature, but I unzipped my hoodie, threw it to the ground, and pulled down my pants.

"I'm ready for ya, Kev," I said, laughing.

Kevin's assistant approached with the dress I was going to wear, a bright pink floor-length gown with a high neck and a plunging back. I'd already had one fitting so it wasn't my first time trying it on, but it never failed to make me gasp. It was beautifully constructed and light as air. I lifted my arms as the dress was hoisted over my head and pulled down over my shoulders. Kevin watched in the mirror as the assistants tugged and pinned in several places.

Kevin pursed his lips and turned me to the right so I was standing in profile.

"Get her some shoes," he barked to one of the assistants. "Size eight! The petal-pink pump with the bow! *Not* the pointy toe. Almond. Four inches. *Not* three."

All of this was communicated across the expansive space of backstage, which was starting to fill up with makeup artists, hairstylists, and various assistants lugging equipment. Kevin's voice carried like it was on a loudspeaker.

It was interesting to see Kevin in boss mode.

When I stepped into the shoes, it was like I was wearing a totally different dress. My posture changed. It wasn't just straighter, but my back arched, forcing my hips forward and my shoulders back. My body looked completely different.

I wasn't really sure what to do, so I started modeling a bit, putting my hands on my hips and tilting to the right. At one point I crossed the right leg over the left and dropped my left arm down so it ran straight along the side of my body. I kept my right arm bent, my hand on my hip.

"That's it!" Kevin exclaimed.

"What?" I looked back at myself.

"That's the pose!" He snapped his fingers at an assistant. "Get the effing camera!"

The assistant produced a digital camera from her back pocket and handed it to Kevin without blinking an eye.

"Look at me—right at me," Kevin said.

I stared back at the camera and smiled as he snapped away.

Kevin put the camera down.

"Never, ever pose any other way," he said. "Ever." He cupped his hand over his mouth. "I'm going to have the models do that at the end of the runway. I'm calling it 'the Minty.'"

At first, all I could do was laugh. I felt so silly and self-conscious. I'd posed this way for a picture before, but I'd never really thought about it. Emily was always talking about having a "signature," something that stood out from the rest, so why not have a signature pose? It was genius, come to think of it.

I clapped my hands. "The Minty," I repeated. "I love it."

I stood still for about half an hour as a swarm of seamstresses sewed me into the dress and made sure every last detail was perfect. I'd never felt more special. I almost had to pinch myself. I had found a mentor—someone who believed in me. While it was one thing to have Tripp, Kevin's wholehearted faith in me made me feel that success—whatever that meant; I still wasn't sure—wasn't just possible, it was inevitable. Kevin felt more like a fairy godfather than a boss. I knew that I was very, very lucky to have crossed paths with him, even if it meant going through some pretty harrowing experiences to get there. And now, New York Fashion Week was about to start . . . and somehow I was a part of it.

When the dress was so perfect I could barely move, Kevin helped me down from the platform.

"Amazing," he said, gazing at me. "Now get over to Damien for hair."

He patted me on the behind and hopped off to greet another model.

Damien the hairstylist was impossibly sexy—French, with dark, Johnny Depp–esque looks.

"Darling, pleasure to meet you," Damien said in his throaty, pack-a-day voice.

I settled into the chair and gazed at myself in the mirror—one of ten or so set up in a row. Damien said something in French to a girl wearing a fanny pack and she started handing him hot rollers.

Within minutes, backstage had gone from calm quiet to borderline chaos. There were barely dressed models everywhere, video cameras equipped with blaring lights, reporters equipped with intrusive microphones, and makeup artists working under the gun to create the perfect cat eye. In the midst of all of that, Kevin and his team were trying to get the clothes not only *on* the girls but styled just so.

"Wow," I said to Damien, "this is intense!"

Damien shrugged. "Always craziness," he said.

Before I knew it, I was being ushered into the chair of the key makeup artist, Betsy McHale. Kevin had mentioned that she was one of the most famous makeup artists in the world. They were friends at Central Saint Martins College in London, where they both studied fashion together.

"No one at my level gets Betsy for their show," he said. "She's like the Jessica Stam of makeup artists."

"Dahling, dahling, dahling," Betsy said, inspecting my skin. "You're a baby, but you're dehydrated."

This was probably true. With the stress of, well, everything, I hadn't really been taking good care of myself.

Within seconds, a girl was standing in front of me exfoliating with one hand and moisturizing with the other. Then she stepped back and let Betsy assess.

"Much better," Betsy said.

She was putting the finishing touches on my makeup when someone tapped me on my shoulder. I turned around to see Spencer, a huge grin on his face. He was wearing a headset and holding a clipboard. Oh my God, I thought. RVPR is overseeing Kevin's show? Why hadn't I thought of that?! I glanced around instinctively. Where the hell was Ruth?

"Look at you, gorgeous," Spencer said.

Betsy smiled as she applied mascara to my bottom lashes.

"There!" she said. "You're all done here, love." She blew me a kiss and moved on to the next model.

Spencer grinned. He was clearly in hog heaven.

"I've missed you!" I said, blowing him an air kiss so as not to mess up the makeup.

"Of course you have," he said, glancing around.

"So tell me," I said, lowering my head. "I totally forgot Ruth was going to be here! Do I need, like, backup security or something?"

Spencer leaned against my chair and shook his head.

"I wouldn't worry about it," he said. "She's so caught up in launching Alexis's 'career' these days. You know, the girl they mentioned in 'Page Six'? Ruth somehow convinced Kevin to let Alexis walk in the show. She doesn't have a good spot in the lineup—she's somewhere in the middle from what I heard—but she's walking."

"Well, that's a relief," I said. "At least she found someone else to torture."

Spencer rolled his eyes. "They get along like two peas in a pod. Each one is more vapid than the other," he said. "Oh!" He jumped a little. "I have a little secret to tell you."

I squirmed in my seat. I desperately wanted to tell Spencer that Tripp and I were married. I had to will myself not to form the words. I decided I'd wait to hear what his secret was first and see if it might be worth the trade. Or not! But then I thought, No, I should wait. Spencer was a lot of things, but a secret-keeper was not one of them.

"Tell me! Tell me!" I said.

Spencer paused dramatically.

"You are looking at the new assistant features editor of *Vanity Fair*," he said.

"No!"

"Yes!"

"Oh my God, Spencer, that's amazing!"

"I know," he said. "I haven't told Ruthless yet, though. And somehow she hasn't found out. Or maybe she doesn't care? God knows I'm dead weight at that place. I think I spent four hours yesterday navigating that new socialite website. Have you seen it? OMG, it's ridiculous."

"What socialite website?" I asked. Kevin was motioning for me to join him on the other side of the tent.

"SocialiteRoster.com?" Spencer said, following me as I made my way over to Kevin. "It's kind of a . . . what's the best way to describe it? It's like the *Blue Book* meets Zagat. It ranks each socialite by how many parties she attends, how many times her picture appears in certain outlets, you know, that kind of thing. You're all over it."

"Seriously?" I said. I couldn't believe I hadn't heard of it yet. It must have been brand-new.

"Minty, babe, we need you back up on the platform," Kevin said, appearing in front of me.

"Later," Spencer said, disappearing into the mob scene.

Kevin took off my robe and smoothed out my dress. I noticed that every person in the tiny space was in a similar state of frenzy. Models were lined up along one side of the room standing still as stylists put the final touches on their looks and sent them to the front, where the rest of the girls were already lining up for the start of the show. Damien came over at one point with a comb, pulled out my rollers in a single swipe, and teased and styled my hair. Betsy's assistant had barely finished touching up my makeup when I heard my name called.

"Minty! Minty! The show is about to start. We need you lined up with the rest of the models in thirty seconds!"

Thirty seconds! I jumped out of the chair and headed in the direction of the other models. I heard the music start and suddenly each was disappearing through the dark hole of the opening of the runway, one after the other. I closed my eyes and took a deep breath, trying to gather my thoughts, and suddenly I was being pulled toward the opening as well. Oh my God, this was it.

"Go!"

I've heard that speaking in public can be an out-of-body experience, like you're hovering over yourself watching, fingers crossed, praying you don't trip over any of the words or die of embarrassment.

Walking in public—walking on a runway, that is, in front of every important person in the fashion industry—is similar. You take that first step into the lights and the crowd and the music and everything goes blank. Suddenly you're taking another step forward, but you're not exactly sure how. And then another and another, until you're nearing the end of the runway and you realize it's almost halfway over. For a split second you might glance at someone in the crowd.

For me that person was Tripp, who was seated front row, looking somewhat bewildered but also amazed and proud. He started whistling and clapping. And then I saw my mother, who was so overwhelmed with excitement she was fanning herself. A row behind her was Emily, slightly more composed but beaming nonetheless.

Suddenly I was a few feet from the end of the runway. All I could think about was remembering to do "the Minty" like Kevin had reminded me a thousand times over. I placed my right hand on my hip, crossed one leg over the other, and struck a pose. Cameras flashed; the audience clapped and cheered. A few people yelled my name. Were they actually cheering for me?

When I made it backstage, the other models were already starting to walk out again for the finale. Kevin grabbed my arm and gave it a squeeze.

"One last time before we can celebrate," he whispered in my ear.

The finale was even more of a blur, as I stood at the end of the runway with Kevin and everyone in the audience gave him a standing ovation. So many camera flashes went off, I started seeing spots!

After, we all surrounded Kevin backstage and raised a glass of champagne as he thanked the production team, makeup artists, hair-stylists, and models who had worked so tirelessly to make the show a success. I was listening to him speak, my heart still racing from the thrill of the runway, when I noticed a girl across the way looking at me—no, staring at me. She was pretty, with catlike eyes, and long platinum-blonde hair. I looked back at her and smiled; it was the only thing I could think of to do. But she didn't smile back. She looked startled for a moment and then turned away.

Kevin came over then and put his arm around me.

"You're a natural, babe," he said, giving me a kiss on the cheek.

Flashes started going off and I realized people were taking *my* picture. Wow, I thought. Just a few years before, I was happy to even be allowed backstage. Now I was part of the show. Richard Fitzsimmons ran up and gave me a quick double kiss.

"Did I not say you were going to be someone?" he said, snapping away.

I laughed and struck a pose. When Richard was finished, he started taking photos of Kevin with the models. That's when I saw Ruth. She was standing just behind Kevin's right shoulder with the girl who had been staring at me!

"That's Alexis."

I jumped.

Spencer was standing next to me with his headset around his neck. As I turned to him, Ruth looked up and our eyes met. She shot me one of the coldest, most evil glances I'd ever experienced. If she had the ability to fly over the crowd at that moment, swoop down and bite my head off, she would have. Then Alexis whispered something in Ruth's ear and they both looked at me. I literally got chills.

"Why are they staring at me?" I asked.

"Who knows," Spencer said. "Ruth is probably annoyed you're getting all of the attention."

Two of the seamstresses came over and started undoing the stitching in my dress. Right in front of Spencer, they pulled it off and handed me a white robe. And, just like that, my Cinderella moment was over. Except I still had the shoes, and *both* shoes at that. I stared down at my feet.

"You think they'll let me keep them?" I asked Spencer.

He glanced around.

"If you make a run for it now, I won't tell anyone."

Put On a Brave Face

The day of the engagement party, I woke up in a cheerful mood. I got up, made coffee, and picked up my newspapers. The review for Kevin's show was front and center in *WWD*, glowing about his fall collection. There was even a note about how I'd modeled the final look. The writer said I'd really "held my own" in comparison to other socialites and celebrities who'd all walked the runway at one time or another. Then there was a quote from Kevin about our meeting that fall and how my personal style actually had a hand in inspiring the fall collection.

"Wow," I said out loud.

My phone rang. I picked it up—it was Tripp.

"You haven't read the *Post* yet, have you?" he asked. He sounded annoyed but not exasperated. Okay, so maybe it wasn't so bad.

"No," I said, "I'm about to though."

"You know where to look," he said. "I'll wait on the phone."

And there it was: QUICKIE MARRIAGE AND RUNWAY DRAMA SIGNAL TROUBLES FOR SOCIAL SWAN.

The story that followed went on for nearly half a page. It started with the "rumor" that Tripp and I had "tied the knot" at city hall a few days before, citing public records and "inside" sources that had tipped them off to the news. It then went on to say that I'd tripped Alexis Barnaby on the runway at the Kevin Park show and insinuated that I'd done it out of jealousy. I thought for a moment. I hadn't, at any point during the show, been within ten feet of Alexis. Who was feeding the *Post* this garbage?

"Holy shit," I said.

"Yup," he replied.

"Are your parents freaking out?"

I was referring to the city hall thing, of course. Bebe and Phillip were already so used to reading gossip about me in the papers, they probably skipped over the whole part about Alexis. That was for me to deal with on my own.

"They're okay," he said. "They were disappointed, of course, and there will be more discussion to come, but they have a cocktail party to host."

"Ugh, why does this always happen?"

"Don't worry about it," he said. "I was planning on telling them after tonight anyway. They just found out a bit earlier. I mean, what can we do?"

"You're right," I said. "I love you."

"I love you too," he said.

The next person to call was Emily.

"Is this true?" she asked. Her voice sounded shaky and shell-shocked.

I was silent.

"Minty." She let out a huge sigh.

"Emily, I'm sorry, I've been meaning to tell you. It's just, we were going to try to keep it a secret for a while. It's really just something we did for ourselves, you know, we didn't plan it or anything."

"I'm just . . . shocked," she said. "I don't get it." She paused. "I mean, what's the rush? You're planning a wedding for June. Isn't that fast enough?"

"Yes, of course it is," I said. I couldn't really explain to her exactly why we did what we did. "Listen, Em, it's just a formality. We're still having the wedding."

"I just wish I didn't have to read about your wedding in the *Post*."

"I know," I said.

There was a long period of silence.

"Anyway," Emily began, "I'll see you tonight at the du Ponts'? I imagine you and Tripp have some explaining to do in the meantime."

Oh God, she was right. Bebe and Phillip were going to be livid. And on top of it I had to face them and a hundred or so of their closest friends and family in a few hours.

"Yeah, I guess you're right," I said.

As I hung up the phone, I heard the lock turn and the familiar click-clack of my mother's Chanel pumps on the parquet.

"Where is my recalcitrant daughter?" her voice bellowed down the hall. She appeared in front of me, slipping out of her mink. "I hope you and Tripp are happy. Your father's gone and canceled his flight over this city hall business; he's furious."

"Daddy isn't coming?"

"Sadly, no," she said. "I knew this would shatter him."

"Mother, he can still walk me down the aisle!"

"It's not the same." She shook her head. "Just not the same."

I groaned. I felt terrible about my father, but at least Scarlett was there to smooth things over a bit. Yes, she was less than pleased about the whole thing, but she would get over it. She'd smile and nod her way through the entire party and convince everyone that Tripp and I were just being silly kids in love. She was good at playing to the public and I was glad to have her on my side.

"Now," she said. "Shall we get down to business before we find ourselves with less than an hour to get ready for the party?"

"Absolutely," I said, sitting down. "Fire away."

She bulldozed through her list of various updates: the service was confirmed at the French Huguenot Church in downtown Charleston; the combination guest present/menu holder would be handmade picture frames made from green velvet Cowtan & Tout fabric to match the wedding colors, pale green, cream, and white. She'd decided on hydrangeas, orchids, and roses for the florals. Each program, engraved by Bernard Maisner, would feature "Minty and Tripp" in a pale green Edwardian script on a cream card, tied with a ribbon at the top. As our four hundred guests arrived in the church, a string quartet would play music from the balcony.

"The reception is a whole other animal, Minty," Mother explained. "I've practically slaved over the menu. We've got waiters standing in the reception area of the club offering mint juleps in silver cups when people walk in. Also, the martini bar will have a big ice sculpture martini glass. I thought that was cute, no?"

I nodded. "It all sounds amazing, Mother."

"We'll have passed crab cakes and tea sandwiches," she continued. "And when the main doors to the ballroom are opened, everyone will see the gorgeous Sylvia Weinstock cake in the center of the room. This cake is going to be incredible, taller than you and Tripp! And I have Sylvia doing lily-of-the-valley flowers wrapping around each tier." She sat down, took a deep breath, and opened up her scrapbook. "And then we have this pale green moiré for the tables covered with this sheer overlay cloth. Each place setting will have a clear square box tied with ribbon and a clear sticker that says 'With love from Minty and Tripp,' with mini three-tier wedding cakes inside."

She showed me a picture of the mini cakes.

"Wow, Mommy, you're really outdoing yourself."

She let out a little "ha!" because she would never think for a minute to not create the most extravagant, amazing, breathtaking wedding anyone had ever seen, including the most jaded New Yorkers. It comforted me to know that she understood how important it was to show them that we southerners were known for our hospitality for a reason. No one can throw a party or a wedding like a southern belle.

"And I've confirmed Peter Duchin, honey," she said, rolling her eyes. "We're flying him and his orchestra down from New York. It's like I'm dealing with a rock star or something. Would you believe it?"

I laughed. "Yes."

"Now," she continued, "when everyone leaves at the end of the night we'll do little cones of Smythson paper stamped with the family crest. We're going to fill them with rose petals and everyone will throw them in the air when you and Tripp leave for the honeymoon. It will be a real 'moment.'"

Oh God, the honeymoon.

Tripp and I had discussed spending a few weeks in the Maldives, but we hadn't had a moment to iron out the main details. It felt like every time I had something crossed off my list, another thing was added!

"Sounds great," I said.

She showed me an example of the Smythson paper, which was no less beautiful than everything else, even though some people might have treated it as a throwaway detail. "Mommy," I said. "It's perfect."

She closed the scrapbook and the buzzer rang. It was Jenny, Kevin's PR director. She was stopping by to drop off my outfit for the evening as well as some sketches for the bridesmaid dresses. I'd always dreamed of a wedding dress from Oscar de la Renta, so when I broke the news to Kevin, I asked him to design my bridesmaid dresses. He was completely gracious and understanding about the whole thing, and anyway, he had a lot of work cut out for him with the bridesmaid dresses alone.

There were twelve—count 'em—*twelve* bridesmaids: my sister, Emily, five cousins, three childhood friends, and two of my best friends from college. I was also mulling over the possibility of asking May to be the thirteenth bridesmaid. Tripp had mentioned a while back that it might be a nice gesture since Harry was his best man and oldest friend.

At first I'd recoiled at the idea. May hadn't exactly been the most welcoming person in Tripp's circle of friends. But in the last month or so (around the time I started working for Kevin) things had started to take a turn for the better. We'd run into each other a few times and she couldn't have been more lovely.

Of course, I had a feeling her recent interest in me had more to do with my rising profile than any heartfelt interest in being my friend, but that was the way things worked in New York. One day, May acted like she could barely believe Tripp was dating someone like me. The next, we were gossiping over champagne.

When the front door opened, Jenny was standing there holding a garment bag and a portfolio. She looked like she hadn't slept in days.

"Oh my God, Jenny," I said. "Aren't you supposed to be relaxing right now? The show is over!"

She laughed.

"The phone has been ringing off the hook since the *WWD* article," she said. "You wouldn't believe it, the collection is such a success. Anyway," she said, handing me the bag and the portfolio, "I have to get going. Kevin said he'll see you tonight."

"Okay," I said, waving her good-bye.

The door had barely shut when it opened again. I figured Jenny had forgotten something. Instead, Tripp was standing there, dressed in khakis, a button-down, and a battered white college hat. The engagement party was supposed to start in less than two hours.

"Tripp, what the hell are you doing here?!" I said.

"Scarlett," he said, walking toward my mother, who was standing near the kitchen with her mouth hanging open. "How are you?"

He kissed her on the cheek.

"Tripp, honey, I'm just fine," she said, her southern drawl a bit more pronounced than usual. That happened when she was either nervous or stressed out or both. "I must mirror my daughter's sentiments. What on earth are you doing here?"

"I just have a few things to discuss with Minty if you don't mind," he said.

She pursed her lips.

"Of course, darlin'," she said, painting a sugary-sweet smile on her face. "I was just going to pop into the powder room anyway and start to pull myself together. You all right, baby girl?"

"I'm just fine, Mommy," I said. "You go get ready."

She disappeared toward the back of the apartment.

Tripp lowered himself into the sofa and rubbed his forehead.

"I know it's barely four P.M. but do you have any scotch?" he asked.

Of course I had scotch. I went over to the bar and poured him a glass. He took it from me, sipped slowly, and sighed.

"Tripp, Christ, tell me what's going on."

"I thought the drama was over with my parents, but then something else came up of course. We just need to address something before tonight."

My heart was in my throat.

"Anyway," Tripp continued, "you've probably heard about this website already."

"What website?"

"The social register one. Social something. I don't know. My mother told me about it. It's got all the girls on it. Even May's on it. And you're on there."

I stared back at him.

"Social Roster?"

Tripp blinked. "Yes. How do you know about it?"

What was that supposed to mean?

"Spencer mentioned it at Kevin's show. What's going on?"

"Some woman from my mother's bridge club just sent her a bitchy e-mail about all of the stuff with 'Page Six' and then mentioned the website, how the site says I'm making a mistake marrying you."

I couldn't help but laugh.

"Minty, I'm serious," Tripp said. "I only say this because I love you and I don't want these people to be saying such terrible things about you at all, let alone to my parents, who are not the most open-minded people, to say the least."

I frowned.

"And," he continued, "I should mention that there's another layer to the story, which, again, is ridiculous and totally unfounded, but you should know what people are saying."

"All right," I said. I steeled myself for part 2.

"There are some people," he began, "who think you might have something to do with it. With the website, that is."

"What?!"

Tripp sighed. "They have this ranking system on it, something having to do with how many times you show up in the press. I don't know. Anyway, some people, I'm not sure who, but this is all according to my mother, so take it with a grain of salt—"

"Tripp! On with it!"

"Some people," he continued, "think that because you're number one on this ranking list, and apparently you've been number one since the site launched, you may have something to do with it. Or at the very least that you're friends with the people who started it and you're supporting it. Or something."

I held my head in my hands. "What else does it say?" I asked.

Tripp just stared at the floor.

"Tripp, do I have to get online now and go through this thing myself or are you going to tell me? What else does it say?"

"There's bad stuff on there, babe," he admitted. "There's a bio of you that has stuff about your family, how your mother claims to be FFV. What's FFV, anyway?"

"First Family of Virginia," I said. (Didn't *everyone* know that?)

"Anyway," he continued, "that story about your father being a door-to-door salesman of course. There's a whole paragraph about Tabitha, which I won't even get into. Then there's a whole other section where people can comment, and let's just say no one's pulling any punches when it comes to voicing their opinion about you."

"Who? What are they saying?"

"All of the comments are anonymous," Tripp said, "but they're just mean. One person went off about how you curse all the time and eat too much Domino's pizza. Oh, and how sometimes you sleep in your makeup from one party and wear it to a party the next night, or something?"

I gulped. All of those things were kinda true.

"Eyelashes!" I shouted. "I keep my eyelashes on!" I was actually pretty angry they didn't get that detail straight. I thought my false-eyelash trick was a pretty good one. "Oh my God, who cares?"

"Mints . . ." Tripp put his hand on my knee.

He looked so lost and upset, I almost felt bad for him when I *should* have been feeling bad for myself. "Like I said, I didn't come over to tell you this to upset you, but I didn't want you to come to the party unprepared. Maybe you should cool off on some of this stuff for a while?"

"What stuff?"

"I don't know," he said. "The fashion stuff? All of the parties you've been attending? It's putting you in this very vulnerable position where people think they know things about you. It doesn't look good."

I couldn't help but roll my eyes. "Babe," I said, "the 'fashion stuff' is kind of my job these days."

Tripp sighed. "Maybe just keep a lower profile for a while. Especially before we get married. You know, my parents will probably lay off once we get through the wedding and the dust has settled a bit."

I buried my face in one of the pillows. I couldn't understand what all of the fuss was about. Why did Tripp's parents care so much about what a few people were saying on the Internet?

"Point taken," I said.

"I love you," Tripp said.

"Love you too," I said. "Make sure you tell your mother I plan on spending the rest of my life sitting in bed with a black veil over my face reading Jane Austen novels."

"I think that's exactly what she had in mind," Tripp said, shaking his head. "You know, I don't think anyone else in this world would handle the pressure of my family as gracefully as you have."

We kissed the kind of kiss that happens only when one person is trying to assure the other person that everything is going to be all right. I walked him to the door.

Once he was gone, I'll admit it, I ran to my computer to check out this SocialRoster.com. I have to say, navigating through page after page of gossipy stories and personal details didn't make me feel any better. It was anonymously written (how convenient) and the home page featured a photo of me, along with nineteen other girls, ranked according to how many times our photo had appeared on Richard Fitzsimmons's website, how many mentions we received in the press each week, and so on.

I pushed myself away from the computer. My mother emerged fully dressed and coiffed from the powder room at that point, wearing her most innocent expression. I'd almost forgotten she was there. It was immediately clear that she'd heard some of Tripp's and my conversation. Luckily, she'd had the wherewithal to wait until he left to come out.

I glanced at the clock.

"Oh, fuck!"

"Minty Mercer Davenport, you watch your—"

16

Boys Will Be Boys

Mother always says that it's in good taste to arrive either on time or a few minutes early if you are the guest of honor at a party, but never more than that. Just to be safe, I'd told Bebe ahead of time that we would be there a few minutes before six o'clock. I didn't want to ruffle any more feathers.

The du Ponts' apartment reminded me of Baron Guggenheim's place. It was like everyone on the Upper East Side had gotten together at some point in the 1950s and decided on one acceptable way of decorating: dark wood, oriental rugs, chinoiserie lamps, oil paintings from the mid–nineteenth century, and so on. Not to say there was anything wrong with any of that. But there was no color! No flair! Standing in the living room, I felt like I was tucked away somewhere in the English countryside, not riding high over the glittering sidewalks of Park Avenue.

"Bebe," I said, kissing my new mother-in-law on the cheek, "I just want to say I'm so sorry for the way you heard about everything." I took a deep breath. "I know you've already spoken to Tripp, but honestly, we really didn't mean to hurt anyone."

She looked at me and managed a patronizing smile.

"No worries at all, dear," she said. "I've dealt with my son already. Unfortunately we don't have the luxury of better timing, but that's life. Shall we step into the library for a drink?"

My mother had a smile painted on her face.

"That sounds lovely," she said.

The library had floor-to-ceiling bookshelves, which were lined in vintage, leather-bound books. Bebe sipped from a glass of what looked like straight vodka on the rocks. When the waiter came over to take our drink order, my mother asked for a Campari and soda.

"To go with my lipstick," she explained.

Tripp walked in wearing his usual uniform of a dark blue suit and a striped tie. He looked so much more confident and assured than he had just an hour or so before.

"The guests are starting to arrive," he announced. I noticed Emily stepping off the elevator. He turned to me and whispered in my ear, "Are we okay?"

"We're fine," I said.

"Good," he said.

Tripp was a smart boy. He knew things weren't exactly "fine," but what were we going to do? The party was starting to fill with some of the du Ponts' oldest and dearest friends. We had to keep our cool. We had to keep up appearances, at least for the duration of cocktail hour.

"You holding up?" Emily asked, kissing me on the cheek. She had on a simple black shift and minimal makeup. I was grateful that she was one of the first people to arrive. I could always escape to her side if I found myself trapped in the middle of a right-wing debate with Tripp's father and his friends. She glanced across the room. "Looks like someone needs you, babe."

Tripp was motioning for me to join him. He was standing with an older gentleman in tartan plaid pants and a navy blazer.

"Oh, awesome," I laughed. I kissed Emily on the cheek.

Tripp had just finished introducing me to the fifteenth family member in a row when I saw May and Harry making their way through the crowd. I steeled myself for a minute and then relaxed. She looked more friendly and enthusiastic than ever.

"Minty!" she squealed. "Sweetie, you look adorable." We double kissed. Harry nodded in my direction and started talking to Tripp. "I'm sure you have about a million people to say hi to, but we need to get together! Breakfast or something? Oh my God! The *Post*!" She leaned in closer. "I knew about the secret wedding all along, you know. Harry told me. Total blabbermouth." She flashed a megawatt smile. "Wait. Are you going to Carolina tomorrow?"

I stared back at her.

"Um, yes, I think so?" I said, dumbfounded.

The Carolina Herrera show was at ten A.M. the next morning. Thankfully, yes, I'd been invited. I had planned on attending with Emily but she'd had to cancel at the last minute because of a work commitment. If I hadn't been invited it could have been a problem; in May's world, not being invited to the Carolina Herrera show was the definition of social suicide.

"Perfection." May smiled. "Palm Court at nine?"

The last time I'd had breakfast at the Palm Court at the Plaza, I must have been no more than twelve years old. My innocent dreams of Eloise's New York life had never seemed so naïve.

"Um, sure."

"See you then, honey," she said, turning to Tripp. "You boys are off to London on Saturday?" she asked him.

"Ugh," I groaned. Tripp had just found out he was going to London on business for two weeks.

"Yeah." Tripp grinned, turning to Harry, who shrugged.

"Danger," Harry said.

I glanced at Tripp. As forgetful as I was feeling, I was certain he'd never mentioned that Harry was joining.

May leaned toward me. "Harry always finds a way to tag along when Tripp has to work out of the London office," she said. "It's like they get separation anxiety."

I nodded.

From what I understood, Harry ran his own "investment firm." I guessed he could work from anywhere. It wasn't like Tripp was keeping the information from me, but hearing that he would be in London with his partner in crime was not exactly the most comforting piece of news.

"Don't worry, Mints," Tripp said. "I'll be on my best behavior."

"Somehow I believe Tripp," May said. "Not so sure about Harry though." She laughed. "Anyway, see you tomorrow, sweetie?"

She kissed me on the cheek and swirled off in another direction as Harry followed closely behind.

Tripp glanced at me and shrugged. "Like, best friends forever?"

I poked him in the ribs. May was one thing. But as I shook hands, smiled, and tried to remember the name of Bebe's second cousin, it was pretty clear that Tripp's family was a whole other story. The way Bebe watched me from the sidelines and hovered with every new person I encountered, it was almost like she was waiting for me to slip up, to offer up some sort of proof that I was the kind of runway-model-tripping, calculating person the press was making me out to be.

Of course, I wanted to change her mind. She was going on the opinions of other people, reporters who'd never met me or catty people who probably had nothing better to do than to tear other people down, and that just wasn't fair.

I knew I wasn't going to win Bebe over right off the bat, but if I could make a good impression on the people who were important to her, maybe I had a chance somewhere down the line. So I put in a little effort. I asked Betsey Stewart about her African safari. I swapped sorority stories with Tripp's cousin Kelly. I listened intently as Phillip's coworker described—at length—the terrain of the Shinnecock golf course.

I told Tripp's uncle Jack a story about how I used to wet my bed when I was little and my mother gave me a "pee pill," which was basically a little Smartie candy, to "cure" me of the habit. I wasn't sure it was the most appropriate story, but I had him in stitches.

I told Bebe's friend Mary about the time I tried to bleach my hair blonde at summer camp in North Carolina and turned it purple instead. My mother drove four hours at two A.M. up to Camp Moorhead, took me to a reputable salon to have it fixed, turned around, and drove back. *That* is how important hair is in the South.

By the end of the evening, Tripp, who was glued to my side at the beginning of the night, had left me to my own devices. Several times I even caught him gazing at me from across the room and smiling. I said good-bye to May, Harry, and Emily, who were headed to a dinner for Valentino downtown. As the rest of the guests started to file out, I actually had a moment to catch my breath. I sat down on the sofa in the living room with a glass of champagne and closed my eyes.

"Well, well, well, look what we have here."

Spencer was standing over me smirking.

"Spencer!" I squealed.

"Sweetie, you look spent," he said, sitting down next to me on the sofa. He already had a scotch on the rocks in his hand. "And . . . married."

"Oh my God," I said. "Sorry."

He waved his hand in the air. "Who cares. You've practically been married since the day you met Tripp anyway." He leaned in. "Did Bebe and Phillip swallow a bottle of Xanax or what? How are they looking so calm and composed?"

I laughed.

"The best part is," he continued, "you know underneath all of that smiling and nodding they're bursting at the seams. How much you want to bet Bebe's got a little Minty voodoo doll stashed in her underwear drawer?"

"Spencer, you're too much," I said. "Luckily Scarlett's here to keep everyone's mind off the scandal."

We both gazed over at my mother, who currently had a small crowd of people roaring with laughter. I was pretty sure I even spotted Phillip in the group, chuckling to himself. Now that was a feat.

"I haven't seen you since the show," I said. "How has the rest of your Fashion Week been?"

Spencer rolled his eyes. "Well, Ruth didn't take the *Vanity Fair* news so well," he said.

"No!" I said with mock surprise.

"I really cried myself to sleep about that one."

"Seriously," I chuckled.

"Actually, it's funny you haven't heard yet," he continued, "I thought for sure she'd already sent the press release out. I envisioned the headline, MEDIA ALERT: SPENCER GOLDIN SUCKS AT LIFE," he laughed. "I have to admit, I was pretty disappointed that there were no burly security guards involved, though. She pulled out all the stops for you. All I got was a cardboard box and a swift kick in the ass." He paused and took a sip of his drink. "Whatever. I'll write about it someday."

"True," I said. "By the way, on top of everything else, Bebe discovered Social Roster today."

Spencer raised an eyebrow. "Oh Christ. Are you okay?"

"I will be," I grumbled. "I mean I'd barely looked at it myself until I was basically forced to read it this afternoon. Tripp said it was like the apocalypse over here today."

"Oh, sweetheart," Spencer said, "what would life be without a crazy mother-in-law? You've got to stand strong, though. Remember, I have to write about you one day. And I want it to be a glamorous and triumphant story. I can't have you go all *Grey Gardens* on me."

"Oh God, no," I said.

Bebe was now standing in the entrance seeing people off. I wondered where Tripp was. I hadn't laid eyes on him in what seemed like almost an hour.

"Spence, can I get you anything?" I asked. "I'm just going to try to find Tripp. I'm exhausted."

"No, sweetie," he said, taking a gulp of his drink. "I'm actually about to head to dinner."

"Anyone special?" I asked, smiling. I still couldn't get over the fact that someone so socially and sartorially driven dated women.

"Nah," he said. "Some girl named Poppy."

"Not Poppy Hansen?" I asked, impressed.

Poppy Hansen got her start in modeling and had just recently segued into a starring role in one of the hottest new TV shows. Spencer was always going out with starlets or models. Being famous was like a prerequisite.

"Maybe." He grinned, puffing his chest out. "Until next time, Mrs. du Pont. Don't let the bottom-feeders get to you, got it?"

"Got it," I said, smiling.

I wanted to find Tripp, but I also had to use the ladies' room. I made a right turn down a long hallway and followed it to the end, remembering a small bathroom somewhere in the vicinity. As I approached a door slightly ajar at the end of the hallway, I heard a muffled male voice speaking to someone. It was unmistakably Tripp's voice. It sounded like he was reassuring someone. He kept saying, "It's not your fault. There was nothing you could do." And then he called whoever was on the other end of what could only have been a phone conversation "sweetie."

Sweetie?! What the hell?

I burst through the door. Tripp was sitting at the edge of a bed in what must have been a guest room. When he saw me, he was so taken aback that he dropped the phone. I could hear a female voice on the other end yelling something back. What the hell was going on?

We locked eyes for what seemed like forever, then I turned around and ran out of the room toward the elevator. I didn't even say thank you or good-bye to Bebe and Phillip. I didn't have time to grab my coat, or my mother for that matter. I just got on the elevator, pressed the "ground floor" button, and prayed that it would spit me out onto Park Avenue before Tripp or anyone else had a moment to catch me.

How many more times could I catch him in a lie and watch as he wormed his way out of it? I was at my wit's end. I wasn't going to settle for a truth that seemed to change with each person who told it.

When I got to my apartment, all I could do was sit on my bed and stare at the wall in front of me. What on earth was I going to do?

"Minty!"

My mother appeared in the doorway.

"What on earth is going on? Tripp followed me out of the apartment and begged me to help him. The boy is a mess!"

In between sobs, I somehow managed to form a sentence.

"He was talking to that woman," I blurted, reaching for a box of tissues. I had a mixture of snot and tears running down my face—not a good look.

"Are you sure?"

"Yes!" I shouted.

"You're a hundred percent sure?"

I paused. "Like, ninety-seven percent!"

"Well," she said, "then there's a three percent chance he was not talking to that woman? And maybe you have nothing to be worried about?"

I blew my nose.

"Mother, he called her 'sweetie'!"

She looked at me and frowned.

"Okay," she said, "but this conversation you're saying you over-heard. Are you sure it was Tabitha?"

"It was a woman," I said, "I heard her voice."

"Sweetheart," she said, her voice calm and soothing. "All I'm trying to say is that these things are not always what they appear to be. Boys will be boys. They make terrible decisions. Then they lie because they're afraid of the consequences. Then they're angry that there are consequences to begin with . . ." She trailed off, shaking her head. "What I'm trying to say is, I know the boy has his flaws. But one thing is clear: he loves you."

If Tripp really did love me, then maybe he had a different definition of love. My definition, for one, did not involve cheating.

"Mother, I really should be getting to bed," I said. "I have the Carolina Herrera show tomorrow morning and I'm meeting a friend for breakfast and, honestly, I'm exhausted."

She frowned at me.

"I'm sure Tripp and I will talk. I just can't begin to wrap my head around this yet."

"All right, sweetheart," she said. "We'll touch base tomorrow."

She kissed me on the head.

The next morning, I was actually grateful to have the Carolina Herrera show—and breakfast with May—as a distraction.

As I hopped into a cab outside of my building, I wasn't sure if I was even going to mention the previous evening's events. But for all I knew, she'd already heard something via Harry.

Walking into the iconic, light-filled Palm Court, I knew it was just what the doctor ordered. Even though I wasn't in my best frame of mind, it was hard not to feel hopeful and optimistic amidst the grandeur of Eloise's room.

May arrived just a few moments after my cappuccino. She was wearing a black, high-waisted skirt; a white silk blouse; a black motorcycle jacket; and taupe Alexander Wang fringed booties. I looked like her polar opposite in a cobalt-blue Carolina Herrera dress and sparkly MiuMius, but who said I had to look like May, or anyone else for that matter? Maybe there was something freeing about the prospect of being completely independent, a single girl in New York.

"Oh, Minty," May said, "you'll have to forgive me, I just got the news on my way over here and I'm not sure it's hit me yet."

What was she talking about? If she was referring to my fight with Tripp, she was being a little dramatic.

"May, I'm sorry," I said, confused. "Is everything all right?"

"You didn't hear?" She gulped. "You seriously didn't hear? Oh God."

I shook my head. "I don't think so."

"Tabitha," she said. "Tabitha Lipton."

"What about Tabitha?"

May took a deep breath. "She almost died last night."

I gasped and covered my mouth with my hand.

"She was vacationing in Anguilla with a few friends," May continued. "And she disappeared from the yacht. She was missing for over an hour!" May's eyes welled up. It was surprising to see someone like her, who was always so composed, on the verge of tears. "Luckily—" She paused. "Sorry, but she's kind of a friend." I shook my head, telling her to go on. "Luckily she's okay, apparently. She's just a bit banged up with a sprained ankle. But she gave everyone a big scare. I thought you'd heard."

Had Tripp been talking to Tabitha the night before? Or had someone called to let him know she'd gone missing?

"Oh my God, May!"

I placed my hand on my chest. I was breathing so heavily, I felt like I was going to pass out.

May nodded, her eyes red and watery. "To be honest with you, Minty," she said, "Tabitha can be pretty dramatic sometimes. I have a feeling it may have just been a cry for help gone wrong. But it's still jarring."

I nodded.

"I guess if we're being honest," I said, "you should know that Tripp and I had a major clash last night, after the engagement party."

May raised an eyebrow.

"I overheard him on the phone with someone," I continued. "He was reassuring someone or telling someone everything would be okay and he called whoever this person was 'sweetie.' I ran out before he could say anything. I couldn't handle it."

"Oh wow," May said. "I would be freaking out if I were you."

"Oh, believe me," I said, "I am. You didn't hear anything, did you?"

I couldn't help but ask. I had no reason to believe that May was completely on my side. She was dating Tripp's best friend. I barely knew her. The little I did know did not paint the most flattering picture.

"About last night?" she asked. "No. The last I saw you two, you looked completely in love!"

Hmmm; it seemed like she was being sincere.

"Listen, Minty," she said, pursing her lips. "I know we don't know each other all that well, but I have some experience with this kind of thing."

I nodded.

"And there's nothing I can say to make this better." She paused. "But there's one thing you should know if you're going to survive in a relationship with a guy like Tripp."

I cocked my head to the side, intrigued.

"Monogamy is not part of the deal," she said.

Wow, I thought. I'd never seen her more serious.

"I'm not saying it's right," she continued. "I'm not saying you should accept it. But it's reality."

I didn't really know how to react to that statement. Part of me felt like she was stating the obvious. Another part of me couldn't help but wonder, Is that really how it works? Is it really just "part of the deal"? Am I being unrealistic?

When I remained silent, May sighed and shrugged her shoulders.

"Anyway," she said, her expression morphing from serious to exuberant, "let's talk about something happy. What's your seat assignment for Carolina? I hope we're together!"

If Life Gives You Lemons,
Make Lemonade

I never made it to the Carolina Herrera show. I finished up breakfast with May, expressed my deepest regrets, and hopped in a cab home.

As excited as I was to even be invited, I just couldn't bring myself to sit and smile at a fashion show when I felt like everything that mattered to me was a lie. I was brought up to believe in things like true love, fidelity, and marriage. Basically, May was telling me those things weren't possible with Tripp.

I had just taken off my coat when the buzzer rang. My doorman said that Tripp was coming up.

"Hey," I said, opening the door.

He was wearing sweatpants, sneakers (never a good sign), and an old overcoat. As he walked past me, I noticed he was holding something under the overcoat and that "something" was moving.

"What do you have under there?" I asked, reaching under his coat.

He swatted me away. "Give me a second," he said.

He sat down. "I'm thinking you've heard about Tabitha," he said.

I nodded. "May told me."

"She's in the hospital but she's going to be fine."

"Thank God," I said sarcastically. I surprised myself, it came out so quickly. Even Tripp looked taken aback. Then again, what did he expect? Was I really supposed to feel sorry for the woman who may or may not have been my husband's mistress?

His coat moved again and he adjusted his hand.

"Tripp, what do you have in your coat?"

He ignored my question. "In a minute," he said, petting whatever was underneath there. What was it? A bunny rabbit? A gerbil? It couldn't have been any larger than a kitten. I narrowed my eyes.

"We've been over this a million times, Minty," he said. "I told you there's nothing going on."

I shrugged. "I'm not sure I can believe that."

I'd read somewhere that when a person is lying and their lie is being met with resistance, they usually react with rage and anger. A person telling the truth will react with sadness, something close to defeat.

Tripp stared at the floor. Then he started tapping his foot, like a nervous tic. The tapping traveled up his body until it reached his fingers and suddenly every part of him was shaking in one way or another. At the same time, his neck flushed red, his face turned the color of a turnip, and he clenched his fists. I instinctively jumped back, thinking there was a possibility he might react physically. I'd never seen him so enraged. I could practically hear his heart beating out of his chest.

"Jesus Christ!" he screamed, standing up. He deposited the tiniest little Chihuahua I'd ever seen in my life on the floor. I gasped. "What the hell do you want me to say? What are you going to do, hire a fucking private investigator to follow me around? Tap my phone? Listen to my voice mails?!"

"What is that?!" I stared at the tiny, quivering animal.

"Should I get up in front of a jury and swear under oath that I am not having an affair with Tabitha Lipton?"

His voice was so loud, so bellowing, I was sure the neighbors could hear. Great, I thought, another item for "Page Six" to run with.

"Tripp, I—I can't," I stuttered, bending toward the ground and staring at the little creature. "Did you get me a—a dog?" Clearly, he'd gotten me a dog.

He ignored me, continuing on.

"The last thing I need is you, of all people, bringing up old bullshit that I thought we'd moved past already." He ran his fingers through his hair. The veins in his temples were popping out. "I haven't seen Tabitha in months. From what I hear, she went on vacation to clear her head and get away from everything. But I only know that because her sister explained everything when she called last night. I was on the phone with Tabitha's sister last night when you walked in."

Tabitha's sister, huh? Wow. Okay, so he'd worked this out in his head. I had questions about that story, too, but I was afraid to speak. He seemed so out of control, so infuriated. I felt like if I said the wrong thing he would really lose it.

"So you were talking to Tabitha's sister in the room last night?" I asked calmly. I picked up the dog and held it to my chest. I guessed we would address the "Chihuahua in the room" at a later date.

"Yes," he said. His chest was heaving up and down. He was finally able to take a decent breath.

"You call her 'sweetie'?"

He looked shocked for a moment. Then he focused.

"She was hysterical," he said. "I was trying to calm her down."

I nodded. "I see."

He finally sat down.

"Tabitha is a very high-profile person. The vultures are going to descend on her, on her family and friends, and it's not going to be pretty." He shook his head. "There are going to be stories coming out, just like the ones people tell about you tripping that girl on the runway—fake stories—and some people are going to believe them." He paused. "Look at me, Minty."

I stared back at him.

"I need you to stand by me on this one. I need to know that my wife is on my side." He gulped. "Because you're all I have right now. You're the only person I can really trust."

I just looked at him. I wasn't sure what to say. Did I believe him in my heart of hearts? No. Did I want to believe him? Yes. And, at the center of it all, I loved him. I hated myself for it, but I did.

"What are you thinking?" he asked.

I shook my head. "I don't know," I said. "I'm stunned. Not to mention this." I held the dog up in the air. I couldn't help but smile.

His body relaxed a bit.

"I was on my way over here and I saw her in the window of that shelter down the street," he said. "I couldn't resist. The people at the shelter have been calling her Tiny, but they said she can probably learn a new name if you really want to change it."

My heart melted. Tripp did know how to distract a lady.

"Mrs. Jelly Belly," I said out loud.

"Mrs. what?"

"After the jelly beans," I said. "She has a round, little white tummy like a marshmallow-flavored jelly bean."

He shook his head. "Okay, then. 'Belly' for short?"

"Exactly," I said. Couldn't we just talk about the dog for the rest of our lives?

"Listen." He leaned in closer, changing the subject. "I can imagine what it looked like, what it sounded like. But Tabitha's sister was panicking. She kept calling and calling from a restricted number so I finally picked up. She was obviously in a state and I didn't want to get you involved so I took the call in the guest room. I certainly never expected that type of news, especially in the middle of our engagement party. And then when you left, I wasn't quite sure how to explain it, to be honest."

"Got it," I said.

Inside, I was numb. I felt like a bad actress reciting her lines. But he didn't pick up on any of the irony in my tone. Honestly, he just seemed relieved I wasn't calling my lawyer.

"I love you," he said, running his hand down the side of my face. I gazed up at him.

I loved him too. But I also hated him. I hated the fact that I had ever met him in the first place, that I'd fallen in love with him when

I was fifteen. I hated that he'd suddenly reappeared in my life. I hated that part of me believed his stories. Part of me rationalized that it was a normal thing for Tabitha's sister to call Tripp in a panic, that it was a normal thing for Tripp to call anyone other than me "sweetie." I had no control over these feelings. They just came to me and I gave in.

He frowned and looked at me, waiting for some sort of reaction, probably hoping that I would reassure him that I believed him and everything was going to be okay. But I couldn't bring myself to go that far.

"I just hate that all of this is happening and I have to leave in a few hours for London," he said.

I sat up, startled.

"Oh my God," I said, "that's right."

"I know," he said, "it's a mess but I have no choice. They're expecting me first thing in the morning. You understand, don't you?"

I nodded. "Of course."

"I promise this will work itself out," he said, stroking my face. "Do you believe me?"

"Of course," I said. It was an outright lie.

After Tripp left, I did what any self-respecting southern girl does when she's feeling like her world is crashing in around her. I packed up my new Chihuahua in a Chanel handbag and went shopping.

———◈◈◈———

On the corner of Sixty-sixth and Madison, the Oscar de la Renta boutique loomed. Just days before, my mother and I had mapped out a plan to spend all of Monday tackling the best ateliers in the city: Vera Wang, Carolina Herrera, Reem Acra, and, yes, Oscar. So many people I knew had gone to large stores to find their wedding dress, but my mother insisted on the personal experience of the New York flagship boutique. You had to make an appointment, of course.

I stopped in front of the window. The clothes were impeccably styled and tailored, right down to the most delicate buttons and nearly undetectable seams. I peered past the dress forms and into the shop. And there, in the center of the room, was one of the most gorgeous wedding gowns I had ever seen.

At first it reminded me of a tulip upside down, the way the skirt bloomed from the pink satin sash at the waist and cascaded toward the floor. The top portion of the dress was sheer, sleeveless, and covered in delicate embroidery. It was love at first sight.

I stood there and stared.

I was standing in front of the window, daydreaming about the dress, when I heard an all-too-familiar voice coming up behind me.

"Why, don't you look like a sad, lost puppy."

"Mother!" I swiveled around and Belly popped her head out of the bag.

"My lord, you've got to be kidding me," she said, glaring at Belly.

"Tripp's guilt present," I explained.

"Christ." She rolled her eyes, looking up at the Oscar de la Renta sign. "What are you going to do with a dog?"

I sighed. "I don't know. I should be furious he got it for me, but there's something comforting about having her around."

My mother's eyes softened.

"Your doorman said you were headed up Madison, so I figured I'd find you here."

"Mommy." My lower lip quivered. She knew me too well.

"It's going to be all right, sweetheart." She put her arm around me.

"No it's not," I said. "I really don't think it's going to be all right."

"We'll make it better."

"How?"

She peered through the window. Her eyes focused directly on the gown.

"By trying on that dress to start," she said, pointing through the window.

"I'd marry pretty much anyone if it meant I could wear this dress," I said.

"Don't say that."

I closed my eyes. "I love him," I said. "I really do. I want this to work, but things are not good."

"Well, every couple hits bumps along the road, especially in the beginning," she said. "Anyway, you do have a wedding in the works that, God willing, will happen. So you need a dress. Better to be over-prepared than underprepared." She opened the door to the boutique. "Shall we?"

Stepping into the Oscar de la Renta boutique on Madison Avenue feels like stepping into an enchanted kingdom. There is glamour, of course, but also a personal touch, as if Mr. de la Renta himself has invited you into his home.

We were immediately greeted by Geny, a petite saleswoman with an Eastern European accent. She had spied us gazing at the dress from the street and knew exactly where to begin.

"A bride-to-be, I see," she said, arranging for the gown to be placed in the private dressing suite.

I deposited the Chanel bag with Belly in it on the floor of the dressing suite (she was sound asleep, already so well behaved!) and we spent a few moments perusing the wedding dresses displayed in the salon. How could we not? It was like standing in the middle of the Costume Institute at the Met. Some of the dresses were so structured and voluminous that they stood up on their own. They made the debutante gown I wore to the Frick look like a fancy nightgown. But I'd always been decisive, and the second I saw the dress with the pink sash in the window, I knew it was exactly what I was looking for. Now I just had to try it on.

The dressing room had its own little settee. The lighting was flaw-less. I made a mental note to ask Geny what kind of bulbs they used so I could get them for my apartment.

She helped me fasten the dress, which had a teeny tiny corset and a hidden zipper up the side. I poked my head out of the room. As much as I loved the dress and felt amazing wearing it, I knew Mother was the final test.

Her initial reaction was hard to read. She pursed her lips, then scrunched them to the side. Then she turned her head and her eyes narrowed into tiny little slits. But I knew the coast was clear when she started nodding. It was a subtle nod at first, almost as if she was trying to keep herself from nodding too enthusiastically. But then she was smiling and clapping her hands. She stood up, ran over, and made me twirl around a million times in order to catch every angle.

She turned to Geny.

"There will be a few alterations of course," she said. "Minty's wedding dress needs to be one-of-a-kind."

Geny jotted down some notes. "Of course, Mrs. Davenport," she said. "Of course."

As Geny walked away, I felt the initial rush of wearing the dress peak and plummet. What was I doing, standing in the middle of Oscar de la Renta in a wedding gown when just a few hours before I was questioning whether or not I wanted to go through with the wedding in the first place? A lump formed in my throat and within seconds I was crying.

"Sweetheart," my mother said, rushing to my side. "The dress is breathtaking, I know, but there's no use crying about it."

"Mother, give me a break," I gulped through the tears.

She cupped my face in her hands. "All I'm saying is, let's not jump to too many conclusions."

"I'm just feeling so unsure right now," I said, pulling away. "I don't even know where to begin to make this better."

"Well, I'm not sure if this makes you feel any better," she said, "but Tripp called me crying last night. He said he couldn't live without you, that he was worried he'd screwed it all up. I would have had to have a heart of stone not to listen to him."

I gulped. "And what did you say?"

"I told him to be honest with you. He said you wouldn't believe him. So I told him he should sit you down, face-to-face, once everyone had cooled down a bit and discuss it. I had no idea that floozy was off on a boat somewhere trying to draw attention to herself."

"Mommy, let's at least try to be civil," I said.

"'Floozy' is the civil option compared to everything else I want to call her. So, were you able to talk to him as well?" she asked.

I frowned. "Yes."

"And?"

"I'm not sure I believe him. Actually, I think he's lying."

"I see," Mother said.

Geny returned. She consulted with my mother about the dress for a few minutes as I pulled myself together in the dressing room and changed back into my clothes. When I came out, my mother was standing there looking very focused, with just a touch of concern. As suffocating as she could be, I knew that she wanted nothing more than the best for her daughters. I trusted her opinion more than anyone's.

"Well," she began, "look at it this way. Tripp is off to London. You have yourself some time to think. Take a few days, breathe a little. And when he's back, hopefully y'all will figure this out."

I nodded. "Okay." I picked up Belly and stroked her head.

As we walked out of Oscar de la Renta, Geny was putting the dress back on display.

I glanced at my mother.

"I told her we have a little more shopping around to do," she said.

18

Keep Your Friends Close
and Your Enemies Closer

May scored an invite to the Marc Jacobs show *and* after-party and she was nice enough to invite me. It was one of the final shows of Fashion Week, on Sunday night. I spent the entire weekend preparing. From what I'd heard, it was nearly impossible to get an invite to Marc unless you were a top fashion editor or a celebrity, so the fact that May had been able to convince her friend in the PR department to give me a seat was a huge deal. Even Emily was impressed.

"I reminded her about the Kevin Park story in *WWD* and she realized you'd be an asset to the front row," May said.

"Wow," I said. "Thank you!"

When I arrived at the Armory on Lexington Avenue, I was horrified to see Ruth standing at the front of the house overseeing the check-in. A long line had already started to snake around the front of the building.

"Minty!"

I turned around and saw May making her way toward me. She was waving dramatically, drawing a lot of attention to herself. She towered over the crowd in amazing Marc Jacobs platform heels.

"Minty, what are you *doing* on that line?" She grabbed me by the arm. "You shouldn't be standing on a line."

She ushered me toward the front—past the bewildered-looking girls from RVPR—without getting so much as a second glance from Ruth. The word "no" was not in May's vocabulary, probably because she had never heard it. May lived in her own world, and that world was filled with last-minute trips to Paris on private jets, multimillion-dollar real estate, a wardrobe of couture, and never having to wash your own hair.

"Excuse me, Ms. Abernathy," one of the RVPR girls said, running after us as we made our way toward the entrance of the show. "We're actually not ready yet. We're going to start letting in VIP guests in the next five minutes or so if you don't mind waiting?"

May shot the girl a withering look and kept walking.

"Oh, it's okay, honey," she said over her shoulder, waving a willowy hand in the air. "Marc won't mind." She burst through the doors, dragging me behind her.

We stood at the end of the runway, where packs of photographers had already set up shop. There was still a long piece of black fabric covering the runway. Girls in black T-shirts were placing gift bags on the first- and second-row seats.

"Every season it's like, blah, blah, blah, we're not ready yet. Well, I'm ready." She turned to me. "Do you know what I mean?"

I didn't really know what she meant. "These shows always start so late, it's annoying!"

"Not Marc," May said, making her way toward our assigned seats, which were thankfully next to each other. "Not anymore. There was a ton of drama one year about how Marc was almost an hour late. Anna got up and left, she was so annoyed," she said, referring to Anna Wintour, the editor in chief of *Vogue,* "and God knows you don't piss Anna off. Anyway, he starts on time now and that's that. But really . . ." She trailed off, glancing around the cavernous space. "OMG, where is the after-party again? I'm pretty sure it's at the Jane. We'll have to ask Judy from PR backstage. Remind me."

"Okay," I said, trying to process everything she'd just rattled off. "Do you know when Emily is getting here?"

Emily had mentioned she was going to try to catch the show as well.

"Oh," May said, "you didn't get her text? She's meeting us at the after-party. Something with her boss. She works like a dog, that one."

I laughed. To May, any job seemed unfathomable, inhumane. We sat down and she placed her gift bag under her seat without so much as glancing inside. It was uncouth to glance inside a gift bag in public. Some people just left the gift bag behind as if they couldn't even be bothered!

People started filing in. The crowd already included every chic and important person on the island of Manhattan. And then the celebrities started to descend. The flash of the cameras growing more frequent was a sure sign that someone famous was entering the room. And, sure enough, there were Kanye, Beyoncé, and J.Lo.

There was a hush in the crowd and everyone started taking their seats. Then the entire room went black. I looked at May, who had already moved into the next topic of conversation and was texting away on her BlackBerry.

"The after-party's at the Jane," she whispered. "Ugh, so fucking far west. And the car situation outside is going to be a nightmare. I'll have Billy pull up right on Twenty-fifth as soon as the show is—"

May was cut off by the sound of thumping techno music. A single spotlight shone on the start of the runway and a model stood still there, wearing a sculptural dress, her hair teased and piled high on her head. The music switched to a less jarring song and she started walking with a completely blank expression on her face. Of the handful of other shows I'd attended that week I couldn't recall one smiling model.

I tried to keep my eyes on the clothes, but Jennifer Lopez was sitting directly across from me, and if Jennifer Lopez is within a hundred feet it's hard to focus on anything else. She was wearing huge Dior sunglasses and her hair was so long, wavy, and thick it was almost otherworldly.

"No one does 'cool girl' better than Marc," May said as a model strutted by in an ankle-length skirt and a structured jacket.

I nodded. I thought the clothes were cute. But there were so many amazing things going on, it was hard to even begin to process what the models were wearing. This was theater and the clothes were the stars. The celebrities, socialites, and various glitterati were part of the production, adding a glamorous backdrop to the stage. Because of the brevity of the show—seven, maybe nine minutes tops—you couldn't help but be distracted by the reactions of the front row.

Was that a raised eyebrow from Anna? Did Liv Tyler just point out that leather skirt to her stylist, Rachel Zoe? Could Gerard Butler wipe that silly grin off his face?

And then, the grand finale. The girls came out for their last walk, one after another, so close together they were like a giant centipede of chic, snaking down the runway and turning, circling back to where they came from. Marc stood at the end of the runway and did a quick wave.

"Wow," I said.

May nodded. "I know. I know. Major, right?" She uncrossed her legs and turned to me. "Shall we, honey?"

Everyone stood up. More camera flashes were going off. I'd always loved fashion. I'd always loved to shop the latest trends, discover new designers, and put together a cute outfit. But *this* is what it was about. Because every single person in the Armory that night, from the students and interns standing on their tippy-toes at the top of the bleachers to the celebrities and editors lining the front row, was passionate about being there. That was it—there was an amazing energy, an enthusiasm that I'd never felt anywhere else. It was a natural high. And all I could think was, This is what I need to do.

As I daydreamed about a future Minty Davenport show, May and I began to weave our way through the crowd. I noticed Alexis Barnaby standing off to the side. We made eye contact, briefly, and then Richard Fitzsimmons asked May and me if he could take our picture.

"Of course, handsome," May said, winking jokingly at Richard.

Richard's flash went off several times, and then it was over.

"Minty!"

A man in jeans and New Balance sneakers came running up as May wandered off to the other side of the runway and said hello to someone in Beyoncé's entourage.

"Minty, Ken Dawson from Gawker," he said. He looked flushed for a minute, nervous even. "I've, uh, written about you a few times . . . ?"

"Oh, really?" I asked.

From what I knew about the website Gawker.com, whatever he'd "written" about me was probably pretty snarky and also just a little bit rude.

He shrugged. "Yeah," he said. "All in good fun."

I shrugged back. "Sure," I said.

"So, uh, do you have any comment on the news?"

I looked back at him blankly. "I'm sorry?"

"Social Roster," he said. "The news that Ruth Vine has been behind SocialRoster.com all along?"

My jaw hit the floor.

"Rumor has it she's going to be on the cover of *New York* magazine next week. A huge exposé on the downfall of one of the city's top publicists," he said, rolling his eyes. He leaned in, lowering his voice. "Supposedly her clients have already started dropping like flies."

I gulped.

"So. Any comment?"

"N-no," I stammered.

"What about you and Tripp?" he continued as I started backing away. "Why did you decide to get married in city hall when you're already planning a big wedding?"

"Excuse me?" I said.

"Are you going to comment or not?"

"No!" I shouted.

I pushed through a crowd of people (which is something I normally wouldn't do) to get to May, who was standing a head taller than most people.

"Minty! Are you okay?"

"Excuse me," I announced to Beyoncé's entourage. "I'm sorry." I grabbed May's arm. "I have to get out of here."

May escorted me in the opposite direction of the crowd, through the little entrance to the backstage area. Behind the black curtain, Marc was calmly answering a few questions from interviewers while the hair and makeup teams closed up shop. As we passed by, May blew a kiss in his direction and he blew one right back, barely skipping a beat in the "deconstructed glamour" sound bite he was giving the reporter from the Style Network. May pointed to a door on the opposite side of the room that was slightly ajar.

"Through there," she said.

When we stepped onto Twenty-fifth Street, the cold air hit me like a jolt of caffeine. I felt like the last five minutes had happened in a terrible nightmare.

"Minty!"

Alexis Barnaby had followed us outside and was standing there in the freezing cold, alone, with no jacket. I stared at her.

"May, hi," she said. "I'm so sorry to bother you both, I just wanted to explain."

"What's wrong, honey?" I asked. She looked like she was about to cry.

"It's just," she began, "I want you to know I had nothing to do with any of the negative press. Ruth was really angry when you left. I was interning a few days a week and she suddenly started inviting me to parties instead of asking me to work them. She was letting me borrow clothes from the closet. She called me her little 'project' and, honestly, I just thought it was fun. And then these stories started appearing out of nowhere, linking me to you and saying you'd tripped me on the runway and all of these things that weren't true." She gulped, her eyes filling with tears. She was clearly overwhelmed. "I didn't know where they were coming from. At first I just thought someone random was making them up, but then I realized it was her! She was using me to get back at you! And honestly, Minty, I had no idea. If anything, I would have loved to be your friend and now we're supposedly enemies."

"Please," I said, attempting to look like I knew all along that Ruth was behind those stories. "I know how Ruth can be." I smiled at her. It seemed like she was telling the truth. "And what is this thing about Social Roster?"

"Ugh," Alexis groaned. "She started it as a joke. But then it became this big thing and I don't think she realized what she was getting herself into."

I shook my head. May frowned, becoming increasingly impatient with the long-winded story.

"Sweetie," May said in a patronizing tone, "tell me: if Ruth was behind that website, why would she put Minty and me as the top girls and you all the way down on the bottom?"

Alexis stared up at May. "I don't know," she said in a shaky voice. "She had some plan about having me climb the ranks. By the time I found out, it was pretty late in the game. I'm terrified of her."

I glanced around the block, which was quiet save for a few passing cars and neighborhood people walking their dogs. I hadn't felt so bullied, so singled out, since junior high school when Amber Macintosh told my whole gym class that I still wore Strawberry Shortcake underwear. But at the same time, at least I had one less enemy than I thought. I guess Alexis wasn't so bad after all.

"Anyway," Alexis said. "I'm freezing and I'm sure you have to get going. I just wanted to say that I'm sorry for everything." She turned around and walked back into the Armory.

May craned her neck down the block and waved her hand in the air as our car approached.

"Oh my God, May, Ruth is evil!"

May just shrugged. "Oh, honey," she said, "aren't you sweet to act all shocked and surprised."

19

If It Walks Like a Duck,
It's Probably a Duck

Tripp was right. The media was having a field day with the news
that Tabitha had "almost drowned" in the Caribbean.

Thankfully, only one or two articles mentioned that Tabitha and
Tripp had dated in the past. One piece in *New York* magazine suggested that Tabitha and I were not the best of friends, but that was
the extent of it. Perhaps I was being spared some drama this time
around.

I called Tripp in London twice over the course of two days to
check in, but I kept getting voice mail. He finally called back to
say he'd lost his cell phone and that I should just leave a message
with the concierge if I needed to reach him. I shook my head. It
was classic Tripp to lose his cell phone. He was always forgetting it
somewhere.

But after leaving several messages with the concierge, I was starting to get angry. I was sure he was busy with work but what on earth
was keeping him from calling me back? Especially in the midst of
the Tabitha media frenzy. He was my husband! And he was skating

on extremely thin ice. I didn't think checking in once a day was too much to ask.

Emily not only agreed, she was aghast.

"You're kidding me, right?" she said when I called to fill her in on the situation.

"Am I overreacting?" I knew I wasn't, but for some reason I needed a second opinion. I needed *her* second opinion.

"Minty, don't make me come over there and drop-kick some sense into you," she said, fuming. "It would be one thing if you guys parted on completely normal, healthy relationship terms, but this is unacceptable. He should be sending you diamonds and filling every room of your apartment with roses right now, not ignoring your calls."

I was silent. She was right, of course.

"Will you let me know the second you hear back from him, please? I'm really curious to hear what he has to say for himself."

"Okay," I said.

"Promise?"

"Promise."

On top of it, Ryerson—of all people—reappeared. I was rushing out of the door for work when my phone started ringing. I hadn't seen his name pop up on my phone in, well, two years. And there it was: Ryerson Bigelow. I nearly dropped the phone on the ground I was so shocked. But I couldn't bring myself to answer the call, especially when I was so wrapped up in the situation with Tripp. I was pretty sure the last thing I was prepared to handle was a heart-to-heart with my ex-boyfriend.

Thankfully, he didn't leave a voice mail. Probably a pocket dial, I told myself. I quickly pushed the thought of Ryerson out of my head.

Luckily, Kevin was keeping me busy. He was so in demand after the success of his runway show that he was getting offers left and right to expand the business and add an accessories line. I was thrilled for him and honored to even have a small role in the building of his brand. The more I experienced the inner workings of the fashion industry, the more I saw myself eventually expanding my role in it. Tabitha had used her boldface name status to start a jewelry line. Why couldn't I do the same? I was in the perfect position to learn everything I could from Kevin Park.

In an effort to make the most of my time with him, I'd been checking in with Jenny and the PR team on a regular basis to see if there was anything I could do to help. Did they need me to do any interviews? Could we arrange for paparazzi to shoot me coming out of a chic restaurant in a Kevin Park design? Maybe I could give some of my friends, like May or Emily, Kevin Park items that they could then wear to the next high-profile benefit? What if I hosted a tea party for a bunch of girls in Kevin's honor? We could get *Town & Country* to cover the event and donate money to a worthy New York–based charity like the Doe Fund or New Yorkers for Children.

Jenny was receptive to my ideas but she was also very busy. Sometimes I wondered if I was being a pest. So when Kevin asked that I stop by his office for a meeting one day, I wasn't sure what to think.

"Minty! How are you?" Kevin stood up and we double kissed. "Have a seat," he said, gesturing toward the chair in front of his desk. He gazed at me. "I feel like I haven't seen you in years. But it's been, what? A week?"

"About a week and a half." I smiled.

"Oh my God," he said. "It's only been a week and a half since the show. I feel like I've aged ten years in that time." He shook his head. "Barneys and Neiman Marcus are taking the line. Can you believe it!?"

"Kevin!" I exclaimed. "That's amazing!"

He nodded. "I owe a lot to you."

I shook my head no.

"Really," he said. "You can't imagine the amount of attention the line has been getting just as a result of being associated with your name and all of the amazing girls you've introduced to the line. It's unbelievable."

"Kevin," I said, "the clothes really speak for themselves."

He grinned. "Well, of course they do, honey. But there have been many talented designers before me who have struggled to get noticed. It takes more than talent to make it these days. I found my muse in you!"

I didn't know what to say. I was so flattered. "You're making me blush, Kev!"

"Well," he began, "I called you in here today because I want to discuss a proposition with you. A business proposition."

My eyes widened. "Go on!"

"I've been lucky enough to secure some additional investors as a result of the success of my show. The clothes are doing well. Saks is already a major account, as you know. But the next step is a solid accessories line." He thought for a moment. "I've done clutches or a scarf or something here and there, but I really want to commit to it this time around, and thankfully now I have the capital to work with."

"I see," I said. What was he saying exactly?

"So I was wondering, would you be interested in designing a line for me?"

I sat up in the chair. "Are you kidding?!"

"Not in the slightest," he laughed. "I'm not saying the entire line, of course. We'd launch with a Kevin Park line of handbags and clutches and whatnot. But I think it would be cute if we had, say, three or four special Minty Davenport designs. They could be limited edition, maybe only sold in the boutique? Something to really get the buzz going. Maybe you could even do a cute dog bag inspired by Mrs. Jelly Belly."

"Oh my God!" I nearly screamed. "And you'd let me design them myself?!" I couldn't believe what I was hearing.

"Well, yes," Kevin said. "In theory. You'd work with a more established accessories designer, someone on my team, to come up with your own designs. You'll need your hand held just a little, especially the first time around. What do you say?"

"Oh. My. God. Kevin!" I squealed. "I would die! I mean, I can't believe you're even saying what you're saying right now! I have so many ideas! When can I start?"

He laughed. "I had a feeling you'd be enthusiastic," he said. "So then it's a deal?"

"Absolutely," I said. "One hundred percent."

———◆◇◇◆———

After my meeting with Kevin, I had plans to see Spencer for a drink at the Waverly Inn, a restaurant that was owned by Spencer's new boss at *Vanity Fair*. I couldn't wait to see him, tell him the news, and catch up on all of the gossip since we'd last seen each other at the engagement party.

The restaurant looked like it hadn't been touched since the early twentieth century, and yet it still had the vibe of a downtown hot spot. A mural along one wall depicted various famous New Yorkers, including Woody Allen and Fran Lebowitz.

Spencer was sitting at the bar looking every bit the *Vanity Fair*-ite he'd become in the last couple of weeks. He had on a dark gray tailored suit that could only have been Dior Homme and a white shirt open at the collar.

"Spencer Goldin," I said, kissing him on the cheek, "you look like you just popped over in your Alfa Romeo or something."

"I'm not screwing around, Davenport—er, du Pont," Spencer said. He was sipping a Dewar's on the rocks. "I'm at *Vanity Fair* now. I have to represent."

"You really look dashing."

"Why thank you, darlin'."

"So," I began.

"So."

"Tabitha!"

"I know," he said.

"Crazy."

"I'll say." He took a sip of his drink. "Have you talked to the Trippster?"

I rolled my eyes. "He's in London."

"And? Have you talked to him?"

"It's been hard to get ahold of him."

"Really."

The bartender came over and took my order, a glass of rosé Moët. In spite of my absentee husband, I was in the mood for celebrating.

"I haven't seen you since the engagement party, and we barely had a moment to talk," Spencer said.

"I know." I rolled my eyes and took a sip of champagne.

"So what's going on? You haven't gotten divorced yet, have you?"

The look on my face must have signaled he'd said the exact thing he shouldn't have said.

"Oh my God." He placed his hand on my knee. "Totally kidding. Are you okay? Did something happen?"

I sighed. "I wasn't planning on getting into this, but yes, something happened the night of the party."

"The same day Tabitha hurled herself over the side of the yacht?"

Spencer mimed a swan dive with his arms and crossed his eyes. He looked more like a crazy cheerleader forming the letter "A" than a glamorous socialite.

"Yes," I said. "It has something to do with that actually."

"Noooo," Spencer said. "She didn't do that because of Tripp, did she?"

"I have a feeling she was trying to get *someone's* attention," I said.

"Holy shit. Do you think he's cheating on you?"

I closed my eyes. "I don't know. It's a big mess."

"So is he?"

"Let's just say I'm at the end of my rope." I looked at him. "He says he's not. He says she's crazy and he wants nothing to do with her. But the pieces don't add up."

He sat there for a moment. And really, it would have been nice if Spencer had told me to let it go and move on, that Tripp was a great guy and I should drown out the noise and live my life. But there was something strange about his reaction. It was almost like he was attempting to hide the fact that he did not approve.

"What is it?" he asked, looking slightly uncomfortable.

"You don't think I should have agreed to marry Tripp in the first place," I said.

Spencer gulped. "I did not say that."

"And it's not even the whole Tabitha thing, is it?" I swallowed. "It's the general concept of Tripp being my husband."

"Minty," Spencer began, "I barely know the guy. I can't possibly have an educated opinion. It's just, it is what it is."

"What is that supposed to mean?"

"Tripp is who he is, and if you're okay with that, then so be it."

I was silent. The whole world knew that Tripp was the kind of husband who went on long business trips to London and rarely returned his wife's calls. The kind of husband who said one thing and did another. I'd given him the benefit of the doubt, but he hadn't changed a bit.

I guess the hurt I felt showed on my face.

"Mints, are you okay, sweetie? I didn't mean to—"

"No, no." I took a sip of champagne. "It's just, sometimes you're the last to show up to a party, you know?"

"Sweetheart." Spencer looked sad. "All relationships are different. They are all complicated. If you're happy, that's all that matters. You shouldn't care what anyone else thinks."

I pursed my lips and managed a smile.

"Tell me something happy," Spencer said. "I mean, something happier than Tabitha throwing herself off a yacht."

I couldn't help but laugh.

"Well, let me think," I began. "Kevin asked me to design a line of handbags for him."

At first, Spencer just looked relieved I'd so willingly changed the subject. Then he literally almost fell off his bar stool with excitement.

"No!"

"Yes!" I said.

"Holy crap!" he shouted. "This is huge!"

"I know," I said. "The bags are going to say my name on them and everything."

"Not to bring up a sore subject, but did you tell Tripp yet?"

"Nah," I said, "I just got out of the meeting and it's already so late there, he's probably asleep."

Spencer took a sip of his drink. "Yeah."

"Screw it," I said, "I'm calling him now."

The phone rang in that funny, droning, echo-y way they do abroad. "Hello?"

He picked up! And he sounded groggy! I sighed. It was nice to know that my husband was actually doing some sleeping, in his room, while he was in London.

"Tripp?" I said.

"Mints?" He groaned. "It's two o'clock in the morning here."

"I know," I said, "but I've been trying to reach you!"

"Work gets crazy when I'm in London; can we talk about this later?"

I frowned. "I have some exciting news."

Spencer looked on, his glass to his lips. "Yup," he said.

I told him about how Kevin wanted me to become more involved with the company. About how he wanted me to actually design my own line of handbags as part of the Kevin Park accessories line. Could he believe it? How exciting was that?

There was silence on the other end of the line.

"A handbag line?" he said.

I felt my heart begin to deflate like a sad balloon, twirling slowly toward the ground and finally settling in a muddy patch somewhere.

"Yes!" I tried to maintain my enthusiasm. I looked back at Spencer, who was nodding along and smiling. "I'm starting next week. I'm working alongside his head of accessories and everything. He's going to let me do a dog bag for Belly. The bags will have my name on them!"

"Wow, handbags," he said. "Really. My parents are going to just have a *field day* with that."

And then, somewhere in my psyche, a grimy boot stomped on my sad little balloon heart until it was so flat and dirty there was no more balloon to be seen.

"Anyway"—I smiled at Spencer as I talked—"you're tired. We'll talk tomorrow?"

"I'm back in a few days, Mints," he said. What was *that* supposed to mean? "But yes, we can talk tomorrow if you'd like."

"Okay!" I continued on in my fake-peppy voice. "Love you. Bye."

I hung up.

"At least Tabitha's in the hospital so you know she's not with him now," Spencer said, half-joking.

I took a sip of champagne and punched him in the arm.

We sat for a few more minutes and made small talk, but I was in another place. Tripp had not exactly reacted the way I expected him to react, to say the least.

After we finished our drinks, Spencer said he was heading over to SoHo for a cocktail party at a friend's house. We hugged good-bye. "I know I joke around with you a lot," he said. "And God, if anyone wants you to be a du Pont—excuse me, to *stay* a du Pont, it's me." He smiled. "But if he fucks up again, in any way, shape, or form, don't let him get away with it. Got it?"

"Got it," I said.

In the cab on the way uptown, I gazed out the window at the sprawl of Sixth Avenue in its mishmash of mom-and-pop hardware stores, fast food restaurants, and big-name retailers. Every person walking down that street had something on their mind. My "something" was Tripp. At some point—now or years from now—I knew I would have to decide if it was worth it. But I hadn't come to that fork in the road yet.

20

Pick Your Battles and Fight Them

In Charleston, March means springtime. In New York, it means at least another month of snow, slush, and below-freezing temperatures.

I didn't even really care so much about the lack of sun and biting windchill. I'd just had it with layering! I think my legs had forgotten what it felt like to *not* wear tights. Also, I don't think I've ever seen so many scowling faces as I did walking the streets of Manhattan after a snowstorm in early March. It was hard not to feel bummed out!

Kevin told me to channel my winter doldrums into ideas for the handbag collection, which was set to debut in the fall, so that's what I did. By the time Tripp was due to return from London, I'd already filled a whole sketchbook with design ideas. I'd never felt more inspired.

Zeke and I met Tripp at JFK. As downtrodden as I was feeling, I was trying my best to stay positive. Maybe things would be better after he came back? Maybe we just needed a little space? Things *had* moved very fast between us.

Zeke and I stood together outside of the gate area and waited while businessman after businessman passed by in their tailored suits with their carry-ons. I held up a sign that said TRIPP DU PONT. We were meeting May and Harry for dinner that night at Cipriani, so I was already dressed up in a bright pink Tibi dress and little black suede Chanel booties. I'd borrowed Zeke's round black chauffeur's hat to wear as a joke. We must have looked like an interesting odd couple, the grumpy old driver standing next to a blonde girl in a goofy-looking hat. When Tripp spotted us, he immediately started laughing. I felt like he'd been gone for years.

"You look adorable," he said.

"Good, that's the point." I smiled.

Zeke took Tripp's luggage and started walking ahead of us. I looped my arm through Tripp's. It was nice to have him back, to have a man in my life again who was not Spencer or Kevin. Spencer and I had spoken once since our drinks date. It probably had something to do with the fact that everything he said about Tripp was right, even though it was the last thing I wanted to hear.

"So, you were able to survive without me?" Tripp asked as we reached the car, a naughty grin on his face.

I rolled my eyes. "I managed," I said.

We stepped into the car and Zeke closed the door.

"Any more drama about the wedding?" he asked.

"Well, Scarlett refuses to acknowledge that we're technically married already. She keeps referring to the fact that I said it was 'just a piece of paper' and changes the subject whenever it comes up. She's never reacted well when I've gone ahead and done something without getting her permission first."

"Her permission?" Tripp scoffed. "You're almost twenty-three years old."

I narrowed my eyes. "As if *your* parents don't still try to control you in one way or another?"

He smiled. "Fair enough."

As we rode toward Manhattan, I snuggled into the crook of his arm, which strangely smelled like some sort of flower. What was that? Maybe he'd had his coat dry-cleaned at the Dorchester.

"You smell different," I said.

He looked at me, an eyebrow raised.

"Nah," he said, smiling. "You probably just forgot what I smell like."

There were a lot of things that needed to be said that weren't being said. About Tabitha, for one. And what about London? We'd talked only three times in the last two weeks. Was it normal for a husband to go on a business trip and basically cut off all forms of communication? I was new to this marriage business, but it didn't feel normal to me.

"So, how was London?" I asked.

Tripp stared straight ahead. "Brutal," he said. "Busy."

"Did you and Harry at least get to have a little bit of fun?"

He shrugged. "A few nights," he said. "Honestly, I was so tired from pulling basically eighteen-hour days that I pretty much crashed straight from work. The few times we went out, Harry had to drag me." He shook his head and glanced in my direction briefly, without making eye contact. "I'm an old married man these days."

I narrowed my eyes and stared out the window. "That you are." I pursed my lips. Why did I feel like we were making small talk? "So did you get a chance to do any sightseeing at least?"

Tripp smirked. "Mints, I've been to London a million times."

"I know," I said, feeling stupid. "Just . . . no museums? Did you see a show in the West End? You were there for two weeks!"

"It's one thing to go there for two weeks of vacation," he said. "It's another thing to go there for two weeks of work." He let out an exasperated sigh. "Anyway, what did I miss in New York?"

"I've been really busy working on my bags," I said. I tried my best to ignore his attitude. "I'm meeting with the design team next week and going over my ideas, and then we're narrowing it down to five different designs and Kevin said supposedly we should have samples by the end of May! The whole thing has just happened so fast and—"

"Whoa, whoa, whoa," Tripp said. "I thought we were going to discuss this. You're off and designing already?"

I stared at him.

"Well, yes," I said. "What do you mean we have to 'discuss' it? What is there to discuss?"

"It's just," he began, "you have to keep in mind you can't just go running around accepting every offer that comes your way."

"But I'm not," I said. What the hell was he trying to say anyway? "Kevin Park is an amazing brand and this is an opportunity that most people would die for. It's not like I'm selling bags on the street. Tripp, what is this about anyway? I thought you'd be happy for me."

He softened a bit and put his hand on my knee. "Mints," he said. "I just thought when we talked about it before, you were going to wait until I got back. I told you that my family can be a little sensitive about this kind of thing. I'm just trying to protect you."

How come every time he said he was just trying to protect me, it felt like he was locking me away in a cage? My husband had just spent two weeks in another country and our communication had been limited, to say the least. If I hadn't had my job with Kevin to keep me busy, what would I have done? There were only so many spa days with Emily and late brunches with May I could take. This was a once-in-a-lifetime opportunity!

"Ugh," I said. "This sucks."

Tripp actually cracked a smile. The nerve.

"Mints," he said, "baby. It's nothing. Let's forget about it, all right? I didn't mean to get you upset."

"Well, you did," I said. "And instead of congratulating me and making me feel good about something that is very exciting and, to be honest, a real honor, you're thinking about how your stupid family is going to freak out or whatever."

There, I said it.

"This isn't about me not being proud of you," he said. "This is just about me . . . well, yes, maybe I do care a little too much about what my family thinks."

I almost wished I had recorded that statement so I could play it back for him the next time his mother freaked out over something that was none of her business.

"Thank you," I said.

Tripp leaned in and kissed me on the cheek. He had been back in New York for less than an hour and we'd already spent the majority of the time bickering. Now we had to go meet May and Harry for dinner at Cipriani. We pulled up to Tripp's building and I waited on the curb as he and Zeke unloaded the luggage.

"Thanks, Zeke," I said, taking one of Tripp's bags.

"You take care of yourself, now, Ms. Davenport," he replied. He held my gaze longer than usual.

"I will," I said.

As I walked through the entrance of Tripp's building, I couldn't help but think, Why did Zeke look at me that way?

Tripp's apartment was more than twice the size of mine with an extra bedroom. The first time I stayed there, back in the beginning of our courtship, I'd immediately started mapping out where I would put my—our—furniture, the prints my mother had painstakingly hung and framed, the rugs she'd spent days on end searching out and sizing just so. Tripp mentioned I could start moving my belongings into one of the closets in the bedroom, although he hadn't gotten around to cleaning it out just yet.

I sat down on the edge of the bed as Tripp unpacked.

"So, no stories at all?" I asked. "No late nights at Buckingham Palace?"

Tripp made a face. "The royals were otherwise engaged."

"Oh well," I said. "I was hoping for a bit of dirt. Maybe Harry will have a story or two to share."

Tripp froze for a moment.

"Doubt it," he finally said.

I watched as Tripp changed out of his traveling clothes and put on a fresh shirt and pants. He seemed worlds away, like he was trying to avoid something.

"What's going on, babe?" I finally said. "You're acting like you forgot my name or something and you're trying to get around it. It's Minty, by the way."

He made a pouty frown and dove in to kiss my neck, blowing a raspberry for comedic effect. "Minty," he repeated in a silly, high-pitched voice, "how could I forget? You're not getting much attention, are you? Let's give you some."

He tackled me onto the bed and nuzzled my neck. It was cute at first, but it also felt like a diversion. We continued on for a minute or so. We kissed. But it . . . God, it felt weird. So after a minute I pulled away.

"We should probably get over to Cipriani, no?" I asked.

━━━❧❦❧━━━

When we walked into the restaurant, Tripp told the hostess we were meeting Harry Van der Waahl.

"Oh! Yes, of course," she said, guiding us toward the back of the room.

As we approached, I saw a group of people sitting around a long table. There were Catherine Dorson and Perry Hammerstein—the girls from Baron Guggenheim's party. And Baron! What were they all doing there?

Before the hostess could even take us to our seats, the entire group erupted into applause.

"Surprise!" they all shouted.

I gaped at them and turned to Tripp. He looked more mortified than I did.

"I have no idea," he said.

Just then, May came gallivanting into the room with Harry trailing behind looking like he'd rather be anywhere else. Almost immediately, I realized that this was May's doing. She had planned a surprise "welcome back" dinner for Tripp and Harry and conveniently failed to let me in on the surprise.

"Sweetie!" she squealed. "How fun is this?"

"Wow, May," I said. "There's like twenty people here."

"I know!" she said, waving to everyone as she spoke. "I hope you don't mind. I wanted it to be a surprise. You know"—she lowered her voice—"remind them what they've been missing."

"Well," I said, "this is definitely one way of doing it!"

She laughed. "Have a seat! Have a drink!"

I scooted into the banquette side of the table, toward the center.
"Good to see you, Baron," I said across the table.

"Stunning as ever, Mrs. du Pont."

"To Harry and Tripp," Baron said, standing up and holding his
glass of champagne in the air. Everyone else followed suit. "For giving
us a reason to celebrate for no apparent reason."

Everyone clinked glasses.

———◆◆◆———

After the appetizers, a few people slipped out to smoke cigarettes.
Perry leaned over and asked if I was ready for the wedding.

In the midst of explaining the color scheme and the florals, I
heard something that was definitely not meant for my ears. It was
Harry whispering to Tripp, clearly louder than he'd intended.

"Dude, that girl in London was hot," Harry said. "Hot! How much
did you pay for that ass?"

And then Tripp replied as if I were not sitting several feet away.

"She wasn't a hooker," he said.

"I figured all of those chicks at the Dorchester bar were," Harry
said, laughing.

I could only think, He must be drunk.

"Shhh," Tripp finally said, barely glancing in my direction. "Jesus,
man, you're pushing it."

"Well, I hope you bought her a nice lobster dinner at least," Harry
replied, unfazed.

Tripp shook his head. His end of the table erupted into laughter
and everyone glanced in their direction except me. I couldn't look at
him. I just stared at my fork and thought, This is the man I married.
Then I glanced around. I was surrounded on both sides by people. I
would have no way of escaping the table unless I asked several people
to get up, Tripp and Harry included. And so, when no one was looking, I slid underneath the table and crawled out, past Harry's and
Catherine's legs, squeezing through the chairs, on my hands and
knees. When I emerged on the other side, no one noticed. I was on
my hands and knees in a Tibi dress on the floor of Cipriani, and not

a soul noticed. I quickly hoisted myself into standing position and bolted for the door.

"Minty!"

Someone called after me. I think it was May, but I didn't turn back to check. Maybe they thought I was going to the ladies' room and wouldn't bother me. All I knew was I needed to get out of there, fast.

It was nearly eleven P.M. when I hit Fifth Avenue. The air was a lot less crisp than a few hours before. I wanted to get on a plane and get the hell out of New York, but I knew that wasn't the responsible thing to do. I immediately texted Tripp and told him to please meet me outside as soon as possible. It had taken me nearly half my life, a whirlwind six-month romance, and a quickie courthouse wedding to realize it, but Tripp du Pont did not deserve me.

"What's going on?"

He was standing just outside the front door, no coat, no scarf. He nearly stumbled as he moved toward me, his arms outstretched, pleading. In the few minutes it took him to say those disgusting words out loud, receive my text, and make it to the door, did he ever get an inkling as to why I was upset?

"I heard what Harry said back there." Tripp opened his mouth in protest but I wouldn't let him speak. I held my hand up in the air. "I don't want to hear excuses. I don't want to hear a convoluted story or some crazy explanation. I'm going to go home right now, book the first flight to Charleston, and take a Xanax. I'll call you when I'm ready to discuss anything further. But I will say, here and now, this has been a mistake."

Tripp stared back at me dumbfounded. "Mints, it's not what you think."

"That's what you always say."

I held out my hand and a cab pulled up almost immediately. If I'd had to wait a second longer standing next to him in front of Cipriani, I would have lost my composure. I'd already lost my dignity.

The cab had two, maybe three blocks to reach my apartment. I could have easily walked. But those thirty seconds of being anonymously sheltered from the rest of the world saved me. It gave me the chance to go from the crippling feeling of being punched in the gut to autopilot, and autopilot was where I wanted to be.

"Sixty-first Street, miss," the cabbie said.

I jumped, nearly dropping my BlackBerry on the floor. I paid the fare and stepped onto the street.

As I walked through the door to my building, the night doorman nodded at me but I barely noticed. It was a lot to take in for anyone, the realization that your current relationship—excuse me, your *marriage*—was a sham. But there was something else I was feeling. It was like I'd been waiting for this moment to come. And that's what got to me the most. How had I let it go this far? How had I allowed Tripp to lie to me time and time again? I was so disappointed in myself I could barely breathe. I walked into my apartment, called my mother in Charleston, and told her I was coming home.

"Good God, Minty, what are you talking about?" she asked in a groggy voice.

"I really would rather not get into it right now, Mother," I explained, "but some things have happened and I can't be here right now. I'm booking the first flight out. I'll let you know when I get in. Will you be able to pick me up?"

There was silence on the other end.

"Of course, darlin'," she finally said. "You're sure you don't want to talk this out?"

I sighed. "Not now. We can talk tomorrow."

I went through my closet and threw together what I could. I was pretty sure I wasn't leaving for good. But I needed to leave the city for a while if I ever wanted to come back again and see it in a new light. I had to rid myself of the grime and grit if I had any chance of seeing it the way I did when I was a little girl and stepped into the lobby of the Plaza Hotel for the first time. I needed to get back to that place, and the only way I could do that was to go back to where I started.

Never Forget Where You Came From

Scarlett was eagerly awaiting my arrival at the baggage claim, wearing a cherry-red Ralph Lauren sundress and matching strappy heels. "Minty, sugar, what on earth is going on?"

"In the car, Mother," I said.

Miraculously, we made it to her BMW convertible without one more peep. But the second we got inside the car and secured our seat belts, she started.

"I can feel it in my gut, I know what's wrong, but I'm going to let you tell me," she said, pulling onto the highway and nearly sideswiping an oncoming truck. Scarlett drove both timidly and recklessly. "Did something happen in London?"

She slammed on the brakes and nearly rear-ended the car in front of us, which was slowing down due to traffic.

"*Mother!*"

"Goddamn SUVs take up so much space. I can't see a thing!"

I braced myself against the armrest and exhaled.

"Tripp is not who I thought he was," I finally said.

Scarlett stared straight ahead.

"Or maybe he is who I thought he was," I continued, "but I just wasn't letting myself see it because I loved him. Because I believed in all of the romance and the idea of us getting married."

She crept past the car next to us, nearly swiping its side mirror. "Spill it, child. What happened?"

"He picked up a girl at the Dorchester . . . in London."

Saying the words out loud, it felt like they were coming from someone else's mouth.

She was silent. I imagined she was even more furious than I was, which was saying a lot.

"There have to be other things going on," I said. The words were spilling out of me. I realized I hadn't exactly had the chance to voice my feelings on Tripp's extracurricular activities until now. "Who knows what was really going on with Tabitha? I can't believe a word he says about anything." I couldn't hold back the tears any longer. "I mean, what kind of person does that when they're in a serious, committed relationship? When they're married!"

My mother remained silent, her hands gripping the steering wheel. She was obviously in shock. We pulled up to the house.

Our house sits on fifteen acres of magnolia-tree-lined land about ten minutes outside of downtown Charleston. I'm pretty sure no one in New York would consider Charleston a "real" city. There's really only one good place to get your hair and nails done. No one honks their horn. In fact, drivers happily wait when people randomly cross the street. Everyone smiles and says hello, even to strangers. It's not small enough that everyone knows one another but it's definitely small enough that most people seem familiar.

For all of these reasons, I couldn't wait to leave Charleston. For the same reasons, it was wonderful to be home.

It took Scarlett a few minutes to process everything I'd just told her. We'd never had such a frank conversation. Of course, we fought openly and she knew more about my life than probably most of my best friends, but blatant infidelity? We hadn't quite crossed that bridge yet. I guess there was a first time for everything.

"That motherfucking prick," she finally said. She turned to me. "You're one hundred percent certain he did this?"

"Well, not one hundred percent," I said. "I overheard him relaying the story to a few friends at the dinner table. He was drunk. He didn't think I could hear. Not to mention, I only heard from him a handful of times when he was in London. I can only imagine what was going on over there. He was there with Harry and I don't trust Harry for a second. The guy can barely look me in the eye. These boys operate in a way I can't say I've experienced before. It's like they almost think it's okay to act that way. They almost think it's . . . expected."

We pulled up to the gate of our driveway, which opened automatically, and pulled in. It had to be 70 degrees. I felt like I'd been living in the tundra compared to what the weather felt like in Charleston that day.

"Just to warn you, your sister has a few days left of her spring break before she has to head back to Ole Miss. The last I heard she's coming in tonight, something about getting a ride with her friend, but you never know with that girl."

"Oh, okay, great," I said. Part of me was excited to see Darby. Another part of me was beyond overwhelmed.

"And we're having dinner at the club tonight with a few people," she continued, referring to the Charleston Country Club. "It's your grandfather's seventy-fifth birthday on Tuesday, as you know, so we decided to celebrate tonight since your sister will be in town and all."

I gulped. In the midst of all of the craziness, I'd forgotten my grandfather's birthday was coming up. I couldn't help but groan a little. I was well aware of the fact that "a few people" meant more like half the town and the majority of my extended family.

We walked into the kitchen and Anna Mae, our housekeeper since I was a baby, was standing there drying a stainless steel pot. She looked at me, her mouth dropped open, and she nearly dropped the pot as well.

"Miss Minty!" she yelped. "I thought you forgot about us down here!" She gave me the biggest, warmest hug I'd had in a very long time.

That was another thing about the South: big hugs were the norm, even when you were meeting someone for the first time. I used to get so annoyed and feel like I was being suffocated. Now it felt like the best thing in the world.

"It was kind of last-minute, Anna Mae," I said sheepishly.

Anna Mae reminded me of comfort food, like grilled cheese and tomato soup, and bedtime stories. She was the first person who introduced me to Eloise. She used to read the books out loud to help me fall asleep at night when my parents were out late.

"Well, it's no matter what got you here. The important thing is you're back." She stepped away and looked at me closely. "My word, what have you been eating up there? You're so skinny you look like you could hula-hoop with a Cheerio!"

"Oh, stop it," I said. "I'm not that thin."

"Don't tell me to stop it," she said, waving a finger in my direction. "Gonna have to stand in the same place twice to get a shadow if you don't start eating something."

"Minty looks just fine, Anna Mae," Mother chimed in. "She's practically Rubenesque compared to most of the girls up north."

"Ruben-whatever. A Reuben sandwich is what you need."

That was a refreshing point of view. I hadn't even thought about eating a sandwich in months.

"Minty, sweetheart, why don't you get situated upstairs," Mother said, changing the subject. "I laid out a few things I thought you might like—just a few dresses I found on sale on King Street. You know, something might work for tonight."

Thank God, I thought. I'd packed so quickly, I wasn't sure I'd brought anything appropriate for dinner at the club. The Charleston Country Club was a coat-and-tie kind of place for dinner. I would have looked completely ridiculous if I'd shown up to my grandfather's party in anything other than, well, something my mother might pick out for me. It was also nice to know I had something brand-new to put on. I hugged and thanked my mother and gave Anna Mae a quick squeeze as well.

"Take your time, dear. We'll head over around six."

My bedroom was exactly as I'd left it: girly and frilly. Lining my book-shelves were copies of *The Baby-Sitters Club* and *Sweet Valley High* books; framed photos of me and my sister as kids; one of me with two of my best friends, Ginger and Mallory; and countless tennis trophies.

The dresses Scarlett had picked out were typical Scarlett dresses: A-line with a nipped waist in bright colors. I went with a polka-dot Michael Kors, which was very simple and classic—perfect for this crowd. It felt nice to let go of all of the trendiness of New York for a few days.

"Minty, Jesus, what are you doing here?" Darby was standing in my doorway, her right hand on her hip.

She had on a striped Splendid T-shirt and cut-off jean shorts that showed off her spring break tan. I was jealous!

She stormed into my room, slammed the door, and plopped down on my bed.

"Mom wouldn't tell me a thing," she said. "Are y'all calling the wedding off?"

"Seems like," I said.

"Holy shit," Darby growled. "Did he cheat on you?"

I gulped, holding back tears.

"Awww, Mints, come on," she said. "Do you have proof?"

I shook my head. "Well. Sort of. It's more . . . a feeling. I overheard something and, well, it's a lot of things that have built up over the last year."

"I hear ya," she said, sitting down next to me on the bed. "Listen, whatever's going on, I want you to know you deserve only the best."

"There was a girl in London," I blurted.

Strangely enough, Darby barely batted an eyelash.

"You're not surprised?"

"Oh, Minty, not really," she said. "Boys like Tripp, they do what they want."

"I'm such an idiot," I said.

"No." She put her arm around me. "We've all been there. When you guys reconnected, I hoped maybe he'd finally grown up, but I guess that isn't the case."

"That is definitely not the case," I said.

She was right. Tripp had always had a dishonest side, a sense of entitlement, as if he not only expected to get away with everything, he felt he deserved to get away with everything. But it was strange. I never thought that Darby would have picked up on that so easily.

"What's happening with the wedding?" she asked.

"Oh God," I said, holding back a lump in my throat. "I can't go there just yet."

"I bet Mom's holding out for a reconciliation." Darby laughed. "Whatever happens with that, you shouldn't worry. Parties get canceled all of the time."

She was trying so hard to make me feel better, which of course made me start to cry.

"Darbs, I really appreciate it," I said, gulping. A few tears streamed down my cheeks. "Honestly, the wedding is the least of my problems. I guess I'm just . . . so . . . disappointed. I expected more. I hoped for more."

"Don't we all," Darby said. "Listen. I don't know about you but I could use a drink. And Mom said the new bartender at the club looks like Cary Grant." She paused. "You know, Cary Grant like sixty years ago."

I giggled.

"I'm going to do a quick change," she continued. "Then why don't we head over a bit early? Anna Mae will drop us off. It will give us some time to prepare before the onslaught of the entire extended Davenport family. Sound good?"

"That's perfect," I said.

⟞⟝

My great-grandparents were among the first members of the majestic, sprawling Charleston Country Club when it opened in 1925. When Darby and I walked in around five thirty, they were just finishing setting up the dining room for dinner. Of course, over the years some of the staff had come and gone, but the core people had been there for decades.

"Hello, Misses Davenport," Frank, the maître d', said as we walked past him and made our way over to the bar. "You'll be joining us for dinner at seven with the rest?" He glanced at his book. "I know your mother is planning a really special evening for Gharland Senior."

"Yeah," Darby said, rolling her eyes, "which is why we're getting a little extra time in at the bar."

Frank laughed.

"Berkeley will take care of you, I'm sure," he said, motioning over to the handsome young bartender. As we got closer, I realized my mother wasn't kidding—Cary Grant was an understatement.

I could see the wheels in Darby's head turning. While I was a relationship kind of person, Darby enjoyed the hunt, the chase. As a result, she also tired of people pretty quickly. Sometimes I wondered if she had the right idea. I got wrapped up so easily that by the age of twenty-three, I'd really only had two serious relationships, Ryerson and Tripp. Maybe this was my time to let out a little of my Darby side, if I even had one.

"Berkeley, honey," Darby said, leaning over the bar. "Allow us to introduce ourselves. I'm Darby and this is my sister, Minty. I think you've already met our mother, Scarlett? She said y'all had a nice conversation last weekend."

Berkeley laughed. "Sure thing," he said. "Scarlett and I go way back."

"Super," Darby said. "Then I'll have a Tom Collins and my sister here will have a . . ."

"Champagne, please," I said.

"Champagne," Darby repeated, "because she lives in New York now, so she's fancy."

"New York, eh?" Berkeley asked. "What brings you back to Charleston?"

I groaned. "A lot of things."

"Well, either way, welcome back," he said, smiling. "Let me know if there's anything we can do to convince you to stay."

"Yes, please do let us know," a male voice chimed in.

I turned around and there he was. Ryerson Bigelow. I gasped. Is that why he'd been contacting me? Because he'd finished up living on a boat in the Adriatic Sea or whatever the hell he was doing the last I'd heard? I immediately wanted to ask him if he'd "found himself" yet but I held my tongue.

"Jesus, Ryerson, you scared the living daylights out of me," I said.

He sidled up next to me, all six foot four of him, towering over me in a pale blue linen shirt, khaki pants, and a navy blazer. His looks had matured in the last couple of years. He was still lean and lanky, but his shoulders had filled out and his skin was a bit weathered now, sun-beaten. And there were those sparkling green eyes, the slightly crooked nose he'd broken twice when he was on the wrestling team in high school. His light brown hair was a little sun-kissed and unruly and he had a few days of beard growth. It was the kind of messy look my mother would describe as "boy needs a haircut and a shave." Anyone in their right mind would have called him handsome.

"Likewise, Minty," he replied.

I narrowed my eyes. "What are you doing home?"

"What are *you* doing home?"

Darby exchanged an amused look with Berkeley.

"Ugh, enough, Ryerson." I took a sip of my champagne. "This is the last thing I need right now."

"Oh really?" he asked, leaning over and resting his hand on the bar. He had a silly grin on his face. He was enjoying seeing me taken so off guard.

"Really," I said. "Literally and figuratively."

"Learning some big words up north I see," he said.

Berkeley narrowed his eyes at Ryerson like he'd witnessed this act before.

"So, Ryerson," Darby chimed in, "we've all been dying to know: have you found yourself yet? Because you're standing right here, in case you're still looking."

I covered my mouth with my hand to keep from laughing. Thank God for Darby.

Ryerson stiffened. "Always a pleasure, Darby." He turned to me.

"I guess you can't ignore me anymore seeing as I'm standing right in front of you and all."

I rolled my eyes. "What was I supposed to say?"

He looked down at the floor. "It's okay. I admit it, I didn't give you much to work with. And I know we didn't exactly end things on the best of terms."

I nodded and we locked eyes. "That's true."

"So anyway," Darby said in a louder-than-necessary voice, "loving the therapy session and all but last I checked we were here to have a drink and unwind before the Davenport crazy train descends." She took a deep breath. "Am I right, Minty?"

She was right. If Ryerson and I were going to have this conversation, it wasn't going to be in the middle of the Charleston Country Club with Berkeley the bartender looking on. I brushed a strand of hair out of my face and Ryerson zeroed in on my bare ring finger. Before I could hide my hand behind my back and change the subject, he'd grabbed it and was inspecting my ring finger.

"The last I heard you were married," he said, letting go of my hand. "Or getting married? Or something."

"It's a long story," I said.

"I'll say that again," Darby said, winking at Berkeley. "Really, Minty, Mother is on her way over here this very second. We really should go."

Ryerson stifled a grin and cleared his throat.

"Well, then, Minty Davenport, it's good to see you. Maybe you'll tell me that story sometime."

I looked down at my drink and gulped. I had mixed feelings about seeing Ryerson. He was a good guy—he was no cheater, that's for sure. And deep down I knew he had a good heart. Ryerson "meant well," even if he didn't always make the right choices. But it was always touch-and-go with him. I was constantly wavering between wanting to kiss him and wanting to wring his neck. He could be charming and sweet one moment and completely distant and emotionally unavailable the next. There was also the fact that I wasn't in the best frame of mind. Tripp had drained me of my desire to give people the benefit of the doubt. And even though Ryerson was back from his globe-trotting, we were still going in totally different directions. My life was in New York now, and Ryerson was a simple southern boy. He hated New York.

"Minty." Darby stared at me, annoyed. She and Ryerson had always butted heads for some reason, and let's just say her opinion of him hadn't exactly improved since he broke my heart.

As I was turning to say good-bye to Ryerson, I saw my mother walk in out of the corner of my eye. She was followed by my father, my grandparents Gharland and Cookie Davenport, and, finally, Darby's godmother, Farleigh Carter, one of the most gossipy, vicious women in all of Charleston. She was going to have a field day with the Tripp situation.

"Anyway, Ryerson, it was good to see you," I said, scrambling to get the words out. My mother had spotted me across the room and was starting to make her way toward us. Knowing her, she would either give Ryerson a piece of her mind and make a scene or try to play matchmaker and get us back together. "I'll, um, Darby and I really should be getting to dinner." I jumped off my stool and grabbed a surprised Darby by the arm.

Ryerson and I locked eyes. Why were we locking eyes? The last thing I needed in that moment was to be locking eyes with Ryerson Bigelow.

"You're just going to run off like that?" he said under his breath.

I clenched my jaw. "You did."

Ryerson took a sip of his beer. He clearly hadn't expected that kind of retort from me. But I was different now.

He opened his mouth to say something and then changed his mind.

"Maybe I'll see you around."

I stared at him. "I doubt that," I said. "I'm headed back to New York, like, tomorrow." This was a tiny lie. "Good-bye, Ryerson."

Darby grabbed my hand and gave it a squeeze. Mother had stopped halfway across the room to say hi to someone. She looked up as Darby and I walked toward her and wrapped up her conversation.

I was pretty sure she hadn't recognized Ryerson. His back was facing the room, so if she had seen Darby and me talking to him she probably just figured he was a random guy hitting on us. We made our way over to the table, where everyone was already seated.

"Minty, darlin'!" my grandfather exclaimed.

He may have been turning seventy-five, but he had the energy and spirit of someone thirty years younger.

"Happy birthday, Grandpa," I said.

"What is this I hear about some Yankee breaking your heart? You know, sometimes life makes decisions for you. And I think your life is saying it's about time you come back and settle down with a nice southern boy."

Wow, I thought to myself. Talk about ripping off the Band-Aid. I guess my mother had brought them up to speed on the state of my engagement.

"Never did trust those du Ponts, sweetheart," Farleigh Carter said.

Farleigh had a house in Palm Beach on the same street as Tripp's family. On one hand, she'd always wished they'd give her the time of day. On the other hand, she had no problem voicing her opinion that the du Ponts were "hypocritical" and "stuck-up" and "not actually as wealthy as they would have you believe." Farleigh had a whole list of complaints about most people, in fact.

"I must say, people up north don't know how to conduct themselves in a discreet manner. If you're going to philander, honey, don't get caught! Not to mention all of that gossipy stuff they've been saying about you all over the Internets. Just disgraceful, really."

I took a deep breath. For all I knew, she was one of the people making those terrible comments on Social Roster. She had a lot of time on her hands and an unhealthy obsession with other people's business. She'd made comments to my mother on several occasions that I was "shaming" the family up in New York, "running around town" and drawing attention to myself. She wasn't the only person in Charleston, of course, who shared that opinion, but she was certainly the most vocal. I was sure she was thoroughly enjoying the fact that Tripp and I were over.

I made eye contact with Scarlett, who shook her head and winked at me in an attempt to brush off the attack.

Darby turned to me and rolled her eyes.

"So you'll be coming back to us, then, dear?" Farleigh turned her attention back to me.

"I'm sorry?"

"Coming back to us. You'll be moving back to Charleston, I imagine? It's the civilized thing to do."

As if fragile little ol' me couldn't handle the big bad city.

"Actually, I'm just planning on staying here for a few days, Farleigh, and it's wonderful," I said. "But New York is my home now."

The entire table grew quiet, even Darby, who cocked her head to the left, scrunched up her face, and took a huge gulp of her Tom Collins. Why was that so surprising? I was tired of people treating my time in New York like it was a flight of fancy. I finished off my champagne and ordered another.

"I think Farleigh here is just saying, baby," my father interjected, reaching across the table and patting my arm, "you might want to think about your options in light of everything that's going on." His tone was soothing, borderline patronizing. "You just might want to think about . . . what do you really have keeping you there now?"

All right, that was it. Now I was mad.

In the meantime, my mother had started up a side conversation with the waiter about the dinner specials. When she was finished and the waiter walked away, she turned back to the table and rested her eyes on me.

"Well, that's said and done," she said, letting out a big sigh. Another one of her famous segues, I thought. "Shall we move on and have a little toast to Gharland Senior's seventy-fifth birthday? No use in getting ourselves in a tizzy over a little canceled wedding, now. After all, there are other grooms in the sea."

We all raised our glasses.

"To everything your mother just said," my father said.

"To everything Scarlett just said," we repeated.

The evening carried on rather civilly from that point on. By the time we got around to dessert, my grandfather was singing Johnny Cash songs and my father was adding a bit of percussion with his fork and knife. As my father signed the tab, Darby and I looked at each other and decided to make our exit.

"Mints and I are going to walk home," Darby announced. "Get some fresh air, you know."

"Is that what they're calling cigarettes these days, Darby?" my mother asked.

Darby scowled.

We each gave Grandfather and Gram a hug and said our good-byes to the rest of the table. Scarlett looked peeved, as if we were up to no good, when the reality was we really were just walking home.

"Want to head over to the gazebo?" Darby asked. "It's en route. We can cut through the seventeenth hole."

"Sure," I said, pulling my cardigan tighter around my body. I'd forgotten how the temperature dipped at night in the springtime. Funny, though, in New York I'd probably have been wearing a full-length coat, gloves, and a hat. As we were making our way onto the green, I got an e-mail from Kevin. He said he'd "gotten wind" of the "scene at Cipriani" and wanted to see if I was all right.

"Oh great," I said.

"What's going on?" Darby asked.

"Word is out about what happened at Cipriani." I closed my eyes. "I can only imagine what kind of story 'Page Six' is drumming up right now."

For a minute I felt like I might have another breakdown. Then I read the rest of Kevin's e-mail. He said he thought my bag sketches were "phenomenal" and that the design team was "eager" to meet with me to get started on production. Could we set up some time as early as this coming Monday?

I closed out of my BlackBerry. I was needed back in New York.

Darby put her arm around me.

"Is everything okay?"

I looked back at her and smiled.

"Yes," I said. "Everything is *going* to be okay."

Make an Entrance

I had a career now. Pretty much my *dream* career. I had a life too, even if that didn't necessarily include Tripp. And it was all north of the Mason-Dixon Line.

So I did what any self-respecting southern belle would do. After some rest and relaxation, I picked myself up, brushed myself off, and sprang for a first-class flight back to New York. The flight was less than two hours. Typically, I was happy to fly coach on such a short trip. But now was not a time for frugality. I deserved the legroom and the free champagne. I owed it to myself.

New York is one of the most magical cities in the world for many reasons, but the view from an incoming plane is, by far, my favorite reason. I'd been visiting the city since I was eight years old, but it still impressed me every time. It was like each structure had fought for its place in the terrain. For a newcomer to stake a claim, you had to knock something down and rebuild. I guess it was my turn to rebuild.

"Hot towel?" the stewardess asked.

I had my forehead pressed to the window, staring out as we circled over the island. I thought I spotted my building for a moment and I surprised myself by feeling all warm and fuzzy inside. I was dreading the experience of walking through my front door. But stronger than that feeling of trepidation was a feeling of . . . home.

"Hmmm?" I jumped, turning around. "Oh yes, thank you."

I took the towel and held it over my face and let it sink in. When I pulled the towel away, I felt fresher, ready to face the Delta terminal and all that lay beyond.

As I walked off the plane and toward the baggage claim, where my driver was waiting for me, I knew the first thing I had to deal with was Tripp. I called him as I made my way down the escalator. He picked up on the second ring.

"Meet me at my apartment in about an hour," I said before he could get a word in edgewise.

"Minty, I—"

"I'll see you soon, Tripp," I said. I hung up.

———⊱❀⊰———

It only took about forty minutes to get from LaGuardia Airport to my doorstep, which was record time. There was something quiet about the city that Sunday. The temperature had started to rise, and at five o'clock the sun was still high enough in the sky that people walking the streets needed sunglasses. I noticed a new energy in the way they walked. There was more smiling, more stopping on a street corner to chat. Some people weren't even wearing jackets. It was like New York had been hosed down and polished while I was away. I guess some-times it takes a long winter to appreciate the benefits of spring. Living in constant tank-top weather had its merits, but there's something to be said for those first few days of spring in New York, when it's pretty clear that winter is gone for good.

I opened my door, thankful for the few extra minutes I had to compose myself before Tripp arrived. Before everything happened, I'd started to accept the concept that my apartment was no longer the place I would call home. And now I'd come full circle.

Since I'd escaped to Charleston, Spencer, Emily, and even May had reached out in one way or another to show their support, which was nice. Emily sent a sweet e-mail saying she hoped I was doing okay and if I needed anything to let her know. Spencer informed me in a voice mail that there had been a few mentions in the press about what happened at Cipriani, but he didn't seem too concerned about it. May sent a BBM that said, simply, *Let me know when you're back in New York.*

The doorman announced Tripp's arrival just as I was finishing freshening up. I had already taken my engagement ring out of my purse and had placed it on the sink as I dabbed concealer under my eyes and fluffed my hair with a little dry shampoo. It sat there next to the soap dish like an afterthought. It wasn't part of me anymore.

Tripp walked into the apartment with his head hung low. He didn't look as homeless and bereft as I had hoped. There wasn't even a sign of stubble, no stray stains on his khakis. All I kept thinking was, Do not let him charm you, he's already made too many excuses.

We sat down in the living room on either end of the sofa. I hadn't felt this much adrenaline surge through my veins since my last tennis match in college.

"We'll start off with this," I said, placing the engagement ring on the cushion next to his leg. A facet was hit by the light coming from the lamp on the side table and sparkled. He glanced at it and gawked.

"Minty."

I took a deep breath. "You were always the one guy I daydreamed about, Tripp. I romanticized you, all of these years. And then when you came back into my life, I was willing to do anything to make it work." I shook my head. "I mean, Jesus, I got married to you in a courtroom!"

He stared at me.

"I was willing to put up with a lot. Looking back, I put up with a lot more than I ever should have. And even after all of the humiliation, the fact that I had to crawl under a table at Cipriani on my hands and knees, I have to say, it's the dishonesty that got me in the end. Regardless of what you've done, who you've done it with, the fact that you've lied to my face about it makes it a million times worse."

Tripp sighed. "I can see why it might be hard to trust me," he began. "I know what you think you overheard at Cipriani, and yes, there was a girl in London but we, we just had a drink!" He gulped and looked around the room. "If you were there you would see there was nothing to it."

"I just can't give you the benefit of the doubt anymore, Tripp," I said. "And I wish I could. I've always wanted to trust you because I love you, but I'm done doing that now. I just can't. I'm done."

Tripp looked at the ground.

"I get it, Minty," he said, gulping. "And all I can say is I'm sorry things turned out this way."

For some reason, that last part really hit home. My entire face flushed with a mix of anger and disappointment.

"I'm glad you're sorry." I gulped. "You should be."

Tripp tried to get me to keep the engagement ring, which made me so angry that I almost threw it out the window.

"I need you to get out now," I said, hoping that he'd leave before the tears I was holding back started to flow.

"Fine," he said, standing up from the sofa and depositing the ring into his pocket. "I wish you wouldn't do this, but you're the boss."

Finally, I thought to myself. As I closed the door behind him, the tears started to fall.

———◦◦◦◦◦———

There's a saying that March "comes in like a lion and goes out like a lamb." I tried to keep this in mind in the weeks following the breakup. Because not having Tripp in my life was definitely an adjustment, to say the least, but things could only get better, right?

The thing is, in such a short period of time, my world in New York had come to revolve around Tripp. His friends became my friends, the restaurants he liked to go to became my favorite restaurants. I even watched the same TV shows as Tripp! I knew if I was ever going to get over him and move on, I had to start over. I had to remove myself from all of the things that reminded me of him and start fresh.

So I reprogrammed my DVR. I went through my closet, weeded out any clothing that reminded me of him and gave it away to charity (and yes, my debutante gown from the Frick ball was the first to go!).

The one thing I couldn't bring myself to do was delete his number from my phone. I called Darby to discuss the matter. I thought it might mean something more, like I wasn't truly moving on.

"Oh please, you're being ridiculous," she said. "Anyway, who knows? I mean, Tripp definitely isn't the right guy for you in the long run but maybe someday you guys can be friends."

Friends? I wasn't so sure. But I also wasn't willing to rule it out. So the number stayed.

In the meantime, I was able to keep busy with my job, which was a lifesaver. With all of the design meetings, leather scouting, and sketching, I barely had a moment to catch up with Spencer or Emily, let alone think about missing Tripp. Before I knew it, April was almost over and the weather was finally turning springlike. March hadn't exactly gone out like a lamb, but it looked like May might be the light at the end of the tunnel.

One morning, I woke up early for a meeting downtown with Kevin. As I got ready to the sound of Z100, taxi horns, and a pigeon ruffling its wings on the windowsill, I realized it was the first time in a while I actually felt normal minus my engagement ring. I felt proud of myself and more ready than ever to face whatever the future had in store.

I was standing on Lexington hailing a cab when Spencer called. It was his work number, the famous "286" exchange of the Condé Nast building. I stared at my phone as his name flashed, one ring after another. We'd been trying to meet up for almost a month now and had only had a few conversations over the phone.

"Hey, honey," I said.

"She's alive," he said.

"Sorry," I replied. "I've been so crazy with work."

"Yeah, yeah, yeah," he said. "I get it. I'll see you when I see you. Anyway," he paused, "I'm actually calling with some good news."

A cab pulled up. I swung open the door and flung myself inside.

"Washington Street and West Eleventh," I said. "Good news? God, I hope you're not kidding."

"For once, no," he said. "I've actually been wanting to tell you this for ages, but I didn't want to jinx it. You know how print is. You never know if it's actually going to happen until you're literally holding a copy of the magazine and there it is."

"What are you talking about, Spencer?" I asked.

He paused. I could tell he was smiling.

"I'm talking about *Vanity Fair,* baby. *Vanity Fair!*"

"*Vanity Fair* what?"

What about *Vanity Fair?* He'd just started; I couldn't imagine he'd already landed his big exposé on the Kennedys.

"You're . . . gonna . . . be . . . in . . . *Vanity Fair!*"

Deep breath.

"What? Are you kidding me?!" I shouted. "I mean, wow. Are you sure? But how? What? Oh God, Spencer, are they going to be nice?"

"That depends," he said, laughing.

"Spencer!"

He stopped laughing.

"Gorgeous," he said, "you're killing me. It's not exactly a feature-length story but it's a start. It's an amazing shot of you in the party pages from the Frick."

"Spencer!" I squealed. "Oh my God, thank you! I can't believe it!"

He laughed. "And you look gorgeous. It's out on Monday, by the way."

The cab pulled up in front of Kevin's studio. I paid the driver and stepped out onto the street.

"Spencer, that's so exciting. Really. I'm beyond thrilled."

"Good," he said. "I can't wait for you to see it."

———◦◈◦———

My mother always says it's better to be overprepared than under-prepared. Ever since I was little, whenever I was given a task, I went above and beyond. This opportunity to create a line of handbags for Kevin was another level, of course, but I also looked at it like any other project. I did my homework, I tirelessly researched the competition, and I gave it everything I had.

When I walked into the design office, Kevin was sitting at the conference table with the two accessories designers, Gerald and Lucy.

"Here's our little designer," Kevin said, giving me a kiss on each cheek. "Minty, you know Gerald and Lucy, yes?"

"Of course!" I said.

Kevin stared at me. "How are we feeling?"

I stared back at him. "Fine," I said. "Just fine."

"Shall we get to work then?"

I never realized how many details went into one bag! It was overwhelming. But at the end of the process, we had three amazing designs that I couldn't have been more proud of. There was the Emily, a sleek shoulder bag with a cross-body strap in a dove-gray shade; the Darby, a going-out clutch that came in black or hot-pink leather and featured stud detailing; and, finally, the Scarlett, a top-handle-style handbag in the most beautiful red leather. The hardware was all gold and each bag would come with a special "MD" charm.

"Minty," Kevin said, "if all goes well I'm going to need you on board for countless more collections, got it?"

"Oh my God, of course, are you kidding me?"

"Also, I'm not sure if you already have a date for the Met Ball, but I'd love for you to join me. It would be a pity if I had to show up stag."

My eyes widened. The Met Ball was the Oscars of fashion, hosted by *Vogue* and featuring only the crème de la crème of fashion, society, and—yes—a jaw-dropping roster of Hollywood A-listers. In fact, the Met Ball was so exclusive and so impenetrable that it was arguably a more glamorous event than the Oscars. The guest list was curated by none other than Anna Wintour herself. To be invited was the New York equivalent of being knighted by the queen of England. I'd secretly hoped I was going to get an invite but at the end of the day I wasn't surprised when I didn't. I was still a relative newcomer on the circuit.

"Kevin," I said. I held my hand to my chest. "You're joking."

"I am not joking," he laughed. "And just to prove I'm not joking, turn around."

I swiveled around in my chair just as two of Kevin's assistants walked in carrying one of the most incredible dresses I have ever laid eyes on. All I can say is this: tulle, embroidery, corset, hand-stitching, hidden seams, fishtail train, backless, and the most amazing shade of peony pink, a delicate, dazzling, barely-found-in-nature-let-alone-on-a-couture-dress color. It took everything inside of me not to faint.

"Stop it," I said.

"No," Kevin joked.

"Stop it!"

"Absolutely not."

Kevin's team carried the dress over and held it in front of me for inspection. It was so beautiful it rendered me speechless. And I have to say, it was a nice alternative to the wedding dress I wasn't going to be able to wear. In fact, it was a better alternative. It was like my wedding dress got a makeover . . . a little dusting of blush, a little nip and tuck. I wrapped my arms around it and took in the smell of a custom ball gown.

"Minty, let's not smother the dress, all right?" Kevin joked.

I turned to him and a single tear rolled down my cheek. I don't know where it came from exactly. It was a lot to process, being back in New York, that final conversation with Tripp, *Vanity Fair*, the Met Ball. Not to mention, an amazing dress made especially for me!

I stepped away from the dress.

"Sweetie," he said. "Don't cry. Oh gosh, please don't cry."

You know things are bad when you start crying and no one asks why.

I took a deep breath.

"I'm not crying," I said, which was a lie, but it made me feel better. And then I brushed the tears away from my cheeks and smiled. "The dress is just so beautiful, it's actually *moving!*"

"Awww," Kevin said. "You're too kind."

As I stood in front of the mirror in my underwear and the dress was pulled over my head, I had to give myself a bit of a pep talk. A special dress can do that to any girl, send her into a tailspin and make it nearly impossible to have a coherent thought.

Once everything was zipped and buttoned and tugged in just the right direction, I allowed myself a glimpse. With one eye open, I saw pink. And then I allowed myself to slowly open the other eye and there it was in all of its jaw-dropping glory.

I clapped my hands over my mouth.

"How do we feel?" Kevin asked, beaming.

I looked at him through the mirror. I had no words to describe how I felt. All I could do was try to breathe. I held out my hand and Kevin grabbed it.

"This is good," I finally mustered the strength to say. "This is *really* good."

Kevin grinned.

"Listen," he said, "I put a lot of thought into who I wanted to bring on Monday night. Anna doesn't hand out those invitations like it's nothing, you know."

I nodded. "Of course, of course."

"At first I was worried that you might not be up for it. I heard through a friend in the industry that Tabitha is taking Tripp as her guest, so odds are he'll be there."

I gulped. The thought of seeing Tripp again at one of these things had crossed my mind, yes. I'd even pondered the possibility of Tripp and Tabitha continuing their romance now that he was pretty much a "free man," but wow. They were going to the Met Ball together? That was a lot to digest.

"Not to mention," Kevin continued, "every single reporter in the world is going to be on the red carpet. And you have about forty-eight hours to get ready." He paused. "I'm not trying to scare you, I just want you to be prepared. The last thing I'd want is for you to feel blindsided in any way."

All right, I said to myself. This is the big leagues now. This is how the game is played. I'm either in or I'm out.

"Let's get one thing straight," I began, looking Kevin dead in the eye. "Tripp is no longer a factor in any decision I make."

"I see," Kevin said. He couldn't help but smile a little.

"But you're right, forty-eight hours is not a lot of time for a girl like me to prepare."

I winked playfully, but I was also serious. The list of preparations immediately popped up in my head: highlights from Kyle at Oscar Blandi, a training session at Equinox, costume jewelry from Kenneth Jay Lane . . . what else?

"Kevin," I continued, "I don't mean to run out on you like this but, holy shit, I have a lot of things to do!"

Kevin laughed. "We'll have the dress messengered over once the final alterations are in place," he said. "See you Monday!"

The morning of the Met Ball, I woke up calm, centered, and ready to face the world. The day before, I'd received an e-mail from Tripp informing me that he would be at the Met Ball, that he'd recently heard I was attending too, and that he wanted me to know he was merely *sitting* at Tabitha's table as one of several guests she'd invited. He was not attending as her "date."

All I could do was sigh. I had moved on. I knew Tripp wasn't a bad person. He was just a spoiled kid who acted on his impulses. I needed a man who was confident and strong enough to make the right decisions, even when faced with temptation, and Tripp was clearly not that man. I thought of my chance meeting with Ryerson at the country club almost two months before. Ryerson was the wild card in my life. He'd hurt me too, but he'd hurt me because he was being honest—at the time, he wasn't ready to settle down. Ryerson had good values. He had character. I needed more of that in my life.

I did not respond to Tripp.

I always start the day of a big event with coffee. I steer away from Diet Coke and anything else with even the slightest hint of bubbles. It's best to keep my blood sugar up without ever feeling full. Honestly, all of those actresses who say they ate a cheeseburger before hitting the red carpet are either superhuman or not telling the truth.

At six forty-five P.M., when I had exactly fifteen minutes before

Kevin was supposed to pick me up, my phone rang. I didn't even say hello before my mother started talking.

"Just remember, Minty, hand on the hip. No one wants to see an arm flat up against your side doing nothing. And smile, smile!" she said. "But not too big. You don't want to come across as enthusiastic. Think something naughty."

"Mother!"

"And if you see that Tripp, you tell him I'm coming for him!"

I couldn't help but laugh. "I'll try to mention it to him if we run into each other at the bar," I said.

"All right, baby, I love you," she said.

"Love you too, Mommy."

"Now knock 'em dead!"

———

Visiting the Metropolitan Museum of Art is special enough when you're squished in with the throngs of tourists and students that come to visit on any given day. But when you're invited to the Met Ball, and you walk up those steps just past dusk with thousands of camera flashes going off, the feeling is indescribable. I'd obviously been on a red carpet before, but this was another level.

"Minty! Kevin!" the photographers screamed.

"We're famous," Kevin whispered, half-joking.

As we walked, I noticed a girl who was holding up cue cards with the name of the designer or actress or model currently walking the carpet so the photographers knew what name to scream: Isaac Mizrahi and Coco Rocha, Oscar de la Renta and Anne Hathaway, Karl Lagerfeld and Blake Lively. I spotted the card for Kevin and me on the ground next to her feet. Ha, I thought, I guess Kevin and I aren't that famous after all.

As I was making my way up the stairs, I saw a woman in a gorgeous, nude-colored dress twenty feet or so ahead of me.

"Emily!" I shouted.

Emily turned around, smiled, and waited for Kevin and me to catch up. She was with the guy from the Frick ball, Nate. They looked cute together, I thought. Perhaps a little romance was blooming after all?

"Minty, you remember Nate," Emily said, winking.

"Of course," I said, introducing Kevin as well.

I nudged Emily in the ribs as we entered the museum.

"Later," she said coyly.

The theme of the evening was inspired by the upcoming fashion exhibit "Neo Victorian." Once we entered the American Wing, which was decorated in moody shades of aubergine and garnet, we were shown to our table, which was in close proximity to the Saks Fifth Avenue table, where Emily and Nate were seated. As Kevin and I got situated, I saw May and Harry making their way through the crowd. May was definitely in her element, air-kissing and laughing and pointing. Just as I was about to sit down, she scooted by my table and patted me on the behind, promising to swing back around in a minute. As I waved her off, I glanced over at the seating card next to me: Spencer Goldin! I breathed a sigh of relief as Spencer appeared, looking dashing in a deep navy blue Tom Ford tuxedo with a crisp black bow tie.

"I pulled some strings so we could sit together," he said as he sat down.

I felt more at ease just seeing him.

"Tripp's over there, BTW," Spencer said, nodding in the direction of a neighboring table.

I spotted him almost immediately. He looked a bit stiff and self-conscious in his usual Ralph Lauren tux. He was standing over a table that included the actress Emmy Rossum, her date, and a few people who looked like fashion executives. Just before I turned away, Tabitha appeared at the table looking slightly unsteady. I was about to make a comment to Spencer about her being drunk when I realized she was on crutches. I spotted an air cast on her left leg. Yikes. On one hand, I felt terrible. On the other hand, she looked completely ridiculous wobbling around on crutches in a ball gown.

"Do you think she'll let me sign her cast?" Spencer asked.

I punched him in the arm and glanced back at Tripp, who was already looking in my direction.

"Shit, he totally just caught me looking at him," I said. When I glanced back in Tripp's direction, all I could make out was the top of his head. I couldn't even see Tabitha anymore.

"Well," I said, "that wasn't so bad."

"Music to my ears," Spencer replied.

He picked up one of the pre-poured glasses of champagne that were in front of each place setting and raised it in the air.

"To finally getting a clue," he said.

I looked back at him and narrowed my eyes.

"To finally getting a clue," I repeated.

⸺◈◈◈⸺

After four courses, three different types of wine, and a "sublime" (this was Spencer's description) performance by Florence and the Machine, I realized we'd been sitting for nearly three hours straight. Kevin was engrossed in a conversation with the supermodel Karolina Kurkova and Spencer was desperately trying to make his way into the conversation. I figured I'd grab a drink and maybe wander around some of the exhibits and get some air.

As I passed through the Egyptian Wing, I stopped for a closer look at one of the mummies encased in glass. A man was standing on the other side of the glass case, his hands clasped behind his back and a sly smile on his face like he'd been there longer than I noticed.

I focused in on the five o'clock shadow, the messy crop of hair, the cool green eyes now starting to twinkle a bit as I slowly came to a realization.

"Ryerson?!"

He tilted his head to the side.

"Minty, we meet again," he said.

A shiver went up my spine. I exhaled.

"What the hell are you doing here?" I said.

He laughed. "Well, I'm going to be up here for a few days checking out some art history programs. You know it's always been an interest of mine even though I got that econ degree at UVA. If I'm going to get a job at a gallery I kind of have to start over." He paused. "Anyway, a friend of mine from Buenos Aires had an extra seat at his table and he said I should come along." He stopped and grinned at me. "I have to admit, I had a feeling I might see you here."

"Wait," I said. "Art history? New York?"

"Yeah," he said. He shook his head. "I don't know, it's never been my favorite place, but if I'm going to break into the art world, it's really the only place to be. I've been struggling with the decision for a while. And then, recently, something just kind of clicked." He held my gaze for an extended moment. "It's exactly where I should be."

"Is that right?" I asked.

"That's right," he said.

We both laughed nervously and stared at the ground.

"You know," I finally said, breaking the silence, "it will be nice to have another southerner in the city. My sorority sister Emily has really been my only connection to the South so far, and she's originally from New York!"

"Don't tell me these Yankees have been giving you a hard time?"

I thought for a moment. Maybe he didn't know the whole story with Tripp? I wouldn't have been surprised. He wasn't exactly the type to be up on society gossip.

"Let's just say," I began, "going from a southern girl to a jaded Manhattanite hasn't exactly been the smoothest of transitions."

Ryerson laughed. "I don't know how to break it to you, Mints, but you don't exactly look like a jaded Manhattanite just yet."

I looked down at my frilly dress and patted my perfectly curled platinum-blond hair. "Oh," I said, frowning a bit. "I guess you're right."

He came around the side of the case and put his hand on my arm. A few people breezed past us in their gowns, holding glasses of champagne and laughing. Not even the security guards at either end of the room were paying us much attention. "But, wow, look at how far you've come," he said shyly. "You're like a—what do they call it—a socializer or something here? I saw everyone taking your picture."

"A socialite," I corrected him, smiling.

"Socialite," he repeated. He looked down and touched my face.

"Whatever they're calling you these days, to me you'll always be the girl I threw into a pile of leaves in high school."

I blushed. "You remember."

⸺◈◈◈⸺

That night, I didn't exactly make it back to my table. With Ryerson gazing down at me, talking about moving to New York, acting like maybe I had something to do with it, suddenly sitting in a room full of fashion designers and celebrities was the last place I wanted to be. The old Ryerson would never have been so brave.

"Do you want to get out of here?" I asked him.

"God, yes," he said.

Ryerson and I walked out of the Met, unnoticed by the paparazzi and press, down step after step until we finally reached the sidewalk, where we hailed a cab in record time.

"Where should we go?" he asked, looking at me mischievously as I squeezed myself through the cab door.

I adjusted my dress until I was semi-comfortable. I thought for a minute, but it didn't take long.

"Fifty-eighth and Fifth Avenue, please, sir," I said.

"The Plaza Hotel?"

"Yes, sir, thank you," I said.

Ryerson raised an eyebrow. "A hotel, huh? What exactly are we going to do there?"

I swatted at him. "Don't be presumptuous, Ryerson Bigelow. There's a nice bar in the Oak Room and it's quiet. We can have a drink and talk. You know, we didn't have the chance to have a proper catch-up when I saw you in Charleston."

"That's very true," Ryerson said.

"And, after all," I said, smiling slyly, "if you're moving to New York you're going to need someone to show you the ropes."

He made a face. "Show me the ropes, huh?"

"Well, yes," I said. "I'm a New Yorker now, after all."

Acknowledgments

Without a doubt, I know whom I need to thank first for the inspiration and inception of *Southern Charm*! Thank you, Charles and Maria, Tanner and Ross Rose, for inviting your southern cousins up to share the city you loved . . . fabulous New York!!! Had I not had the opportunity to truly experience the city at a young, very impressionable age, I might never have fallen under the spell of the most magical city in the world. I consider myself the luckiest girl in existence to live in New York City with all the passionate, intelligent, and glamorous people who inspire me every day.

However, I must send extra hugs to a few people for their unfailing friendship and support! First, thank you to my publisher, Jon Karp, for believing in me, and to my editor, Trish Todd, who gave me wonderful suggestions and never failed to get back to me quickly when I had a question, no matter how busy she was. I might never have had the confidence to begin *Southern Charm* without Bryn Kenny and Dianne Vavra at Dior, who provided me with tons of support and friendship, for which I am most appreciative. I send huge magnolia blossoms to my agent, Mollie Glick, without whose enthusiasm and support I most certainly would have lost the strength to complete *Southern Charm*. Thank you, Kerri Kolen, Tracey Guest, Amanda Ferber, Christina Papadopoulos, Raina Seides, and Pat Hull, for all your help and guidance.

To Kazu Terada and Tobias Buschmann from Samantha Thavasa I send big hugs and kisses for providing me not only with the opportunity for the designing job I adore, but more importantly for the support they have given me through the years. And to my first business mentors I send my undying respect. My professional life would be far different had Elizabeth and Lara at Harrison and Shriftman not believed in me, giving me the confidence to believe in myself. I also want to thank Amy Astley, who made my dreams come true by hiring me as her Beauty Assistant when she was the Beauty Director at *Vogue* magazine.

On a more personal side, I want to thank my "babies," BB, Bella, and Bambi. My life would mean nothing without my little family and all the love and strength you give me every day! Kisses to my sister Dabney and my dad. I love you both very much. And lastly, I send my love to my mother, who inspired me to follow my dreams.